Seer Society

Book Two: Broken

Jenna Kay Pridgen

First Edition 2014

ISBN: 0988298255
ISBN-13: 978-0-9882982-5-5

Edited By: Heidi Pittman

LIFELINE Press
Gainesville, Georgia
Printed in the United States of America

Stay alert! Watch out for your great enemy, the devil. He prowls around like a roaring lion, looking for someone to devour.

1 Peter 5:8

For Christopher and Faith

Prologue

Livian

The steps that lead down to Hell's torture chambers are soaked with blackened agony. Ash from the upper chambers lazily dust the air, sticking to my body. Wails of pain can be heard in this lowest region of the pit, though it does not give me a feeling of great satisfaction. The cries saturating the air isn't from lost human souls. Rather, they are pitching from my demon brethren.

Unity in Hell is hard to come by, but I believe in it. We work diligently as a unit to please the master, all striving toward the same goal. That one goal is to destroy the human race, consuming them with the fires of Hell.

The sad fact is, and I hate to even speak it, we demons fail – a lot. Failure results in heinous punishments, though our master doesn't delve out inflictions for every soul we lose to The Light. He only punishes the demons who neglect to derail the humans who work for God, who devote their lives to spread the *Good News*.

The deepest part of Hell's torture chambers are reserved for the workers of the dark who have failed tremendously, bringing shame and disgust to our lord of iniquity. The dark ones who have failed miserably to destroy a Seer, a foot soldier for The Light. And right now I am heading to talk with one of Hell's biggest losers.

A demon known as Lukus.

With my bare feet touching the rocky base of Hell, my flowing black dress swishing delicately around my ankles, all goes quiet with my arrival. The prisoners know exactly who I am. One of Satan's Generals – a high ranker. They all know I rule over them, and they fear me. I smile at that thought.

I pass cell after cell, not bothering to glance inside. Most prisoners are chained to the wall, given no sustenance to thrive upon. If a demon isn't around human suffering and grief, they will not be fed. They can't die, because my kind is immortal. Though, like a flower that thirsts for water, our bodies shrink, dry out, and wilt if not fed. Without a drink of constant misery, we are depleted of energy, becoming weak and useless.

Coming up on the last cell on the left, I slow my steps.

Gently grabbing a steel bar with one hand, I gaze into the jail cell, finding its prisoner. Instead of chained to the wall, the red demon is laying in a heap on the rocky floor. He has withdrawn into himself, his body shaking and quivering. I frown at the heartbreaking display. So sad, so tragic, so...

Vulnerable.

"Oh, Lukus, what have they done to you?"

His red eyes crack open, the light completely vanquished from them. "Livian, have you come to gloat?"

The demon has lost all his valor, thanks to his demeaning dwellings. His muscles have deteriorated, with skin hanging loosely from his bones. The structure of his face has shrunk, his eyes sunk in and his mouth hanging open. He can't die, though his body shows signs of decomposition.

"I don't gloat, Lukus," I reply, with both hands grasping the cold steel bars.

He releases a dry, coarse laugh. "Give me a break! Everyone down here knows that you've been assigned the Seer in Garlandton. The one I failed to extinguish."

"That's not why I'm here," I tell him innocently. "In fact, I've brought you a gift."

"Really?" he scoffs with a curled-up lip.

"Yes." Not breaking eye contact with the underling, I reach into the hidden pocket of my dress and bring out a jar of blackened torment.

Showing him the bottle I say, "Just dipped this out of the River of Desolation. If you look closely you can see it's still churning – will you accept my gift?"

With wide, wild eyes, his answer comes in the form of jagged claws digging into the ground, dragging him toward the jar of demon nourishment. Bending to one knee, I extend my arm through the bars, jar in hand. He reaches out and greedily snatches it from my possession. Sitting up, he hungrily devours the blackened ooze. I smile, watching as he enjoys every last drop of calamity in the jar. When he's finished, he throws it against the wall. The jar explodes into glittery shards of glass.

Standing to his feet, his black leathery wings suddenly release from his back. His mouth opens wide as a howl rips from his lips. Muscles grow and ripple under his skin, the small provision instantly revitalizing his weakened vitality. As he quiets down, his eyes fall on me, glowing slightly.

"Don't overdo it, Lukus," I warn, rising to my feet. "That little bit of human affliction will not sustain you long."

"What do you want from me?" he swiftly inquires, balling his fists at his sides.

I grin. "You're a smart one. How did you know I was after something?"

"Because," he smirks, starting to pace his cell, "you never come down to these parts unless you're after something. You don't belong down here, with your white hair and eyes – you may become stained with a slave disease if you stay much longer. And another thing..." He walks over and grabs the bars in front of me, getting in my face. "Most Generals don't bring prisoners sustenance. That kind of defeats the purpose of punishment, don't you agree?"

I sigh. "Yes, Lukus, that is true. I do have a reason for coming to visit you, and it is for my own gain, but I brought you a gift. And if you give me what I'm asking, I'll have someone bring more *gifts* to you."

"Is that a fact?" He appears suspicious, and for good reason. Demons are not ones you can trust, even if we're on the same side.

"Yes," I assure. "Not only that, but if you help me with what I'm asking for, I'll put in a good word to the master, possibly getting you out sooner. And possibly moving you up in the army."

"Yeah right," he snorts. "How is lord Satan going to take me seriously? A *Ra'ah* marked me – marked me!" He raises his arm, and I'm appalled by the Seer mark on his arm.

Crosses, wings, crowns – so *revolting*!

"Lukus," I say softly, "that can be fixed."

"By ripping the skin from my bones!" His yell reverberates off the walls of his cell.

"Your skin will regenerate – "

"Yes, I know, *Livian*," he nastily spits out. "Have you heard how horrible the pain is? I have. I've heard it first hand."

Becoming impatient, I ask, "Do you want to stay in here forever? For all eternity? Do you want to be known as the demon marked by a Seer? Is that what you want? Or," I palm his cheek, "do you want to overcome this and become triumphant, receiving another chance to climb the ranks of Hell?"

He gazes into my eyes. "I want out of here."

"Then help me," I say, adding, "so I can help you."

"What do you want from me?" he questions with narrowed orbs.

"Only this." I smile maliciously. "Information."

"Like what?" he wonders.

"Tell me about her weaknesses, her friends, her family..." Narrowing my white eyes I order, "Tell me how to destroy her."

Chapter One

Kora

A freezing cold wind drapes around my body as I meander up the broken path that leads up to the trailer. There's one light on, dousing the small porch with its orange gleam. The sky is clear, sprinkled with numerous stars. The moon glows down upon the revolving earth.

That's the thing about earth. It spins continuously – it has to. If the earth suddenly stopped its ongoing rotation, all life as we know it would die. Mankind would cease to exist, along with animals, vegetation, water … if God deemed it into existence, he could absolutely deem it *out* of existence.

A few weeks ago I felt the hand of God lift off my life. The night He took Kevin away was the night my world stopped spinning. It came to an actual halt, leaving my reality in shambles, in even more disarray than before. Every morning I wake up is a struggle. It's hard to see light through all the darkness that shrouds my vision. And now, as I open the door to the decaying trailer I share with my alcoholic mother, an undeniable realization hits me square in the face.

My life sucks.

Walking over the threshold, onto the stained brown carpet, cigarette stench bombs my senses with a vengeance. I slam the door behind me, rattling the windows. I'm not worried about disturbing my mother. Pretty sure she's passed out for the night.

As soon as I see her still form stretched out on the recliner, my thoughts are confirmed – she has already drank herself into an unconscious reverie. A lit cigarette rests between two of her fingers, with ashes dropping onto the chair's fabric.

Sighing, I gently take it out of her possession, squishing it into the overflowing ashtray. Taking a blanket off our worn-out, faded plaid couch, I cover her robe-wearing body. I stand there a moment, gazing down at the woman who brought me into the world.

Many years ago, when I was just a little girl, she'd been very attractive. Petite like myself, with silky black hair, vibrant green eyes, and a spunky smile. That all changed when she started hanging out with the drug crowd.

Now her appearance is that of an old lady, though she's only thirty-eight years old. She'd gained over one hundred pounds, which kept her bound with pain in her joints, knees, and back. Her hair no longer held a silky sheen. The natural shade had turned to a coarse gray after years of trauma. The green in her eyes had dulled tremendously, with no light gleaming from them, while her smile had shrunk to half its size, all thanks to the drugs that had rotted her teeth from the inside out.

A pang of sympathy kicks at my gut as I look at her. Brushing her bangs to the side, I lean over and kiss her forehead.

"Goodnight, Mama," I whisper. "Happy New Year."

A half-full bottle of tequila sits on the small television, immediately catching my attention. Figuring I need some self-medication, I grab the bottle. I step over trash and dirty laundry, which litters the path to my tiny bedroom.

Closing my door, I don't turn on the light. The moon is shining in through my small window, giving off enough light for me to see. Plopping down on the floor underneath the window, I unscrew the cap from the bottle and start my nightly ritual of escaping reality.

Drinking is the only remedy for my insomnia. It takes me to a place where there's no more sadness, no more pain. A place where Kevin is still here, on earth, with me. I dream of him a lot, about how happy we were together, and about how things could have been if God hadn't snatched him away.

What hurts the most is waking up the next day and realizing that even though my life is cluttered with misfortune, it continues to push on. To move forward – to *thrive*.

In a way I want to move on, but then an image of Kevin floats across my vision, bringing back the night of his murder. Like a revolving wheel stuck in the mud, I'm trapped in the past, with no way of escape. With no possible way to move forward.

With the continuous spin of my life completely stopped, how can I move on?

It will take a miracle. A mega-sized one.

Clarity

The vibration of my cell phone shakes me from a deep slumber. On the nightstand the digital clock reads three in the morning. I jerk myself up, which is a bad idea. Thanks to the arduous self-defense techniques Sam has been teaching me, my body is a big mass of pain.

It may seem crazy for a country girl like me to be learning to fight, but since the Thanksgiving dance it has become a necessity in life. Knowing that demons had used Nick Reece as a pawn in their deadly game, there really wasn't any other choice. Plus, knowing that the enemy is always devising new plans of attack, another tragedy could be waiting just around the corner.

Picking up the caustic-sounding phone, I answer with a groggy, "Yeah?" No one replies, though I hear someone breathing heavily on the other end.

"Hello?" I say forcefully, the beginnings of anger hitting its peak. If this is a stupid prank call or pervert interrupting my much needed sleep, I'm about to totally go ballistic on them.

"C-Clarity..." The voice is soft but loud enough for me to recognize.

"Kora?" I am fully awake now. "What's wrong with you? Do you know what time it is?"

"Can you come over, please?" she inquires, surprising me with her defeated tone.

A familiar heat starts to tingle in my palms, signaling that something has happened. Since learning of my Seer abilities I've slowly began to trust the little "alarms" tattooed in my palms.

If they glow green, it symbolizes that angels are near. When they glow red, that lets me know that demons are close by. A bright white light explains that the "Big Man" upstairs is by my side. Sam, my Guardian, informed me that the white light is the most important light of them all.

The worst color is black, which doesn't glow but covers the entirety of my Seer marks (crosses, wings, and crowns). My heart falls to my toes when I see my hands are black, like I'd stuck my hands in tar.

Springing from bed, cradling the cell phone between my cheek and shoulder, while pulling my long hair back in a ponytail, I tell Kora, "I'll be right over." Pausing, I close my eyes and take a deep breath.

"Kora, what's happened?"

"It's Mama," she gently speaks. "She's dead, Clare. Dead."

***

The scene at Kora's trailer park is simply surreal. The Garlandton Fire Department is in attendance, along with the police department. Flashing red, white, and blue lights have the park lit up as if it was the fourth of July.

A coroner's van is parked next to Kora's trailer. Two EMT workers walk down the crumbled pathway carrying a stretcher that I presume holds the body of Ms. Dodd. That's when I realize something...

Today is New Years Day.

Yet another horrible day to remember.

A lady reporter from the newspaper is busy questioning the coroner in hopes of squeezing out a juicy scoop, which is ludicrous. Our town must be the most boring town in the world if the local newspaper thinks a trailer park death is newsworthy. I mean, everybody dies.

Thanks to the sea of people drifting in and out of her yard, finding Kora is proving to be difficult. It's almost impossible to spot my best friend in the maze of bodies.

Almost.

Kora sits on her porch steps, surrounded by two guys in suits wearing badges on their belts. Some of her fellow *Trailer*

Parkers (Kora's neighbors) are hanging around as well, appearing emphatically nosy. They're all speaking at one time, bombarding her with question after question.

On observing the clean-cut vacancy evident in her eyes, I know for an absolute fact that she's not comprehending anything spurting from their fast, blithering mouths. A stark white blanket is draped around her shoulders, helping her to stand out in the crowd.

Shoving through the huddled masses of meddlesome people, I'm finally able to reach her side. Though I don't escape the ugly comments and angry grunts from the trailer park peeps.

Kneeling down in front of her, face-to-face, I wipe tears off her rosy cheeks with the back of my finger. A cringe sneaks up in me as I study her deer-in-the-headlights expression. Reminiscent of a lost child in a department store – scared, confused, and helpless.

"Kora," I say lightly, gazing into her bloodshot eyes. There's a slight hint of alcohol laced with her breath. Again I try, "Kora, can you hear me?"

She doesn't acknowledge me at first. Rather, she continues her unblinking stare, resembling a porcelain doll with pale skin, blushing cheeks, and glossy green orbs.

Our surroundings melt away into a dark oblivion. For a brief moment in time we're the only two people in the world, the droning noise in the background a distant echo. After what seems an eternity, she blinks as recognition flits across her countenance.

"Clare?" she drawls in a quivering voice.

Pushing a strand of red hair from her forehead, I take hold of her hand and say, "I'm here."

A tear spills over her eyelid, sliding down her cheek.

"Mama. She's..." Her speech drops off a mountain of disbelief, the realism of what's happened sinking in. She leans forward and falls into my arms.

"It's going to be okay, Kora," I attempt to reassure.

"What am I going to do?" she sobs, her tone drenched with despair.

Pondering a few ticks, raking my teeth over my bottom lip, I tell her with finality, "For now, you're coming home with me."

Livian

The scene set before my eyes is simply delightful. Weaving in and out of the crowd, passing humans in many degrees of hysteria, I savor the grief and death hovering thick in the air. I halt my steps directly in the middle of the turmoil, sucking in a long, deep breath. Releasing the air from my lungs, I sigh, feeling an extreme high from all the human despondency.

Flashing lights bounce off the faces of frantic mortals that busily buzz around. They're looking for answers, attempting to figure out this whole mess, but it's a waste of time. Aimless, even.

"Smell that, Monty?" I ask my favorite little *Tsipor* minion, who is perched on my shoulder. "Sadness, anguish, sorrow – doesn't it just energize your tiny dark heart?"

The bird demon grunts a reply, grinning with his top fangs resting above his black bottom lip. Greenish drool drips off his chin, wetting my shoulder. I am not bothered by it. Not at all.

"And look over their, my little bird." I point at the two female mortals huddled together on the steps in deep conversation. "There is our targets. The supposedly strong Seer, and the broken soul."

Monty squeals, flapping his black wings with excitement.

I chuckle. "No, my dear Monty. It is not time for them to meet us." Lovingly, I pat his head. "But it will be soon. The Seer will lose everything, and this town will burn."

Watching the pair of humans stand to their feet, I add, "Yes, this town will burn, and lord Satan will be pleased. Very pleased."

Clarity

Pulling out of the trailer park, Kora and I cruise silently down the road. One of the paramedics had given her a little pill to calm her nerves. Whatever the pill was, it's working. Sneaking a peek at my best friend, I notice she has her head leaned back and eyes closed. I tear my gaze away, concentrating on my driving. I jump a little when she speaks.

"Go ahead."

"Go ahead and what?" I inquire, my attention strictly on the road.

"I know you want the details," she idly answers. "You know, the whole *shebang*."

Looking her direction, I find her glazed eyes staring back, glistening with tears.

"There's no rush. When you're ready, I'll be here to listen."

She closes her eyes and sighs, replying, "How about the short version?"

"Only if you feel up to it," I tell her. I'm uncertain if she can handle reliving her most recent trauma. Her voice is slurred, leading me to believe that soon she will be taking a stroll in prescription drug land.

"I want to try," she insists, clearing her throat.

"Okay, I'm listening," I promise, giving her an encouraging grin. She doesn't see it, though – her eyes are pinched shut.

"Here goes." She clears her throat once more. "So, I get home from work, usual time, which is a little after midnight. Mom was asleep in the recliner, just the way I'd left her before I'd gone to work. I didn't think anything was wrong. I'd figured she was passed out from all the booze she had downed."

She pauses, becoming quiet. The slur in her voice is getting worse, and I'm about to tell her to stop, but she continues before I can say a word.

"I escaped to my crappy hole of a bedroom, shut the door, and started my nightly dose of liquor. Not long after, my brain numbed enough to switch off the Kevin channel in my mind. That's when I was able to fall asleep."

When she pauses again, I glance over and see she's hastily wiping tears off her face, using the sleeves of her black hoodie.

Kevin had been Kora's first real love, and it had hit her hard when he was killed by Nick Reece, her ex-boyfriend. Since that horrible night I rarely see Kora completely sober.

"Anyway," she presses on, "I woke up to her fist pounding on the door of my room. When I opened it, Mom was there, spazzing out. Blood was pouring from her mouth, nose – I think blood was coming from her eyes, as well."

Another pause and she goes completely still. That's when I realize she's about to break. Racking sobs burst forth from her lungs and she loses control. Reaching out a hand, I rest it on her shoulder, giving it a squeeze.

I can't imagine what she's going through. Though I had lost both my parents years ago, I'd been fortunate not to watch them die. And no matter how dysfunctional her relationship had been with her mom, Ms. Dodd had still been her mother. The only mother she'd ever known.

"Kora," I say after she settles herself, "it's going to be alright. I promise. May not seem like it at the moment, but you're going to make it."

Kora doesn't respond. She doesn't say anything else the rest of the way to my house. All she does is stare straight ahead, unblinking and mute. Like a drugged-up mental patient.

A mental patient with no hope for recovery.

Chapter Two

Sam

The sun hovers slightly above the horizon, preparing to wake the earth. Orange and red hues of morning light slowly extend across the region, overtaking the darkness, so as to unveil a brand new day.

Observing Clarity, my Charge, assist a staggering Kora up the porch steps, I can't help but ponder on what the future holds. I know there is another evil on the way, another strategy of attack Satan has cooked up. What I don't know is how and when the attack will take place. We as angels are not allowed to know the future, or to intervene in certain situations, dire as they may be. All us Guardians can do is stay by our Charge's side, and be there when they fall.

All we can truly do is trust in The Father.

Challenges, even harder and more substantial than ever,

are coming Kora's way. Her life has been one disappointment after another, and following tonight she'll either choose to rise above the tragedy, or drown in it.

"It's time for Clarity to meet me, Sam."

Twisting around, I find a fellow angel standing stiff and straight, his expression stone-cold.

"How do you know?" I inquire.

He promptly responds, "Orders from The Throne. Gabriel has visited me."

I nod. "You have information?"

"Yes," he says in a grave tone. "I know what the enemy has planned."

"Is the enemy on the way?"

"No." He narrows his glowing blue eyes and adds, "The enemy is already here."

Clarity

"Almost there, Kora."

We have made it up the stairs and are now trudging to the guest bedroom. She falls limply onto the mattress, her eyes closed and her moves sluggish. A groan flees her lips as I place her legs on the bed.

"I-I'm so sleepy," she grumbles, her head sinking into the pillows.

Covering her with a quilt I tell her, "Don't fight it – go to sleep. You're safe here." She doesn't hear or respond. I know this because she has started snoring lightly.

Sitting down next to her, I push the bangs off her forehead. A sadness circles around the both of us as I realize that she's exactly like me now – an orphan.

Ms. Dodd had not been the best role model for Kora, which had earned her the worst parent award in our little town. Just recently I learned that my parents had saved Kora many times over from the foster care system. After the death of my parents, A.C. took it upon herself to watch over Kora.

Not only had my aunt taken responsibility for me, but she'd also decided to look after my closest friend. A.C. watches over her from afar. If Kora has ever needed anything, she's always the first one to respond.

Yes, I've just realized all of this, because for the longest time my head was filled with so many convoluted thoughts which didn't include the people I love. In other words, I have been selfish, and one pathetic person. It's funny how fast life changes when disaster strikes.

The sunrise drips its colorful rays onto the drab white walls of the guest room. Reading the clock on the wall, I'm shocked to see that it's six in the morning.

Yawning, I stand to my feet, deciding that I need to try and get a couple hours sleep. I walk to my bedroom, feeling exhausted. I'm pretty sure I'll be able to get some rest, even with all the excitement I'd just undergone.

After all, today is the first day of the new year. Later today, Kora, A.C. and I will have much to discuss.

So, so much to discuss.

***

"Psst! Clarity, wake up!"

Startled, I come to, staring into the sleepy face of my aunt, Caroline. Working the graveyard shift at Garlandton Medical is taking its toll on her. She wears her mousy brown hair in a loose ponytail, with a couple of stragglers dancing around her face. Dark circles shade the underneath of her eyes, which paints the perfect picture of a workaholic.

"What time is it?" I ask, rubbing sleep from my swollen eyes. Sunlight streams through the curtains of the bedroom. Dust particles float in and out of the beam – I really need to clean my room.

Funny thing, I don't remember making it to my bedroom. I must have fallen asleep on my feet, sleepwalking the whole time.

"It's nearly noon," she informs softly. "Come downstairs to the kitchen. We need to talk about Kora." Spinning on her heel, she tromps out of my room and down the stairs.

Yawning, I stand to my feet and stretch. I'm amazed at the cracking sounds my bones make – I sound old way beyond my years.

After a quick trip to the bathroom, I walk down the stairs, yawning the entire time. As I enter the kitchen, A.C. inquires, "Want some coffee?"

"Oh, yes please!" Another monstrous yawn attacks my body as I pull my hair back in a ponytail. I plop down on the nearest chair to the kitchen table. The chair grunts in response.

"Great." She pours two steaming cups of love, handing one of the mugs to me. "Cream and sugar?"

"Nope," I reply, immediately sipping the hot cup of joe. "I like it black."

She tiredly smiles. "Me, too."

A few quiet moments tick by with the two of us sipping the coffee, staring into space. I can tell she's got a lot on her mind, most likely struggling to get it out. She feels a heavy burden for Kora, even more now that her mother has passed. I know exactly what she's thinking.

How can we help Kora?

"We need to discuss Kora," she finally speaks, confirming that my thought train is right on track.

"Yes, we do," I agree wholeheartedly. "We need to help her however we can."

"I'm glad to hear you say that," she continues, "because it's going to take the both of us to convince her to move in."

"Convincing her won't be a problem. She has no where else to go."

A.C. sighs. "Kora's eighteen, hon. And even though her

mother was around, she financially carried the both of them. She may think she can handle living on her own, but she has no idea how hard that will be." She narrows her hazel eyes and adds, "We will have to convince her, and it won't be easy. You and I both know she's as stubborn as a mule."

I ponder that last statement, then mumble, "Yeah, she's a hard-headed Miss Independent, that's for sure."

"She needs to surround herself with positive people," A.C. says, gingerly rubbing her temples. "We need to get her thinking about the future – do you think her grades are good enough for New York State?"

Inwardly, I laugh at A.C.'s inquiry. Kora is and always has been a straight-C student. There's no way she'd be able to get into that university. Instead of pointing out the obvious, I decide to appease my aunt.

"When we get her settled in and all, I'll bring up the college and future subject. Pretty sure right now is not the time."

"You're right," she agrees. Getting to her feet, she yawns and stretches. "Guess I better get a couple hours of shut eye. The three of us will have a sit down talk here in a little while."

"Yeah," is all I respond. I watch as she lazily trudges out

of the kitchen and up the stairs to her bedroom.

When I turn around, my eyes spot Sam sitting across the table where A.C. had sat moments before. I suck in his lavender scent, the smell calming every synapse I possess.

Abruptly another scent barges in, smelling a lot like freshly cut grass. My heart skips a beat when I see a muscular redheaded angel appear in the seat next to Sam, his celestial blue eyes piercing straight through me.

Sam

Clarity is caught off guard for a split second, but quickly rebounds with her quick, sardonic thinking.

"Hello, Sam," she greets with an over-the-top grin. Shifting her gaze to Christopher, she says, "Hello, angel I've never met."

Before I can stop myself, I roll my eyes at her snarky salutation. Clarity is as shocked as I am. I hear it in her thoughts.

Sam just rolled his eyes at me. That's so … human.

She is so right in her thinking. Eye rolling is a human

trait, predominately with the female gender. However, as I spend more time conversing with my Charge, I find that some of her mannerisms are catching. I can only hope that some of mine are catching, as well.

"Clarity," I say, keeping my tone neutral, "this is Christopher, Kora's Guardian."

"Nice to finally meet you," Christopher tells her, nodding his head forward.

Expecting Clarity to be cordial, I'm shocked when she snaps, "Where have you been?"

Christopher, seemingly taken back, wonders, "What do you mean?"

"Clarity..." I start to warn, but she presses onward.

"With everything Kora has gone through, where were you?" An expression of anger consumes her countenance, her eyes wide with frustration. I watch on as Christopher handles the situation.

"I've always been with her," he answers, his voice firm and even. "Since the day she was born, I've looked after her, guarded her. When she dated Nick, I stood back as he hurt her over and over again. I wanted to step in and remove her from the position she'd fallen into, but I couldn't. It wasn't my call. She had to make the choice for herself."

"But – " Clarity tries to push in, but Christopher isn't finished.

"I wanted to step in the night of the dance, to remove her from the dangerous situation, to keep her from seeing someone she cares about die, and to keep her from getting hurt, but again, I couldn't. It was out of my hands, just like it was out of Sam's and every other Guardian in attendance that fateful night."

Still, Clarity persists, "But why did God allow all that to happen?"

"We don't question why," Christopher promptly states. "God doesn't create chaos, and He surely didn't create chaos that night – the enemy did. And when Nick Reece used his freewill and chose darkness, he took a life and then his own. If he'd been a godly person, the enemy wouldn't have succeeded in polluting his mind."

Clarity has many thoughts tumbling over each other in her brain. She knows that Christopher is stating the truth – she's already heard this from me. Still, in her humanness, she has a hard time believing it all. Even though she's seen, heard, and felt more of the spiritual realm than most humans her age, her faith wavers.

"Okay, fine," she grumbles after a few seconds. "I get it. Really, I do. And it's nice to finally meet you, too." Pausing, leaning her elbows on the table, she gets serious. "There's something you need to tell me, I can feel it. Go ahead."

Clarity's forthright, eager attitude warms my spirit. She's grown so much over the last month, becoming bolder and more in tune with the gifts The Father has blessed her with. But nothing she's ever been through will compare to what's on the way. She'll have to become even stronger to fight the evil that Satan has sent to this town.

"You're right," I admit, nodding. "You need to know what's coming."

"You mean what's already here," Christopher deplorably pipes in.

"What are you two saying?" Clarity inquires, looking from Christopher, then to me.

"There's a new demon in town who preys on the young ones," Christopher says with a frown.

"Teenagers," I clarify.

"Her name is Livian, a General in Satan's army," Christopher educates, "and she doesn't stop until she gets what she wants."

"And what does she want?" Clarity questions with raised eyebrows.

Christopher leans across the table, gets in her face, and replies, "The Seer she's assigned to destroyed."

Chapter Three

Clarity

"Wonderful," I mumble sarcastically. "Just great."

"Clarity..." Sam starts, though I press forward.

"No, it's great, really," I remark, shrugging my shoulders. "I mean, I don't understand why I've become such a threat in *Demon Land*, but –"

"Every Seer poses a threat to the enemy," spells out Sam, his voice strong and stern, yet remorseful. "Just like every human who follows God's laws, the ones who know right from wrong – the ones who know the difference between good and evil."

I sigh. There's a heavy, sinking feeling balanced on my shoulders, trying to capsize my unconventional life. The past few months have been surreal – truly eye-opening. Knowing that angels guard us night and day doesn't camouflage the fact that demons reside in the shadows.

Still, I struggle with not having a say so in the Seer matter, even though God has chosen me for a purpose. His hand, his actual *hand*, had lifted me out of the freezing depths of a raging river. He had saved my life when I'd done nothing to deserve it.

God sees something in me, while I see nothing.

Sam reaches a hand over, covering my own. Lavender goodness and calming warmth kisses every nerve my body holds. I gaze into his crystal blues, swallowing down a self-pitying sob.

"Yes, God sees potential in you, because He put the potential there," Sam, who had been listening to my thoughts, assures. Softly he adds, "And I see it, too."

Shaking my head, I reply, "Maybe one day I'll see it."

We stare at each other a few ticks until Christopher clears his throat.

"I think we should inform Clarity on what we know of Livian, instead of wallowing in pity and doubt."

Christopher's words sting – a lot. But he's right. Really, I should feel guilty for being so down on myself. Kora has lost her boyfriend and mother just a few weeks apart. Though I've gone through some major issues and changes, I've come to a place where I'm accepting them. Kora's problems are just beginning, and she'll need me to be optimistic.

Worrying accomplishes nothing. I know this first hand. Plus, with a new evil in town, I must prepare myself for what's coming. No one wants another tragedy like the Thanksgiving dance.

I have eyes that see what no one else can. Might as well use them.

"Christopher's right," I willingly acknowledge. Shifting my gaze to the redheaded angel, I say, "Go ahead. Tell me about Livian."

Christopher gets right down to business. "Livian has skin as white as snow, the same can be said for her eyes and hair. Her voice sounds like a chorus of angels, which she uses to entrance unsuspecting humans."

"Sounds sweet," I mockingly say.

Christopher ignores my fruitless remark and continues. "She is beautiful on the outside – that's how she captures souls.

Underneath all the beauty and tenderness resides a darkness so venomous, an evil so ancient and pure, that it is nearly impossible to free a broken soul."

He hesitates, casting me a strict look. "Livian is a demon of persuasion, a demon of sheer manipulation. A demon that seduces the bodies and controls the minds of humans, molding them into her slaves. She is very proud of what she does, bent on the destruction of young lives, though her main mission is to destroy the foot soldiers for The Light. The Seers. *Your* kind."

"Livian never travels alone," adds Sam darkly. "She has her own band of devils at her disposal, and they do whatever she commands. They are called *Tsipors*. In English terms they'd be called bird demons."

"*Tsipor* demons are extremely weak-minded." A frown captures Christopher's lips. "The easiest to command and manipulate."

With all the information downloading in my brain, I inquire, "Do these demons look like birds with human heads?"

The mental picture that floats through my brain is comical, so comical I start to laugh. I expect Sam to join in, but by his dismal countenance I realize he's not the least bit amused. The look he wears cuts my laughter clear off. I've seen that look before – it's telling me to shut-up and learn something.

"It doesn't matter what they look like," Sam speaks, cool and even. "You'll see them soon enough. All you need to know is they're nasty, ugly, and love to clasp their claws into lost, defeated, and tormented souls. And as you know, this town holds many."

"There's a storm coming to this town, one that no one will see coming," Christopher dreadfully says. "No one will be able to escape the wrath Livian and her army will bring, unless someone stops her. That someone is *you*."

"Me?" I lift an eyebrow, giving my best *do huh?* expression. "But there's only one of me! How on God's green earth can I go up against a demon General and an army of … what are they called again?"

"*Tsipors*," replies Christopher.

"Yeah!" I exclaim. "Her army of *Tsipors* – what can I possibly do?"

"Help is on the way," updates Sam.

"Help?"

He smiles. "Others like you."

About to ask a slew of questions, I never get a word of it out because Christopher abruptly says, "We have to go."

Of course they then vanish right in front of me, taking their unique smells with them and leaving me in a perplexed state. Before I could inquire on the "help" Sam mentioned.

Typical.

I stare at the empty chairs, wondering why they had to disappear in such a fleeting manner. Two seconds later I get my answer.

"There you are," a groggy-sounding Kora says. She walks into the kitchen wearing her pink *Hello Kitty* robe, her short red hair a big mass of bedhead. Her mouth stretches out into a quiet yawn.

"Hiya, Kora, how are you feeling?" I watch her, silently praying she hadn't heard me conversing with angels.

"I guess I'm feeling better," she responds, slumping into the chair next to me. Sporting a curious look my way, she asks, "So, I went to your room, trying to find you, and I just have to ask..."

"What?"

She explains, "The punching bag – what up with that?"

I only grin.

Kora

I can't sleep. Not a wink. Too many thoughts twirling batons in my mind. Too much grief for one person to handle. Not enough sanity left in this person.

My life has come to a stand still, with no light at the end of the tunnel. Actually, there is no tunnel. There's nothing but miles and miles of stark darkness.

This darkness that surrounds me is thick and heavy, with no way out. No way.

Peering at my haggard reflection in the mirror, I don't recognize the girl staring back.

Who is that girl? Her skin is pale, with eyes swollen from shedding many tears. So, so, many tears. There's no light in her green eyes – they appear dark and lost. Her red hair is greasy and unkempt, the ends sticking up like little twigs.

Sleep is not within her grasp. She's weak and wasting

away...

Who is that girl?

"You're beautiful, Kora," Kevin says. He's appeared behind me, watching me through the mirror. He looks the same, wearing a t-shirt, jeans, and baseball cap. The difference is in his eyes. They used to be vibrant and happy, though now they hold a profound sadness.

For a brief moment, I'm happy. Kevin is here, talking to me, saying all the things he used to say. But there's a problem...

He's dead.

Pinching my eyes closed, I tell him, "Go away. You're not really here. You're dead."

I give it a minute or so, letting my mind take a rest. My imagination has been getting the best of me lately, causing me to see people who aren't here anymore. I know deep down that, with all the death I've endured lately, my mind is fabricating what I want to see. I can tell that the fringe of reality is slipping through my fingers, one inch at a time. I've lost all hope, all faith … I'm not sure I have it in me to move forward in life.

I'm not sure I want to *live* any longer.

Scissors.

Instantly my eyes pop open. I glance around the small bathroom, but there's no one around. Where had that voice come from? It sounded like a woman's voice.

Open the drawer.

My heartbeat races, my eyes opened wide. No one is in here with me. No one! What is wrong with me? Am I finally going insane? Hearing disembodied voices can't be a good thing. Pretty sure that's a prescription to the insane asylum.

Sad thing is...

I do as the voice says, and I open the drawer.

Livian

The human Kora stares down at the scissors in the drawer. They gleam brilliantly, as if they are being spotlit by the bathroom light. Her heart is beating triple its time. I suck in a breath, inhaling the solitariness and despair in the air.

"Go ahead," I whisper gently in her ear. "Pick them up."

Her breath comes out fast and raspy, the air in her lungs releasing hefty pants from her mouth. Like dragonfly wings, her heart flutters in her ribcage. I can hear every erratic pulsation her heart makes. What a glorious sound to my ears!

"Go on, Kora," I press. "Pick up the scissors."

"No," she murmurs. Though with a trembling hand, she reaches into the drawer and picks them up. She flips them over in her hand, observing their sharp edges with acute interest.

"Now," I say softly, knowing I'll be triumphant, "go on ... dig them into your delicate skin."

"No, I can't," she speaks, her focus strictly on the sharp object in her hand.

"Please do it!" I plead. "You'll feel better if you go ahead and *do it!*"

She shakes her head. "But I haven't cut myself in years. I've been happy – "

"You are not happy now," I remind her. Pacing behind her, I deplorably point out, "You've lost everything, Kora. Your boyfriend, your *ex*-boyfriend, your mother, and your own place to live – you've lost your freedom!"

"No," she whimpers, with tears cascading down her face. Though she's protesting, she opens the scissors wide.

"Yes," I hiss. "You've lost *everything*! Now you have all this pent-up grief and sadness. You must release it from your body or you will drown in it. You must..." Again, whispering in her ear, I instruct, "Slide the blade down your arm, deeply, and let your sorrow bleed out."

A sob breaks loose from her chest. "But I don't want..."

I laugh as she takes the sharpest part of the scissors and rips them across her skin. Like a *pro*.

Victory.

Kora is mine.

Chapter Four

Clarity

New Year's day rushes by in a fuzzy mist, making the second day in January a busy one for Kora, A.C. and myself.

First off, we went to the funeral home to discuss the plans for Ms. Dodd's body. Her wish had been to be cremated, which cut down on the funeral expenses. Kora told the owner to keep the ashes; she explained that she didn't have any use for them.

Secondly, it wasn't hard to convince Kora to move in with us, though she insists she pays A.C. rent, stating that she's not and never will be a freeloader. Like A.C. and I had talked about, she's being extremely bullheaded. We're still trying to work the kinks out of that one.

Later that afternoon, we drove over to Kora's trailer to gather up all her belongings. After being there a total of three minutes, she decides to set up a yard sale. A.C. was unable to stay, thanks to her upcoming twelve hour shift. That left Kora and I to work an impromptu sales event in the trailer park.

We found out super fast that there was no way we could lift all the heavy furniture and appliances. Thankfully, Brenton stopped by to lend a hand. Thank *God*.

So this is where we find ourselves – having a spur-of-the-moment yard sale that includes furniture, mattresses, appliances, jewelry … you get the picture.

"When did you decide to have a yard sale?" Brenton questions Kora as he sets a box full of clothes down on a picnic table.

"As soon as we got here!" exclaims Kora, who is acting unusually chipper. Sorting through Ms. Dodd's lingerie, she adds with a snicker, "I really don't need all these granny panties." She snaps a silky red pair at Brenton's face, which he deflects with the flick of his wrist.

"It's all her Mama's stuff," I whisper to Brenton. Kora shoots an eye full of daggers my way.

"You don't have to whisper, Clarity. Everyone knows she's dead!" She pauses, examining her mother's belongings.

"Really, guys! How many *Georgia On My Mind* shot glasses does one person need?" She lifts her hands, eight of her fingers cradling a shot glass.

"Hey, I'll take'em!" an old man in overalls announces. He spits tobacco into a white Styrofoam cup. "I'll give ya two dollars for all eight."

The old man slaps two dollars on the picnic table, like he's just poured out his entire life savings. Kora contemplates, arching a thin eyebrow.

"Make it four, Dwight, and I'll throw in this practically new trucker hat my mom kept from her last boyfriend."

They stare at each other a few seconds before Dwight concedes.

Sighing and slumping his shoulders, he says, "You drive a hard bargain, little missy." Again, he spits another load of brownish muck into his cup. Reaching a hand in his pocket, he pulls out two more wrinkled bills. "Alrighty, four bucks it is. Now don't go a spendin' it all at one place, ya hear?"

Kora smiles, taking the cash. "Don't worry, Dwight, I'll make you proud. I'll put it all toward my drug and drinking habit."

My mouth falls open at my friend's response. Surely she's kidding about those certain habits. Before Kevin, she'd dabbled in some drugs and drank up a storm, but I'd thought she had quit. However, with all she's been through the last few weeks, who knows what she's getting herself into.

At least she will be living with A.C. and me. We can keep an eye on her – I hope.

Dwight laughs at Kora's words, placing his toothless grin on display. I cringe, then quickly recover, hoping the old man hadn't seen my horrified expression.

"Thatta girl!" he loudly guffaws. He grabs a plastic bag full of his yard sale goodies. Putting his *like-new* green and white trucker hat on his head, he turns and strolls away.

Catching Kora's eye, I give her a peculiar look. She shrugs, watching Dwight leave.

"Dude's been like a grandfather to me. Gave me my first shot of Tequila." She continues to sort through all the miscellaneous junk. "There. I think that's all." Shifting her gaze to Brenton she says, "Thanks for all the heavy lifting. We couldn't have done it without you."

Brenton blushes, lifting a shoulder. "No problem, Kora."

A lady walks up to us with a handful of jewelry in her hand. She's wearing a pink floral gown, dog-faced slippers, and curlers in her hair. I recognize her as a regular at Baker's Supermarket.

"Excuse me, young lady," she says sweetly to Kora. "Are these real gold?"

"Let me talk to this nutcase," Kora mumbles to us, rolling her eyes. Then with a smile on her face she remarks, "Now come on, Miss Vicky! Don't you think if these were real I'd be taking them to a pawn shop?"

Kora and Miss Vicky walk away, deeply conversing with one another. Brenton and I are alone, standing amongst the shoppers. Letting my eyes roam over his form, I take in his apparel of long sleeve shirt and jeans. I smile, realizing how lucky I am to have him. He's quite a catch in this town … or any town, for that matter. And to drop everything to help a friend – not many men left in the world like that.

Brenton catches my eye and smiles.

"Will you come with me to the truck?"

"Sure," I answer, smiling back. "But why? What is it?"

He runs a hand through his light brown hair. "I want to

talk to you. In private."

We walk hand in hand to his truck, with silence smothering the air around us. Each step we take causes the noise of the yard sale to slowly fade away.

A few footsteps later, we're inside the truck. I watch as he once again rakes a hand through his thick hair. It's a nervous habit he's demonstrated for as long as I can remember. I also notice the darkness under his eyes, a telltale sign that he has suffered a few sleepless nights.

"Why aren't you sleeping?" I hurriedly interrogate.

His mouth drops open.

"How did you know I wasn't sleeping well?" he inquires, seemingly startled.

"I've known you all my life, Brenton," I respond, gifting him with a hearty eye roll.

He chuckles. "Nothing gets by you, does it?"

I sigh, dryly remarking, "I wouldn't go that far."

A few seconds flick by before he admits, "You're right. I haven't been sleeping well." He clears his throat, his eyes the saddest I've ever seen. "To tell you the truth, I haven't had a full night's sleep since the shooting."

I reach over and squeeze his hand, attempting to comfort him.

"Every time I close my eyes," he continues, "I go back to that night, replaying everything that went down. First we're dancing, then the first gunshot, and then I'm shot..."

"It was a horrible night," I tell him, not knowing what else to say.

"I miss him, Clarity. He was my best friend."

"I know," I say, leaning my head on his shoulder.

"There's something else that's been bothering me," he says, placing his chin atop my head.

"Oh yeah? What?"

He hesitates before replying, "It's kind of about you."

Right away my stomach knots up with pure queasiness. My breath stumbles out of my mouth, shaky and inconsistent.

"M-Me?" I stutter out.

"Well, it's probably going to sound stupid." A nervous chuckle rumbles in his chest. "The thing is, right before Nick ...

shot Kevin, you were sort of having a freaked out moment."

Slowly, I lift my head off his shoulder, raising my gaze to his. His eyes have zoned in on mine, attentively awaiting my reaction.

Of course I don't know what to say. That night I had truly suffered a *freaked out* moment. That's for sure. Before the shooting, I had doubled over in pain, like I'd been kicked in the gut by a mule. That was part of my being a Seer, one of those crazy side effects that inform me that trouble's ahead.

Instead of speaking, I remain quiet, at a complete loss for words. His brown eyes soften as he soaks in my confused expression.

"What I mean to say is," he begins in a gentle tone, "right before the shooting happened, you looked like you were in pain, and your eyes – it's like you were a million miles away. Your body was in my arms, but ... uh, I can't explain it!"

I gasp out loud as he punches the steering wheel, clearly irritated.

"S-Sorry," he contritely declares. "I just can't figure nothing out anymore."

Clearing my throat, I fight to slow down the erratic beat

of my heart. I inhale a rickety breath, hoping my face is blank of anything suspicious.

"A lot of things that occurred that night are unclear," I indicate, trying to reassure his distraught thinking.

"Did you see something before Nick shot Kevin?" he blatantly questions. His tired eyes observe me carefully.

Staring into his gaze, I battle all the thoughts zipping back and forth in my brain. Should I tell him the truth? Tell him *everything*? What would he think? Would he believe me? Or would he think I was making it up?

The hardest question of all...

Could he handle the truth?

"No," I reply a few eye blinks later. I withdraw my eyes, peering down at my entwined hands. I'm praying he believes me, while at the same time asking forgiveness for the lie I just told. What else can I do? I can't tell him the truth, because it isn't time for him to know. At the same time, it's a sin to lie. Any way you look at it, I'm backed in a corner of my own making ... sort of.

"I believe you, Clarity."

Shifting my eyes to his trusting ones, I force a small smile. He lifts his hand and lightly touches the sunflower necklace hooked around my neck. The necklace that he gave me.

I feel sick. I had lied to Brenton, my best friend and the man I plan to marry one day, possibly soon. Living the double life of Seer and normal human is starting to wear my emotions down. I know I won't be able to keep this facade up much longer. One day he'll hear the truth, and the unknown is the scariest component of it all.

With complicated thoughts and feelings spinning around like a carousel in my skull, I'm startled when Brenton pulls me into him and kisses me. Usually his kisses are tender and soft, but the ones he's dishing out now are rough, filled with an intense urgency I've never experienced before. He's kissing me so hard it hurts, causing me to slam on the brakes.

Softly pushing him away, I tell him, "Slow down."

"Sorry," he says breathlessly, his forehead pressing against mine. My lips pulse along with the beat of my heart. They'll most likely be swollen tomorrow.

"I better get back to Kora and the yard sale," I say, turning away from him.

"Yeah," he mutters, his voice emotionless. "You do that."

My hand pauses on the truck's door handle as I glance back at him. "Are you okay?"

He stares at me, the edges of his eyes sharp and cutting. "Yeah, I've got to get back to work."

There's a tinge of anger clinging to his tone, but I keep quiet. He's going through some major issues, just like the rest of this town. It's out of my hands.

"Okay." I hop out of his truck. Before closing the door I ask, "Will you call me later on?"

Surprising me, he breaks out into his dimpled grin. "I will. I love you."

I smile back. "I love you, too."

Closing the door, I start making my way back to Kora's trailer. When the screech of tires sound, and gravel hits my back, I swing around in shock. Brenton peels out of the trailer park, his engine roaring as he rips down the road.

I stand there, watching as he disappears around the corner. A heavy, depressing sensation clouds over my existence.

My Brenton is changing, and not in a good way.

Livian

The Seer's boyfriend searches for the right radio station to fit his mood, but he's unsuccessful. In the end, he turns the radio off by hitting it with his hand. The round knob breaks, falling to the floor and rolling under the driver's seat. He lets out a curse, and I laugh out loud.

Monty thinks he's funny, too. The little black bird cackles and points at the puny, retched human.

"Yes, Monty, he's quite funny." I pat the little demon's head. "He's also ripe for the picking."

Focusing all my attention on the mortal named Brenton, I scoot over until my thigh is flush with his. He doesn't know I'm here, but he's about to get an ear load of thoughts that he will believe are his own.

"What is her problem, Brenton?" I query in a musical tone. "Why is it that when you try to get closer to her, she pushes you away? Why is she so afraid of intimacy? Doesn't she love you? Doesn't she care?"

His eyes remain on the road as he speaks aloud, "I don't

know anymore."

"You two love each other," I persist, continuing to plant seeds of confusion and strife. "You guys plan to get married one day, so what's her problem? Why doesn't she give in to her desires and sleep with you?"

"I don't know," he mumbles, pausing at a stop sign. He takes a sharp left turn, his tires squealing in response. I smile at his reckless driving.

"You know what I think?" I get right in his ear and whisper, "You should find someone to sleep with, just to show Clarity that she doesn't control you."

He sighs, striking his palm against the steering wheel. Though he is considering what humans call a "one-night stand", he's clearly flustered by that thought. There's plenty of girls in town that find him attractive and would give anything to be by his side.

Anything.

Just when I think I've got him hooked, he disappoints me.

"No," he says with finality. "Clarity and I have been through too much to just throw it away. She's worth the wait."

Glaring at the weak-minded fool, a frown captures my red lips. This one will be a challenge, no doubt about it. More so than the defeated, useless Kora Dodd.

Monty pats my head, grabbing my attention. I smile at the little minion.

"Don't worry, Monty," I assure, rubbing my nose against his flat one. "This is the first step of destroying the Seer. I have many tricks up my sleeve, and don't forget that I always get what I want."

Cutting my gaze to the Seer's boyfriend, I scowl, "Always."

Chapter Five

Sam

Christopher and I stand in front of Clarity's house, gazing up at the dark, clear sky. Images of Heaven cross my mind, leaving me with a homesick feel. Streets of gold, rivers flowing with milk and honey, the sheer magnificence of being in the presence of The Almighty – for some reason all these things are fresh in my mind right now.

"We've a job to do here on earth, Sam," Christopher comments beside me. "It's what we were created for."

"I know," I tell him, shifting from one foot to the other. "I just … miss home sometimes. There's no fear or violence or death. There's only joy, peace, and constant worship."

He cuts his eyes my way and says, "The reward will be great."

I nod my head in agreement. "Yes, it will."

With our gazes back on the star-filled sky, a few seconds of blissful silence pass between us. It's well after midnight, and all is calm, except for the slight breeze that brushes against the bare tree limbs.

"Livian has started sowing seeds of ruin," he abruptly discloses.

"I know," I reply.

"She's getting to Kora. She was in the house with her."

This instantly snags my attention. Grabbing his arm, I exclaim, "Livian was in the house? How? *When*? You and I have been guarding the house together."

"Sam." His eyes have narrowed, glowing slightly, and his lips are a straight line. "You know as well as I that we have limitations when it comes to a mortal's freewill. Kora allowed Livian to enter her life when she believed the lies the demon dispersed in her mind. In her brokenness it's easier to give up the fight than to strive to live."

"Limitations," I grunt, releasing his arm and stomping at the gravel on the driveway.

"Livian has also gotten to Brenton," Christopher grimly speaks. "Though he chose to ignore the deception she spoke in his thoughts. But she's devising a new plan as we speak."

"Where are you getting your information?" I curiously inquire, with one eyebrow raised.

"A reliable source," he answers, the corners of his lips curling up.

That's when I have a light bulb moment. "You've been conversing with Gabriel, haven't you?"

"Maybe," he slyly replies, shrugging his shoulders.

The sound of a window sliding open breaks into our conversation. Clarity steps out onto the roof of her house, tightly wrapped in a blanket. She sits down and leans back, looking up at the sky. Listening in on her thoughts I find out why she's outside, and why she can't sleep. She's never been successful at flipping the switch to her rambling mind.

"I better go check on her," I tell Christopher.

"And I'll check on Kora." He places a hand on my shoulder. "Oh, and Sam?"

"Yeah?"

"Be careful not to say too much."

I grin, shaking my head. "Yep, you *have* been talking to

Gabriel."

Clarity

"Shouldn't you be in bed?" Sam inquires, appearing next to me on the roof.

My head rolls lazily to the side, my eyes focusing on him. He's wearing his usual wardrobe of white tee, jeans, and bare feet.

"You know I can't sleep," I say, my gaze floating back to the stars. The sky is clear, the moon full – a perfect night to stargaze ... and to think.

"What about school?" he pushes. "You have to go back tomorrow."

"Don't remind me," I mutter, shooting him a droll look. Then, changing the subject, I ask, "Where's Christopher?"

"With Kora," he replies. He leans back on the roof, lacing his hands behind his head.

"Rest is very important for a Seer," he continues. "Rest is important for all humans. Without rest your mind will stall, keeping you from making the best decisions and adapting to sudden situations and, most crucial for Seers, deciphering between the spiritual realm and the reality of earth."

I sigh. "Please don't preach, Sam. I'm *sooo* not in the mood."

"Why can't you sleep?" he persists.

I release a sardonic cackle. "Why don't *you* tell *me* why I can't sleep?"

"Okay, then." He chuckles, tapping his chin and studying my face. "You are worried about Kora because she's lost her mother and is still mourning Kevin. You are thinking about Brenton because he, like you, is unable to sleep at night, and that he seems distracted and angry.

"To top it all off, you keep replaying the conversation between Christopher, you and I over and over again. You're anxious about Livian and her army of *Tsipors*." He throws a smile my direction. "You're hoping the other Seers are close."

My jaw goes slack. "I have no secrets, do I?"

"None whatsoever," he quips back. "You know what you need to do, right?"

"What?"

"Give all your worries and cares to God, for He cares about you."

"Sam..."

"When you're weak, God will be your strength."

He stands to his bare feet, staring directly into the night. Suddenly, his wings explode from his back, stretching to their fullest. The moon illuminates every single white feather, their appearance shiny and radiant. It's a wondrous sight to behold.

Giving me a sideways glance, he reaches down a hand and demands, "Fly with me."

Stunned I reply, "Do w-what?"

He grins, his blue eyes aglow. "You heard me."

A tremor of anxiety hopscotches through my veins, causing shivers to assault my spine. I've flown in Sam's arms before, but I had been out of it during the flight ... *mostly*.

Truth is, the thought of flying makes me want to hurl, even though I'm probably safer with Sam in the air than by myself on the ground.

I've said it before and I'll say it again – I'm a *wuss*, with a capital *Wimp.*

"No, you're not," Sam says, making a *tsk tsk* noise. Again, he'd been listening in to my thought train.

"Yeah I am," I argue, elevating to a standing position. I throw the blanket through my open window. It lands in a messy heap on the floor.

"C'mon, Clarity," he beckons with his hand, his lips forming a goofy smile. "You know you want to."

Squaring my shoulders with his, I express, "For someone who can read minds, I can't believe you think such a thing."

We stare at each other a moment, his blue eyes glowing along with his bright white teeth. The ray of the moon falls on the roof, wrapping its beauty around us. Shivers skitter up and down my spine as my heart rate nervously accelerates.

"Why are you scared?" he softly asks.

"Because," I answer, my heart still a fluttering mess, "I've never even flown in a plane, Sam. Do you know how weird it is to fly with an angel when I haven't flown on a plane?"

"Color yourself lucky," he jokes – or at least I think he's joking.

I cackle. "I didn't know lucky had a color."

He takes a step closer, his features soaked with unrelenting sincerity. I force myself not to flinch, because the wuss in me is threatening to run to my bedroom window and jump in.

"Lucky has a color," he tells me, his face unreadable.

"What is it?" I wonder.

Gazing down, then back at me he instructs, "Look at your hands."

So I do, and I see that my palms are glowing green.

Green means go, Sam's voice echoes in my head.

I don't have time to lift my gaze, because Sam yanks me into his arms and shoots us straight up into the sky. My heart becomes lodged in my throat, while my stomach lurches to my chest and my brain falls to my toes.

Yes, a mighty weird sensation.

Eventually, my body levels out enough for me to scream, "Why did you do that?!" My eyes are glued shut. Too afraid to open them. Too afraid of what I'll see.

"You were about to chicken out!" he responds, just as he

begins doing flips in the middle of the flight. I scream like an infant, clutching him tightly; he laughs in return.

Gritting my teeth I demand, "Stop *flipping*."

Sam immediately does what I say, and we start flying normally.

"What's wrong?" he wonders.

"I wasn't expecting acrobatics in the air!" I directly spit out, my eyes still shut.

Once again, he laughs, then replies, "Okay, I'm sorry. I'll stop showing off."

We fly in silence, the steady beat of his wings a comfort to my frazzled brain. Daring a glance down, I'm surprised to spot the town square. It's empty of cars and people, since everyone in town is snuggled in their warm beds.

I swallow the bile that's rising up my trachea, shocked that I haven't puked all over Sam. I am also shocked that I'm enjoying the flight. That is, until the tops of the buildings start getting closer and closer, one in particular. I realize that we're about to land, my eyes once again closing. Sam is lowering us – *fast*.

He lands us lightly on the pebble-covered roof, his arm still wrapped around my waist to keep me steady. After making sure I'm not going to fall over, he drops his arm. Upon opening my eyes, I see him taking a couple steps back. His glowing blue orbs are fixated on my face.

I know he's wanting to talk, to get something off his chest. There's an urgency written on his pale countenance. We study each other silently. My heart finally chills out behind my ribcage, making it easier to breathe. Tension has formed around us, a sort of raw knowledge wanting desperately to be freed.

With my patience wearing thin, I say, "Go ahead and tell me what's on your mind."

He smiles. "You've always been so perceptive, you know that?"

Opting not to respond, I cross my arms at my chest, giving him a *get on with it* look. Tapping my foot impatiently on the pebbles that pave the roof, I wait for him to speak.

"Alright," he sighs, his joyful grin fading. "I've got something to tell you, though it may be hard for you to hear."

Nonchalantly, I shrug and point out, "I'm a smart, tough, confident girl. Pretty sure I can handle it."

"I hope so," he whispers, his blue eyes piercing right through me.

"I can," I assure, my foot halting its incessant tap. "So just … talk."

His features turn grim. "There's a battle coming… "

"I already know that," I quickly interpose. "A demon General named Livian and her mutated army are coming – er, well, are *here*."

"This isn't about Livian," he corrects. "It's about *you*."

Puzzled, I remark, "Okay."

"Yes, there's a battle coming with Livian," he iterates, "but there's also a battle you are going to have to fight within yourself." He pauses, his gaze a solid lock on mine.

"A struggle," he continues, "that you will have to fight on your own – a struggle that I can't help you with. Only God will be able to save you."

I shiver, not from the cold, but from his uneasy words. Then I softly ask, "What kind of struggle?"

"That I am not sure of." The sadness in his tone deepens. "All I know is that it's coming, and it's your battle."

"That sure is comforting," I sardonically react, releasing a shaky breath.

"God is your strength and comfort," he states, his eyes looking to the skies. "You have come a long way, though I'm afraid you're not prepared for what's going to happen."

Becoming irritated, I point out, "I'm learning to fight. I'm getting in shape ... what else do I need to be doing?"

"You need a personal relationship with God," he strongly responds, his gaze floating down from the sky. "You need to be exercising your faith."

Sam's answer punches me in the gut. Though my faith is growing day after day, I still struggle with trusting that God is always there. My fear is that I'll put every ounce of hope in Him, and He'll let me completely down.

Yes, this is coming from the girl He saved by literally taking his hand and lifting me from the bottom of a raging river to the surface, saving me from certain death. And yes, tragically, my faith in Him still buckles...

"His word says that in all your ways acknowledge Him, and He will make straight your paths." He takes my hand in his. "His word never changes, and as long as you seek Him, He will never let you down."

Not wanting to be preached at, I appease my Guardian by saying, "I know this, Sam. I know." I wrap my arms around me as a cold breeze hits my bare skin. "It's getting colder by the minute. Maybe you should take me home. I think … I think I can sleep now."

He remains silent, knowing every thought in my head. Circling his arms around me, he gently picks up my body. His warmth closes around my existence, scaring off the chill that had been attacking my bare flesh. I close my eyes as he shoots us up high in the air, my stomach once again rolling.

I try not to dwell on the conversation. Instead, I enjoy Sam's body heat and inhale his lavender scent. His calming concoction slowly takes hold of my senses, every part of me relaxing, becoming as loose as a cooked spaghetti noodle.

Mid-flight, I drift to dreamland, secure in the arms of my Guardian.

Livian

The Guardian lands on the roof of the house, the Seer safe and sound, asleep within his embrace. Careful not to hit her head against the window sill, he steps into her room, now completely out of sight.

Perched high on an oak tree situated in the field beside the *Ra'ah's* home, I'm able to observe the love and care the angel of light possesses for his Charge. It's sweet, it's heartwarming, it's thoughtful...

It's *nauseating*.

Patting Monty's head I say, "After all this time, the sight of such compassion these holy angels show their humans completely disgust me. Humans are puny, cold-hearted, greedy flesh mongrels. They thrive on manipulation, and do whatever they can to get what they want, and you know what?" I stop the petting and narrow my eyes at the Seer's home. "He forgives them. They sin over and over again, and He forgives them over and over again. His shows them grace, and mercy ... *redemption*. They stomp on His heart, but they get chance after chance after chance. Makes no sense to me. None at all."

The skies above rumble, thickening with dense

blackness. My gaze watches the night scenery. A smile tugs at my lips.

"Humans have no respect, show no respect, give no respect," I say, my fangs elongated, touching my bottom lip. "But it's almost over for this little town."

Monty squawks, bobbing his head up and down in excitement.

"Yes, my little bird. This town hasn't seen anything like us. And the best part is, they won't see us coming."

Chapter Six

Clarity

The sun shines upon the lush green field, the scenery bright and peaceful. A light breeze gently strokes the fresh grains, the wheat field rolling like ocean waves. The fresh smell of an early spring buzzes in the air, causing a joy to immerse my soul.

Strolling through the knee-high field, I let my hands caress the tops of the grains tenderly, my feet feeling light and airy. The long white sundress I wear dances easily through the field with graceful movements.

I feel beautiful, I feel light.

I feel renewed and refreshed.

I feel free.

This place, this heavenly place – I never want to leave this place that's teeming with everlasting joy. It's a place of grand nourishment for a soul riddled with turbulence.

A child's voice catches my attention, being carried on the breeze. A voice that's calling my name.

"Clarity...Clarity..."

Turning toward the voice, I change direction from the serene likeness of the field to a path that is dark and desolate. A little girl, around five or six, stands in the middle of a dark field, which is bare of any live vegetation. It looks like every inch of the ground has been torched, leaving it blackened and empty, except for the regrowth of weeds and thistles.

In the distance a tree is on fire, blazing a deep red. Grayish black smoke litters the air, thick and extremely gloomy. This field appears dead, trapped in a deep-set mourning.

My feet come to an abrupt halt as I glance down at the ground where the warm, alive field ends and the dead field begins. There's a dark line separating the two contrasting fields. Gazing behind me at the cheery landscape, a deep depression tries to tunnel its way into my heart. I don't want to leave the sunshiny field full of security and peace. I don't want to cross the line where the light meets the dark...

But I have no choice. A little girl with green eyes and a sing-song voice is beckoning, calling out to me with a fierce neediness. Stepping carefully onto the darkened ground, my body convulses with shivers as a severe change takes place.

Where the other field has clear blue skies and rich grains, this one has rumbling storm clouds that sates the air with impending doom. The wind howls viciously, swishing my hair side-to-side. My dress hugs tightly to my legs, as if trying to stop me from advancing. The burning tree scent is so overwhelming that I'm forced to suppress a cough. The dead ground crunches gratingly beneath my feet, what used to be lively vegetation now a dried-up memory. A biting frost clings to the air, so cold I can feel its icy fingertips poking into the marrow of my bones.

My steps gradually come to a halt as I approach the little girl. She wears a dirty white dress that's stained and infested with holes. A black ponytail falls down her back, and now that I'm closer I find that her green eyes are glowing and vibrant. Though they are eyes way too mature for such a young child.

"Are you lost?" I inquire of the girl. My voice sounds like one big echo, like I'm talking into a hollow passageway.

"Yes," she answers in a small voice. Her eyes peer out at me from a very pale face.

Reaching for her tiny hand, I say, "I'll help you."

"No!" she shouts, swiftly jumping backwards. I jump as well, surprised by her sudden outburst.

"They won't let you," she expresses sadly, her body trembling.

"Who?" I curiously wonder. "Your mommy and daddy?"

"No," she woefully replies. "Mama is dead, and my daddy is gone."

My heart breaks in two. "My parents are gone, too."

"They told me you were coming," she continues in a soft whisper. "They told me that you were going to try and help me, but that you wouldn't be able to because you aren't strong enough."

"Who told you that?"

She darkly responds, "The monsters."

Suddenly, a gust of wind picks up around us, sending white thistle seeds into the air. They swirl and sashay in an upward motion, like a slow, deplorable dance. I feel like I'm inside one of those glass snow globes, though instead of snow gracing the air it's fluffy white dandelion seeds.

"Oh no ... they're here!" she caustically cries, watching the flying thistles.

"Take my hand," I order, reaching out for her once again. "I can help you."

She backs away a few more steps. "No, it's too late — see!"

As she points her tiny finger at the sky with an expression of terror plastered to her face, fear takes hold of all my synapses . The dandelion seeds are no longer white – or seeds. They have transformed into what the little girl mentioned a moment ago.

Monsters.

More commonly known as demons.

Covered with shiny black feathers, these demons are three feet tall with black bat wings. Their faces are human-like, their eyes a vivid yellow. They appear to be a grotesque mix between a human and a crow. Like vultures circling a dead carcass, they circle us in eerily graceful movements.

"You must leave!" urges the little girl.

"Not without you!" I shoot back.

For a third time I try to grab her, but I'm too late. The demons snatch her by the ankles, digging their black claws into her soft flesh. I watch helplessly as they drag her up with them, disappearing inside the dark, growling clouds.

I wake with a start, my hands burning and glowing red.

"Livian," I whisper in a pant. Then, feeling extra exhausted, I fall back to sleep.

***

The first day back to school after Christmas break always stinks, but this one will take the whole cake. Yes, the most horrific first day back in Garlandton High's history.

News of Kora's mom has spread through the school like a vicious disease, the rumor mill entering its maximum capacity. Like a raging wildfire, mouths are moving at the speed of light.

"Wow, how sad."

"What's going to happen to her?"

"I heard she's moving in with Kevin's parents."

"Nah, they moved last month."

"Well, I heard she was kicked out of the trailer park and is now living in that nasty motel on Pine Street."

"Kicked out of a trailer park? Only trash gets kicked out of a trailer."

I've always been amazed at how people take the truth, put their personal spin on it, jumble it together, and spew the exact opposite. Gossip mongers thrive on the less fortunate, the ones who, no matter how hard they try, always get burned.

Take a gander at Kora's life. She's eighteen and has been

through more tragedies than most people do their entire lives. If she can make it after this last bit of trauma, she may have a chance to rise above the garbage that's been dumped on her. Maybe, just maybe, she will have victory in life, which could quite possibly inspire others.

Not only are the Garlandton halls blabbing about Kora, but Janey is also a topic of interest. She'd been pregnant, though lost the baby after being trampled the night of the Thanksgiving dance.

"How embarrassing, right?"

"I heard she'd been planning an abortion, anyways."

"She's such a slut."

"I heard her parents took away her Mercedes and credit cards, and now she has to pay her own way."

Why can't people mind their own business? And what gives them the right to be so judgmental? I know for a fact that the ones doing the most talking are far from perfect. Half the school does drugs and drinks alcohol, which leads to one-night stands with strangers. That one scenario can trigger countless unwanted pregnancies, not to mention certain, um, *diseases.*

The bible verse that talks about the log in the eye and

hypocrites come to mind.

Sam's voice suddenly pops in my head.

How can you think of saying to your friend, "Let me help you get rid of that speck in your eye," when you can't see past the log in your own eye?

Another thing that totally bunches my shorts is the fact that Casey, Janey's boyfriend, isn't a topic in the gossip cesspool. Why is Janey the slut? Casey had been an extremely *willing* participant in the whole devastating situation. Why isn't he being called a slut?

Slamming my locker door gains me a few curious looks as I start making my way to World History. Anger and anxiety has already beaten me to a pulp today. I'm mentally and physically drained, and the day is just starting.

Also, the peculiar dream I'd experienced a few hours ago hasn't helped with my constant perplexity.

Who was the little girl? And are the demons I'd seen dragging her away a preview of Livian's army?

I anticipate that the answer is yes, and that I'll see them soon enough.

Walking into the classroom, I find Brenton, the love of my life, slumped down as far as his body can go in his chair. His clothes are rumpled, and his light brown hair is unkempt. There's evidence of a sleepless night written on his pale face. His cheeks are sunken in and dark, with black circles resting under his eyes. The white long sleeve shirt he wears does nothing but enhance his pallidness.

I'm saddened that he doesn't look up at me when I enter the room. Usually he's on the edge of his seat, eager to see me, donning his signature dimpled grin. Even as I take a seat directly in front of him, he keeps his fatigued eyes on his entwined hands that lay on the table. His features are flooded with saturated depression – so unlike his usual happy-go-lucky attitude.

Slowly, carefully, I place my hands on top of his and ask, "Are you alright?"

Brenton jumps at the sound of my voice, a look of astonishment strolling across his features.

"Clarity?" he says.

"Are you alright?" I question again, closely studying his face.

He grimaces and replies, "Didn't sleep last night."

Before I can ask him why, the bell sounds for class to begin. Mrs. Taylor promptly strolls in, seemingly eager to start her lecture. I turn around to face the front, though my gaze lingers on Kora's empty seat. Where in the world could she be? She'd woken up late but promised she would make it to school.

"She's in the girl's restroom."

With Sam's sudden appearance in front of me, I almost fall out of my chair. I want to scold him for just showing up out of thin air and scaring me to death, but there's a fierce urgency glowing in his blue eyes that causes my heart to tumble in my chest. Even his calming lavender scent does nothing to smooth out my crumbling nerves.

What's going on? I inquire, using my thoughts.

He frowns. "Just go to the girl's room. *Now.*" With that said, he vanishes.

"Mrs. Taylor?" I speak, raising my hand.

"Yes?" she replies, not bothering to look at who is speaking.

"May I go to the restroom?" I quickly question.

"Sure, sure," she tells me, her tone bored.

Flying to my feet, I walk slowly up the aisle, though my body is screaming at me to sprint out of the room. Once in the hall, I run as fast as I can to the girl's restroom. I sling the door open, hurriedly checking each stall until I find Kora. She's in the last one, and it sounds like she's crying – it's reverberating off the cream-colored concrete walls.

Thankfully we're alone. I lean back against the locked stall, my heart breaking to pieces as I listen to her soft cries. Just four days after her mother's death, she somehow has gotten to school, only to lock herself in a nasty bathroom, crying her eyeballs out.

What can I say? What can I do? Her life is falling apart at the seams, and I have no clue on how to sew the pieces back together. Not one clue.

"Kora, I'm here if you need me," I let her know. I wait for a response, but all I get back is more sobbing and a clinking sound, like something made of metal has dropped to the floor.

Turning around, touching my forehead and hands on the door, I plead, "Kora, please talk to me."

This time I'm hit with a response, but it's not the one I

was expecting. The middle of my hands heat up, alerting that something is up.

Becoming curious, I try peering through the cracks of the door, but I see nothing. Dropping to my hands and knees, pushing the thought of how nasty and disgusting the floor is right out of my mind, I peek under the door ... and freeze. Concerned dread percolates inside my veins, my hands big scorches of fire.

One single razor blade lies in my line of vision, along with blood droplets. The blood appears vibrant against the harsh yellow tile.

Bounding to my feet, I bang on the door and shout, "Kora, open the door!"

Tears burn red hot stripes down my cheeks as I throw myself against the locked stall door. Then, with a strength I never knew existed in my body, I pull the door open, breaking the lock and almost ripping it off the hinges.

How in the world...?

Nope. Not dwelling on what I'd just done. Or how.

When I see Kora, a hand flies to my mouth to stifle the building scream in my lungs. I can't believe what I'm seeing.

This can't be happening. It's not happening...

Kora has her long sleeves pushed way up, exposing cuts and gashes running down her petite arms, open and bloody. Sitting on the toilet, lid closed, I observe as she rocks back and forth with her chin resting atop her knees. Tears are smeared on her flushed face, and taking in her dilated eyes I know she's unaware of her surroundings – that she doesn't realize what she's done.

Kora has locked her mind behind a door of wicked illusion, somewhere dark with no light at all.

Breaking out of my stunned reverie, I hug Kora to my chest and cry, "Kora!" I'm not bothered by her blood staining my clothes, or her tears drenching my shoulder.

"Oh, Kora, what have you done?"

Chapter Seven

Kora

Waves crash onto the sandy beach, leaving behind white foam as it recedes. A slight breeze is in the air, ruffling my short hair. I'm wearing a sundress, which is extremely odd. I never wear dresses.

Squinting up at the blue sky, I watch as white fluffy clouds amble by. The warmth of the sun tenderly caresses my flesh with a calm sedation. I listen as wave upon wave crashes against the sand. A wonderful, relaxing sound.

My own private island. Ah, finally I have peace.

Wait a minute ... how did I get here?

"You created it," a soft, lyrical voice speaks.

My gaze drops from the sky and falls onto the most beautiful woman I've ever seen. She's walking, almost floating, toward me. Her hair is as white as the clouds, and her white dress sways with the wind. As she sits beside me, a calm flows over my body.

"What do you mean I created it?" I wonder, peering into her light blue eyes. They are so light the blue is almost non-existent.

She smiles, flipping her long white hair over her shoulder. "In your mind. You've been through so many horrific things, and now you are searching for help to get through them. You crave stability and peace, so your mind made up this place. And I have to say, you've done a marvelous job."

My lips start to curve upward, then I look down at my arms. They're cut and bleeding, the blood staining the white sand.

"I've ... I've done something terrible," I somberly say, my eyes staring at the affliction carved on my arms.

She lifts my chin with her finger. "Don't worry, dear. I'll take care of it." Then, rubbing my arms with her hands, a burn pours over my skin, so hot I almost scream.

Before I holler, she says, "There. All done."

My eyes widen as I take in my arms – my cut-free, non-bloody arms. No more scars, no more...

Studying her, feeling confused and discombobulated, I inquire, "What, how ... who are you?"

She grins. "Your savior."

Clarity

Being in the sterile confinements of the hospital brings back all the atrocious memories of that horrible November night. The doleful surroundings, the steady beeping of machines, mediocre voices sounding over the intercom, the gross medicine odor ... *ugh*.

The only comfort I can muster is the sad fact that it's not me hooked up to those obnoxious machines, lying in that uncomfortable bed, trapped in the out-of-date hospital room.

Rather, I'm stuck in a waiting room, flipping through antique magazines, listening to the beeping machines and sad voices, and inhaling the over-sterile environment. Plus I'm stressing over my best friend, who went mental at school and decided to mutilate her body with a razor blade.

I know Sam is around, and I want so badly to talk to him, but I have a constant human by my side.

A.C. has turned into a fanatical mess, her eyes watching me like a hawk, as if I'd been the one to butcher my flesh. At this very moment she's pacing the floor, wringing her hands, leaving me with a perpetual reminder of what has occurred. Her mousy brown hair is flipped up in a clip, and the sweats she wears are mix-matched.

Unable to stand it any longer, I tell her, "A.C., *please* calm down. Watching you pace manically back and forth is totally grinding my nerves!"

"I'm sorry, Clarity," she apologizes, her pacing coming to a halt. "I'm just worried. Why in the world would Kora damage her body that way?"

"Maybe because she's damaged?" I answer dryly, rolling my eyes. "She's still not over Kevin, and with her mom..." I trail off, not bothering to finish the thought – A.C. is not stupid. She's educated on the situation.

"I just don't get it." She plops down in the seat next to mine, staring at the wall. Jerking her head my direction she asks, "Did you know that she was a cutter?"

That question punches me square in the chin. If I wasn't already sitting down, those words would have knocked me off my feet. Catching Kora cutting herself has made me realize, again, that I've been a crappy friend.

"No, I didn't," I reply, avoiding her stare. "But I

should've known."

"Clarity, don't think for one minute that – "

Before she finishes her point, Kora's doctor strolls into the waiting room. A.C. launches from the seat, me following right behind.

"Dr. Reinhardt, how is she?" she queries nervously, once again wringing her hands.

"She's resting now," says Dr. Reinhardt. His glasses slide down the bridge of his nose, but it doesn't seem to faze him.

I quietly study him a moment, disbelieving that he's a doctor. At the most he's thirty, wearing dirty sneakers with his blonde hair tied in a loose ponytail. His appearance doesn't fit your typical "doctor" look, but I guess as long as he paid attention in medical school, there's nothing to worry about.

"We've given her a sedative," he continues, "and patched up her wounds. She'll need to stay a couple of days under strict observation. I also recommend that she see a therapist twice a week, just until we're positive she's not a danger to herself."

"How long do you think she's been doing this?" A.C. questions.

He blows out a breath. "Well, not sure exactly, but by the scars I'd say at least five years."

"What?" I exclaim loudly, floored to the ultimate limit. My stomach ties itself into a distressing knot. Looking to him I wonder, "How could I have not known?"

"Don't feel bad," he says, placing a hand lightly on my shoulder. "She's a classic case of a closet cutter; being a good actor goes along with it, masking emotions and scars. Most of the scars are on her stomach, back, thighs – places that can be hidden. She has no old scarring on her arms. Of course now she'll have many. But I tell you, the scars on her body cannot compare to the emotional scars she carries."

Perplexed by his words, I inquire, "What do you mean by that?"

He drops his hand from my shoulder and answers, "Her emotions play a big part in her cutting. Relationships, peer pressure, feelings … let's face it, she's been put through the ringer the past couple of months."

I hate it, but everything he's saying makes perfect sense. In all the years I've known Kora, she's never undressed in front of me. If she ever changes clothes, she always makes sure she's behind a closed door. When swimming she wears shorts and a tank top, claiming it's more comfortable than bathing suits.

Now, with the truth slapping me in the face, I realize that she'd been suffering then, too. I'd never caught on to her misery. Yet another example of how lousy a friend I've been.

Looking to A.C., then Dr. Reinhardt, I ask, "Can I see her?"

Sam

Christopher and I stand over Kora Dodd's unconscious body. White bandages cover her arms, and a tube sticks out of her hand, sending a calming medicine through her veins. Peering up at her Guardian, the anguish is easily read on his countenance. There's also another feature written on his face...

Anger.

"Livian did this to her," he scowls, his eyes aglow with solid fury. "She made Kora damage herself."

"Christopher," I say calmly, "Livian didn't physically pick up the razor and slash her flesh. She simply put the thought in Kora's head. Kora chose to damage her flesh."

"But if the thought wasn't put there in the first place, this wouldn't have happened. She wouldn't be laying here in this horrible place."

I shake my head. "The enemy wants to destroy the human race – you know that. He wants to destroy their souls, as well. He'll use any method he can to bring God's greatest creations pain and torment. This isn't the first time Kora has cut herself. Livian found a crack in Kora's heart, and went on from there."

"We can't let Livian win," seethes Christopher, his eyes closing. "She can't win."

Placing a hand on his shoulder I say, "Start praying now, friend. Start praying now."

Clarity

I stayed by Kora's side most of the afternoon, and would have stayed longer if A.C. had not ordered me to work my shift at Baker's Supermarket. She had stated that following a traumatic experience life must go on, and *blah blah blah*.

Yes, life goes on, though sometimes not like you plan.

At this very second my own life is a big chaotic pile of muck. I say this because as I'm walking into work, Janey is walking out, her face flushed like she's been crying.

"Hey, what's up?" I ask, gently taking hold of her arm. "You're on the schedule tonight, right?"

"Not anymore," she counters quickly. She shrugs her shoulders, her strawberry blonde hair falling in her face. "I quit."

Shocked, dropping her arm, I react with, "You gotta be kidding me!"

"Nope. Just hung up my yellow apron." She sighs deplorably, swinging her hair out of her face. "My days of cashiering are over."

We both jump as banging sounds ring out from the stockroom, though Janey doesn't seem as startled as me. Casey, apparently, is attempting to make as much noise as possible, obviously upset about her quitting.

"Oh, I get it," I say smugly, putting the pieces together. "You guys are in the middle of a lover's quarrel and you're taking a few days off. Then the two of you will kiss and make up." Smirking, I can't help but think how childish they are being, though Janey's stone-cold expression shouts otherwise.

"No," she opines, her lips in a straight line and eyes narrowed. "Not this time. He's shown me his true colors ... I deserve better than Casey Anderson."

"Wow," I express with true stupor. "What happened, Janey?"

Pain and sadness stretches across her face.

"Did I tell you how Casey reacted when I told him I was ... *pregnant*?" She whispers the last word, her gaze shifting across the store.

I shake my head, replying, "No, I just assumed you didn't want to talk about it."

"You assumed right," she confirms, pushing a wayward strand of hair behind her ear. "After I told him about the baby, he completely freaked, claiming that it couldn't be his. He insinuated that I'd been sleeping around. Then when I lost the baby, he told me he loved me, acting as if nothing had happened, that everything was okay. Like he'd never broken my heart." She pauses, wiping a tear off her cheek. "I see now that what Casey and I had was purely physical. Nothing more."

"You don't really believe that, do you?"

"Yes, Clarity, I do."

"But Janey," I protest swiftly, "I know what Casey said and did was insensitive, but he was most likely shocked. You guys can work it out, I know y'all can."

"Put yourself in my shoes for half a second!" she viciously bursts out. "What if Brenton got you pregnant and denied the baby? How would you feel?"

She pushes on. "I don't care if he was shocked, because so was I. It doesn't change the fact that he was going to dump me because I was pregnant."

I stare at her, open-mouthed and speechless. The thought of being in her shoes, alone and pregnant, causes my stomach to churn. Also, she had miscarried. In all honesty, I don't know what I'd do or how I would feel.

"You're right," I admit, my head nodding. "Casey shouldn't have treated you that way. It's just so weird – you guys have been together forever. Y'all seemed so *happy*."

Janey smiles wearily, her anger quickly melting away. "At one time we were happy, but now it's time for us to move on."

I remain quiet, not having any words to speak – not having the right words to say. Then she brings up another subject.

"How's Kora?" she suddenly asks.

I grimace as an image of Kora lying in the hospital bed flashes in my mind.

"She's going to be fine," I respond. "They want her to stay in the hospital a few days for observation."

"I'll go see her."

"Good, she needs her friends right now." I pause, then softly say, "Janey, I'm sorry about the baby."

Smiling sadly, she gives me a quick hug. At that moment I get a whiff of peaches. For a second I think it's Janey's perfume, but when I spot an angel standing behind her, I know exactly where the smell is coming from.

This angel is petite with auburn-colored hair, blue eyes, and, of course, totally gorgeous. The length of her purple dress is so long it hides her feet. She gifts me with a radiant smile, then disappears.

Janey walks out the doors and climbs into her Mercedes.

Guess all the gossip mongers were wrong about Janey's parents taking her ride away.

In a weird sort of way, Casey and Janey's break up is like a divorce. A slow, painful death taking place in front of everyone. Casey's reaction to the whole mess was all kinds of wrong, though I am not surprised. He's a kid himself, and truthfully, I can't see him as a father. Immaturity holds him in a tight, unrelenting embrace – he has a lot of growing up to do.

The rest of the week goes by in a complete blur, with my reality and everyone in it trapped in a dreary, endless fog. Brenton and I continue all the motions of a normal couple, holding hands and talking about unsubstantial topics. Casey and Janey ignore one another, keeping out of each others paths. As the weekend approaches, Kora comes home, sleeping most of the time.

When Monday arrives, I can't help but notice the whole school is zombified. Something dull and dark clings to the air. A heavy feeling of doom appears to creep all over the walls and throughout the school. No one speaks of parties, dates, or ballgames. Even the most outgoing students seem sluggish and unresponsive, like all the light has been sucked out of their lives, leaving them shells full of darkness.

Something evil is near. I can feel it. And when Garlandton High welcomes three new students to its clan, my suspicions are confirmed.

Wickedness has arrived, and Sam is right.

I'm not fully prepared for this battle.

Chapter Eight

Kora

I lay back in the sand with my hands behind my head. I'm back at the peaceful place I'd created in my mind, one where no sadness, loss, or despair shrouds my reality.

As before, the sky is blue and cloudless, the sun a big orange ball hanging in the air. Here, on this private island in my head, the weather is perfect. Not too hot, not too cold – just right. The waves crash over and over again onto the white sand, the breeze carrying a salty scent.

I know this place isn't real. I'm dreaming. It's all in my head, a place my subconscious created for me to escape my plagued existence. I only wish I didn't have to wake up.

"Hello, my child."

Startled, I quickly rise to a seated position. The beautiful woman with long white hair is back in all her wondrous glory. I still don't know her name, but when she had informed me she was my savior, I believed her. I do believe her. Even without knowing her name, I trust her with all my heart.

"When did you get here?" I curiously ask, eyeing her with strict interest.

She laughs softly. "Oh, Kora, I'm always with you. Why, I never leave your side!"

Her words warm my heart, pleasing my spirit. A bright aura surrounds her body, causing her to appear like an angel bathed in light. Maybe she is an angel, sent from above...

"I wish I could stay here forever," I admit, baring my soul.

"And why is that, my child?" she wonders.

"Because there's no pain or sorrow here. Only happiness and unending peace."

Taking the crook of her finger, she lifts my chin and says, "Look at me, my child."

Being obedient, I gaze into her eyes, which are different today. There's no blue at all in them. They're eerily white, and I find myself thinking that this isn't normal. This whole place isn't normal. But when the next words leave her mouth, any nagging thoughts I may *have or fears I may suffer instantly delete from my mind.*

She says, "Tomorrow, when you wake, you will go to school. You will feel renewed and refreshed – like a whole new person." She pauses, then sweetly smiles and adds, "Tomorrow a gift will await you at school. A very pleasing gift. Just what you are searching for."

"What kind of gift?" I inquire, totally entranced by her beautiful countenance.

Again, she smiles. "Oh, you'll know when you see it. Or better yet, who you see."

Clarity

Three new students have enrolled at Garlandton High and are starting today. At least that's the word bouncing off the halls of the school this morning.

Everyone appears infatuated with the newcomers, as if they're gods or something. Clusters of students brim over with excited, delusional talk. When I walk past a group of guys, I hear a pig-headed boy exclaim "Dude, the new girl is hot!", while a couple of air-headed girls fan themselves, saying the new guys are "totally fine".

Ugh. Teenagers. Can't stand them.

Even the teachers, acting extremely unprofessional, speak amongst themselves in front of the office, right where the new students are becoming acquainted with the principal.

Why is everyone so enamored by three new students? It's not like Brad Pitt is enrolling in our school.

Still, my curiosity is peaked, and before I know it I'm standing in front of the office window. I peer through the blinds, surprised to find that I'm eager to get a good look at Garlandton's newest members.

My first impression of them is that they appear to be rich, wearing preppy designer labels. From my vantage point, I discover that they all have blonde hair, with severely pale skin.

The two boys wear their hair in similar styles, both messy and wild. They're dressed alike, too, with khaki pants and blue collared shirts, which are untucked. Though they are dressed alike, their statures are opposite. Where one is tall and skinny, the other is short and stocky.

The girl's hair is straight and long, flowing way past her shoulders. She's of average height, wearing a skirt that is way too short for school, but neither the principal nor the secretary seem to notice or care. To me she looks a little trashy, though in a wealthy sort of way.

Glancing down at my blue V-neck sweater over black leggings, I instantly feel boring and out-of-date compared to the new girl.

Wait a minute … why am I worrying over my wardrobe? I've never cared before. Shaking my head, upset at myself for caring what other people think, I study the three new students who are still busy in the office.

A pinch of hope sprinkles upon my heart, a part of my brain conjuring up the thought that maybe these are the Seers I've been waiting for. Maybe they're Seers posing as students to battle the demon infestation in our town.

Oh, man, that would *rock*!

My hope is dismally crushed when the shorter of the two boys reaches out for his schedule, which in turn gives me a view of his open palm. No Seer mark rests there, though another mark sits right below his wrist. My hands start to burn and tingle when I grab sight of the round black mark seared on his flesh. Lifting my palms to my face, my breath hitches in my throat at their red glow.

Suddenly all surroundings fade, along with all sounds, disappearing until it's just me and the new students, who are clearly not Seers. Before I can contemplate why my alarms have been set off, all three of them raise their heads and sniff the air. I watch as their bodies are consumed with spasms. My heart all but stops when they simultaneously turn their heads my direction. A gasp breaks loose from my mouth as I stumble backwards, shocked when I see their eyes are completely white.

"Hey, watch it!" a girl bellows gratingly.

Reality comes crashing down like a ton of bricks, pounding me from head to toe. Realizing I've just bumped someone's shoulder, I quickly become contrite.

"S-Sorry," I stutter, attempting to find my balance.

My visions starts to blur, leaving me wholly disoriented. The fast *thump-thump* of my heartbeat obsessively pounds in my throat, while my stomach ricks itself into a thousand knots. The only sane solution is to escape from school, the strict need to run forcing its way through my veins. Got to get out, get away from this madness. So I begin retreating, pushing through the masses, pushing through the exit doors and...

Fall right into Sam's arms.

Hugging me tightly to him, Sam extends his wings and shoots us upward. With the sudden movement, I clench my eyes shut, burying my face in his chest. We land on the school's roof, though he keeps my body in his safe embrace. I take this time to release all my emotions, my fears, my confusions, anxieties – all of these feelings burst forth in his strong, comforting arms.

Sobbing, shaking like a dried-out leaf, I start to worry that someone might have noticed my disappearing act.

"No one saw," he murmurs in my ear, listening to my thoughts. "No one knows we're up here, so please calm down."

It takes a full minute for Sam's calming confection of lavender and solace to settle my frayed nerves. Behind my closed eyelids, I still see the new student's white eyes peering at me, glaring with their robotic expressions.

Eventually, Sam frees me from his arms. I open my eyes. Sam is taking a couple of steps back, his blazing blues regarding me with love and concern. Thunder rumbles above, the air scented with rain. A storm is brewing … or maybe it's already here. Not sure of anything anymore.

Regaining my will to speak, I stammer out, "D-Demons. There are demons enrolling at my school."

He frowns. "No, not demons. *Humans*."

"Then why did my hands burn and glow red – " I come up short as comprehension pummels me over.

"They're possessed," I say after a few silent ticks.

He nods.

"They're human pawns, Livian's puppets, and she's in control of them."

He nods again.

I hesitate before asking, "Are they willing participants?"

"They are runaways," he replies, his gaze searching the dark rumbling clouds above. "They got trapped within Livian's deception when they were at their most vulnerable. What some would say wrong place, wrong time."

His response is perplexing, prompting me to ask, "What does that mean?"

He sucks in a breath, then responds, "It means they had no idea what was in store for them when Livian came into their lives. They come from broken homes, unloved by the people who *should* love them. Most likely Livian welcomed them using an illusion of love, giving them the comfort and peace that had been absent from their lives. Though with Livian she doesn't love or care for them. She's using them for her own personal gain, but they can't see that. They can't see through the deception. They're blinded by the enemy, their minds have been erased from reality. They see her as their beautiful redeemer, unable to see her true self."

"So, they're brainwashed?"

"You can say that."

"Give me a straight answer, Sam, please!" I frustratingly express. "Have they completely lost themselves or not?"

"No," he replies, "but they are close. They can still be saved."

"How?"

His serious expression deepens. "You've got to help them."

My mouth drops open. "What?! You mean along with all the junk going down in my life, I've got to help – "

The bell sounds off, interrupting my immature rant and signaling that class will start in three minutes. Though there's no way I can go to class today.

"You're going to class today," proclaims Sam, lifting me in his arms. "You can't run away from your problems."

"Wait!" I try protesting. "We're not done – "

"For now we are," he strongly dictates, his blue eyes glaring. His lavender-spiked breath grazes my face. "And just a warning – things are about to get a little *weird*."

I snort, his statement extremely amusing. Things are about to get weird. Yeah, like they're not already.

He grins at my thoughts – I really have no secrets.

A cyclonic wind revolves around us, the sound almost deafening. Then we're moving in the air, so fast my stomach drops and my head spins. One minute I'm on the roof with Sam, the next minute I'm standing in front of the school's entrance. Sam, not surprisingly, has vanished. People scurry past, rushing to class so as not to be tardy.

Reluctantly pushing through the doors I'd just escaped from minutes before, I walk in a muddled daze to World History. That's when it hits me that I haven't seen Brenton, Kora, or any of my friends this morning. Worry hums in my chest at the thought.

Once I arrive to class, my worries dissolve. Both Kora

and Brenton are sitting in their seats. When Brenton spots me, a smile lights up his face.

"Hey there!" he greets as I sit down. "Where have you been? I waited for you at your locker, but you never showed." The brown jacket he wears enhances his muddy brown eyes, which are vibrant and awake today.

"She's been a little standoffish lately," Kora states with a grin. "By the way, did you know she has a punching bag in her bedroom?"

I grin back at my friend, happy that she's acting like her jovial self. She hasn't been the same since losing Kevin and her mom, which lead her to do unspeakable things to her body. Not to mention bringing things out of the darkness she'd had hidden for so long. Thankfully the anti-depressant the doctor prescribed is working wonders.

With Kora on this medicine, she's now taking better care of her outward appearance. Like today she's wearing a red long-sleeved peasant dress with black knee-high boots. Her hair is no longer that bright red color, but back to black, which is her natural shade.

All in all, I can see a positive change in Kora, and for that I'm truly grateful. Also knowing that her angel is by her side helps to release some of my wrought-up tension.

For a second I think maybe Sam was wrong in saying things were about to become weird ... well, weirder than usual. Brenton is back to normal, Kora's on the road to recovery – the pattern of our young lives is getting back on the right track.

Of course, such as life, changes happen in the blink of an eye. As the bell rings for class to start, my hopes for less weirdness are diced to bits. Everyone – and everything – changes as one of the new students walk through the doors of World History.

Yep, what happens next gives new meaning to the word *weird*.

Chapter Nine

Livian

The clouds rumble in, thick and black, at my arrival. There is no light shining down on this section of earth. The sun is blotted out by Hell's dark iniquity.

"Yes, the time is now!" I robustly declare. Outstretching my arms, my gaze lifted high, I add, "My children, do what you do best!"

With that stated, the sky rips open and out pours my army.

"Yes, yes, yes!" I cackle loudly, watching as my *Tsipor* minions infiltrate the school building. Monty, my beloved sidekick, makes a grunting sound. Instantly understanding that noise, I say, "Go ahead, Monty. Join the fun." The *Tsipor* flies off my shoulder and into the brick building.

Pleased with myself, I cross my arms at my chest and

smile. The plan is going great, right on time. The Seer, along with every soul at Garlandton High, doesn't stand a chance.

"You think you can win, don't you?"

Immediately, my reflexes kick in, interrupting my gleeful moment. My arms fall to my sides as my body drops down to a crouch. I hiss at the blonde angel that stands just a few feet away; an angel I've known my entire existence.

Gabriel, one of the archangels. One of God's favorites.

"What are you doing here?" I snap angrily, my fangs elongating. To my displeasure, he laughs.

"You think The Light is just going to let you in without a fight?" he inquires, making an annoying *tsk tsk* sound. "Every soul in that building has a Guardian, and all are in attendance today."

"You can't interfere, Gabriel," I snarl, my tongue flicking out. "None of you can."

"You are right, demon," he agrees, surprising me. "We cannot interfere when a human's freewill is in play. Not yet, anyway."

Relaxing, I straighten up, resting my hands on my hips.

"So why even try? Why even show up? Why waste your time on these pathetic humans who will most likely choose darkness? It's inevitable, and you know it."

The jovial grin he had moments ago has vanished, his glowing blue eyes narrowing.

"The only *inevitable* around here is your future," he scowls. Taking a few steps closer, towering over me, he says, "There's no redemption for you or the rest who rebelled against The Father."

Fury burns from deep inside, but I calm it down. Though the archangel is correct in his thinking, I should not allow it to hinder my extremely important mission. Yes, I already know my kind has a short period of time to devastate the human race, but one thing is certain.

If we're all going to be thrown in the lake of fire for eternity, if there is no redemption in store for us, we will make sure millions of God's greatest creations follow directly behind.

Clarity

The temperature warms tremendously as the new boy walks through the doors of the classroom. A familiar heat tingles in the palms of my hands. I struggle to calm my fluttering heart. Different fragrances clog the air as angels materialize around the room. Not just a couple, but twenty. At the least.

Everyone's Guardian has appeared, all standing next to their Charges.

My heart is beating so loud and so hard, I'm worried people can hear it.

With all the celestial beings, invisible to all but me, it takes all I've got to not fly off the handle. The angel's eyes glow that heavenly blue, their gazes strictly on the new guy. As I survey the room, my eyes catch sight of a few angels I've met before.

Tiny Mary Beth stands still and pristine at Daria's side, while Christopher stays close to Kora, crouched in a defensive stance. He reminds me of a football linebacker, hunched over and waiting to move in for the kill.

All the kids in the room are staring at the new guy in amazement, even Brenton. A brown-headed angel is posed next to him. Her face is emotionless, her focus also fixated on Livian's pawn.

Sam walks in with a female angel, a new Guardian. She looks Spanish, with black hair, dark skin, and naturally beautiful. Just like Sam – well, actually like every angel in the room – she's wearing dark jeans and a black t-shirt.

Mentally I ask Sam, *Who is the new angel and why is she here?*

Her name is Rebecca and she's here because of him, he answers, without a glance my way.

Suddenly another mixture of smells sate the air. I have to clamp down the shriek itching to break free from my body. Demons start to pop up all over the room, bringing with them their signature sewage scent. Maybe ten or fifteen of them.

Another scream rocks my entire system as I catch sight of these monstrosities. Thankfully, I find the strength to hold it in and compose myself.

The demons are like the ones from the dream, having stubby arms and legs, black wings, yellow eyes, and covered in black fur. They hiss at the Guardians, but make no move to attack. Their sharp claws dig into the tile ceiling, their heads turned almost completely around, staring at every being in the room. Thick saliva drips from their long yellow fangs.

A smell of rot and decay mixed with perfume consumes the air. I fight the urge to gag. They speak in low tones, conversing in a language I don't understand.

I know what kind of demons they are – *Tsipors* – Livian's favorite.

Focusing my attention on the human beings in the room, I marvel at how everyone is completely bewitched, their eyes wide and mouths hanging open. Even Mrs. Taylor is taken back by the new arrival, though I'm the only one who sees the *other* arrivals. I try not to make eye contact with the *Tsipors*, but unfortunately one of them catches my attention. It giggles, waving its tiny hand and wiggling its clawed fingers. Quickly, I avert my gaze and battle to settle the slamming beat of my heart.

I guess this was what Sam meant by things becoming weird.

A few uneasy seconds of enraptured staring rolls by before Mrs. Taylor breaks free from the trance.

"C-Class," she stammers, then clears her throat. "It appears that we have a new student. Everyone say hello to

David White."

My body jerks when the entire class utters in unison, "Hello, David White."

Murmurs ripple the air, not from the students, but from the angels talking amongst themselves, which intermingles with the demon's weird foreign tongue. My head pounds with the chatter. Try as I might I can't make out what is being said, and Mrs. Taylor continuing her dazed expression doesn't help at all.

"We have one empty seat," acknowledges Mrs. Taylor, pointing to the seat next to Brenton, located behind Kora.

David smiles, and all the girls in class gasp, like he's Johnny Depp or someone equally as handsome. Sure, this David guy is cute, and sure he has a contagious smile, but jeez! He's only a guy!

A guy who is possessed, Clarity.

Sam's voice leaps around the inside of my head like a bouncy ball. I look up to find him staring at me, nodding.

Why is everybody acting so stupid? And why am I not affected?

It's true. I am not spellbound like the others. While they

are slobbering over David as if he's a juicy piece of meat, I'm not at all impressed.

I will explain later, Sam responds. *For now, act normal.*

I scoff out loud, momentarily forgetting about the classroom full of people. Luckily no one takes notice. They are too entranced with this David dude.

All eyes, human, angel, and demon alike, watch as he walks to his seat, which happens to be Kevin's old seat. I half expect someone to say something in honor of Kevin, but no one speaks up.

A chill flows through my body as David casually saunters to his seat. As he comes closer, I get a good look at the black circular mark under his wrist. From what I can tell it's a small black circle, nothing more, nothing less. *Definitely* not a Seer mark.

Nausea hits me as I observe his making eye contact with Kora, who is wearing a captivated expression on her face. When his finger lightly grazes her hand, her body jolts like she'd been struck by lightning.

Christopher tenses, his arm muscles tightening as he stands in front of David. A strong intensity slides down his features, firm and unwavering. A terrifying view for David ... if he could see the hulking celestial being staring him down.

Rebecca, David's Guardian, follows a few steps behind, her face expressionless. A demon appears on his shoulder, hissing at her. She says nothing – I guess she doesn't have to. The narrowing of her eyes with their glowing edge says it all.

David nods at Brenton as he glides into the seat. Then, noticing that I'm staring at him, his dark eyes regard me with amusement. I quickly turn away, a sick feeling growing within my stomach. Fear begins to crawl up and down my spine like cold, prickly fingers, as ice fills my veins. Wrapping my arms around myself, I struggle to keep my teeth from chattering. My only warm spots are the palms of my hands, which are glowing red.

Though my gaze is directed to the front of the class, I can feel David's eyes burning holes in the back of my skull. I'm nervous, knowing of the possessed human behind me, along with despicable monsters surrounding the room. A wet blanket of dread, with a hint of fear, fastens around me, keeping me cold and miserable. What makes me less anxious are the twenty or so angels watching over us closely.

Don't let fear overtake you, Clarity. Remember what God's

word says – This is my command – be strong and courageous! Do not be afraid or discouraged. For the Lord your God is with you wherever you go.

Sam stands at the front of the room, his back casually leaned against the blackboard. His eyes are right on top of me.

I glare at him. *But I am afraid, Sam.*

His expression softens. *Please don't be afraid. Look around you! You are not alone.*

Releasing a breath I hadn't realized I'd been holding, I give him a nod of confirmation. I know I'm not alone, so why am I so fearful?

Pray and hold on tight, Sam says, eyes narrowed. *It's going to be one bumpy ride.*

Kora

There's something about the new boy, David. Something different and familiar at the same time. He reminds me of ...

Kevin.

I watch him from a distance. He's surrounded by girls acting all giggly and stupid. The hallway is jammed pack, so I stand on my tiptoes to get a better look. He pays the girls no mind as he digs in his locker. When he's done, he shuts his locker and pushes passed them as if they're not there.

Wait a minute. He can't remind me of Kevin. They're polar opposites in looks and attitude. Where Kevin had been tanned, muscular, and athletic, David is tall, skinny, and pale. Where Kevin had dark hair, David has blonde hair. Where Kevin had blue/green eyes, David has dark, almost black eyes.

As for attitude, Kevin had been a pleasant, easy-going person who never met a stranger. David has an arrogant, almost hostile aura around him, so really...

They're nothing alike.

So why am I drawn to him so strongly?

He will give you the love you crave so badly.

That voice. Inside my head. The voice of the lady in my dreams.

My savior.

"Is he the gift you spoke of?" I ask in a whisper, careful

not to draw attention to myself.

Yes, my child. You are no longer alone in reality.

A sheer bliss surges through my veins at her words. At the end of the hall I find David, and start seeing him in a new light.

My savior has sent my rescuer.

Chapter Ten

Clarity

The school day goes by at a snail's pace, leaving me trapped watching my friends drool and act foolish over the new students. I never thought the day would end.

At lunch Brenton had made fast friends with Darren, the shorter kid. David's brother ... well, a possessed kind of brother, I suppose.

Brenton found out that they shared the same passion for cars and mechanics. They spent the entire lunch period discussing transmissions. For the first time in months Brenton totally ignored me, as if I wasn't sitting right next to him.

Darren's angel, a little blonde boy named Zachary, had stood directly behind him, making faces at the grotesque *Tsipor* demon perched on his shoulder. The demon whispered in Darren's ear the whole conversation. It appeared that Darren hadn't heard its whispers. I'm sure talking about brakes and rotors was much better than the poison pouring from the demon's black lips.

The other brother, David, seemed to be fitting in quite well, mostly with the ladies. Throughout the day girls had him surrounded, though he paid them no attention. His flippant attitude and total disregard didn't sway the female population. His good looks were enough for them, I guess.

Kora had been one of the girls hanging around David, though she'd remained on the outside of the circle. I knew right then and there that I would have to keep an eye on her. With the recent events in her life, the last thing she needs is a possessed boyfriend.

The truth is, nobody needs to hook up with these possessed pawns. If people could only see the ugly half crow, half human demons balanced on their shoulders, they most definitely would find them less appealing. The black-feathered, long-fanged, yellow-eyed monsters are enough to make anyone want to empty their stomachs.

I have yet to meet David and Darren's sister, but from the gossip I'd been able to gather throughout the day, her name is Danielle. She likes to cheer and, per a few jocks, she appears to be quite, um, *trampy*.

Usually I'm a tired wreck after school, but now, as I drive to work, I find myself eager to be at the dinky supermarket. It has been a weird day, seeing angels and demons all over the school and on a few people. I'm ready for a few hours of normalcy. All the tedious tasks I perform at Baker's should keep the weirdness at bay a few hours.

Today I'm prepared to do a workload meant for two people, since Janey no longer works alongside me. I've done it before, so it's no big deal. Used to it, really.

My shift starts out slow, so I busy myself with sweeping the floors. When Mr. Baker taps my shoulder, I get another shock, which erases the normality I'd been so craving.

"Miss Miller, I have found Janey's replacement."

Swinging around to face him, I exclaim, "Oh great! Who is – "

The words I'm about to speak becomes one big lump in my throat. The broom slides through my fingers, clanging loudly when it hits the floor. As I come face to face with my new co-worker, I'm floored. Sufficiently and completely bowled over.

Danielle, the new girl, is already decked out in the gross

yellow smock Mr. Baker forces his employees to wear. She looks at me doltishly, with her long blonde hair pulled back and lips a glossy pink. Bending over, she picks up the broom and hands it to me.

"Here you go," she says, her voice quiet and soft. "Sorry to startle you."

A shiver rakes down my back when the black circle below her wrist comes into view, the same mark as her "brothers". My heart leaps in my chest as a demon appears on her shoulder, then vanishes just as fast.

Great. Great. *Great*. Not only will I be forced to work with one of Livian's pawns, but it looks as if Baker's will have its own *Tsipor* demon infestation. There's no place of normalcy left in this town.

I can't catch a break!

While those thoughts ring around my mind at a vigorous pace, the smell of fresh baked cookies fill the air. A female angel, wearing normal angel garb of jeans and t-shirt, appears next to Danielle. She's redheaded, a few inches shorter than I, and has a pout painted on her lips.

"I'm Lara," she greets tonelessly, her arms crossed at her

chest. "I'm Danielle's Guardian. Yes, I know who you are, and yes, she's in a heap of trouble."

Sam's lavender scent makes its appearance as he materializes beside her.

"Lara," he says, his tone cool, "let's go have a chat, just you and I." And with that they vanish, taking their scents with them.

I stand there, mouth agape, staring at the spot Lara and Sam had just stood. I can't believe the attitude on that angel! What was her problem, anyway?

"Mr. Baker, I really didn't mean to frighten her!" expresses Danielle, her voice tugging my brain back down to reality.

Quickly, I snap out of it and take the broom back with a shaky hand. "No, you didn't frighten me. You see, I-I was so busy sweeping the floor I forgot I wasn't alone in the store." A lame excuse, I know, but what else can I say?

"This is Danielle White," continues Mr. Baker, still speaking like a robot. "She will be taking Janey's place and I need you to train her." His gaze is glued on her, and his amorous smile is enough to make me retch.

"Nice to meet you, Danielle," I say, trying my best to ignore Mr. Baker's grotesque display of affection. "I'm Clarity. Welcome to the team."

"Thanks!" she replies cheerfully, grinning widely. "I'm so excited! I've never had a job before."

"Oh, that's, uh..." Wow, her first job. I get to train her. And she's possessed. Yay me.

A few awkward moments pass before Mr. Baker says, "Alright, you ladies get to work, unless – Danielle, would you like me to stay and watch over the training?"

Again, his look of acute yearning makes my stomach tense with repugnance.

"That's okay, Mr. Baker," Danielle hurriedly replies, backing a couple of steps away. "I'm sure Clarity will do a good job."

"Oh, uh ... okay, then." He frowns, slumping his shoulders and turning around. Shuffling to his office, he walks in and shuts the door behind him.

Danielle blows out a loud sigh of relief.

"Oh, wow! That dude gives me the creeps!" She shakes

her head, her blue eyes glancing my way. "Is he always that scuzzy?"

"Um," I start, swallowing the hard lump in my throat, "I've never seen him act that way. And, I *really* don't want to observe that again."

"I know, right?" she giggles, blowing a huge pink bubble of gum, then popping it with her manicured nail. "When he handed me this nasty smock I couldn't get it on fast enough. He kept eyeing my chest! Totally gross. Plus, someone should tell him that pants are made to fit around the waist, not under the armpits."

Laughing, I give a nod of agreement. Who can argue with that?

At that moment a *Tsipor* demon appears on her shoulder, its yellow eyes burning into mine. It smiles viciously, showing off its slimy fangs. The smell of raw sewage wafts through the air, making me long for Sam's lavender scent.

Danielle's countenance shows that she's oblivious to the demon perched on her shoulder. It makes me question whether or not she knows she's possessed, though her happy-go-lucky expression reveals that she has not one clue. She's blind to her own dark reality.

We stare at each other a few ticks, until she breaks the weird silence by clearing her throat and inquiring, "So, you gonna train me or what?"

"Uh, yeah," I rebound quickly. Then I add with a laugh, "Sorry, but this time of day I'm ready to space out."

She rolls her eyes. "Yeah, I see how easy that can happen in this town. It's so drab and small."

"I agree," I say, watching her skeptically. "Though there are certain things in this town that can only be described as *unbelievable*."

"Oh, I doubt that," she scoffs. Turning her attention to the cash register, she asks, "How does this thing work?"

The training goes amazingly well, even with the knowledge that Danielle is one of Livian's pawns. I have so many questions for Sam, but one keeps tossing about in my head.

How do these people not know that they're possessed? Because if Danielle knows she's been taken over by darkness, she doesn't show it. In my eyes I see a normal teenage girl attempting to learn the ropes of a boring, tedious cashier job. Though the demon that appears and disappears on her shoulder throws out the whole *normal* scenario.

The rest of the evening flies by, and everything runs smoothly ... until closing time arrives. That's when Casey realizes Mr. Baker has hired a busty blonde to replace his ex-girlfriend. Again, I witness yet another one of my friends slobber and stumble over a new kid in town. And once again I think that if Casey could see (and smell) the ugly, rank demon roosting on her shoulder, he would sprint the other way. Fast.

But no, he can't see. He's blind like everyone else, with the exception of me. Lucky, *lucky* me.

"Uh, hey, my name's, uh..." Casey struggles to get his name out. After a few tries, he stops his stuttering and smiles stupidly at her.

She bats her eyelashes at him. "Well, nice to meet you, *Uh*. I'm Danielle. Wanna walk me to my car?"

"Sure." He's blushing, all the while offering his arm. "And my name's not *Uh*. It's Casey."

"Hmm, Casey," Danielle purrs, linking her arm with his. "I like that name." She winks, and Casey's blush deepens. Without a glance back she says, "See you later, Clarity."

"Yeah, night," Casey says, also not looking back. They

seem, at this particular moment, to only have eyes for each other.

A foreboding feeling constructs in the pit of my stomach as I watch Casey walk across the parking lot, with Danielle attached to his arm. The demon sitting on her shoulder twists around and smiles, waving, its yellow eyes a big glow. I hear laughter being carried in the wind, human or inhuman, I can't be too sure.

A big chill slices straight through me. My thoughts turn negative when I get in the car and start for home. Why is this happening? Is it some kind of twisted test, one that God has purposely set up to see if I succeed or fail?

"It's not a test."

Chapter Eleven

Clarity

Caught off guard by Sam's abrupt appearance in the passenger's seat, I panic, jerking the wheel and swerving into the other lane. Luckily there's no oncoming traffic, and thankfully Sam grabs the steering wheel, instantly pulling the car back in the right lane.

"I thought you'd gotten used to me popping in whenever I feel like it!" he exclaims, with amusement dancing in his blue eyes.

I glare angrily at him. "I thought you knew by now not to show up in the middle of my thoughts!" Sharply, I turn my head away from him and place my full attention on the road. "It's kind of been a rough day and you, out of all the angels in town, should know the pressure on me at this moment."

He sighs. "You're right. You feel attacked, threatened,

and confused." He pauses before adding, "You have loads of questions, too. Go ahead and unload."

Getting down to business, I begin my first round of questions. "Why is everyone's brains turning to mush? Why am I not affected by them? Why is it my friends, even my boyfriend, are drawn to Livian's pawns? And why are angels and demons all over the place? Also, as you already know, I'm working with one of the possessed and a demon is always hanging around her – actually, demons are hanging on all of them – I feel like I'm going nuts! And what are those black circles just below their wrists? And Danielle's angel, Lara – what's her problem?"

I pant, totally out of breath from all my questions. Sam reaches over and squeezes my hand, his calming essence surging through me, while his lavender scent mellows my nerves. Tranquility flows throughout the car, causing a massive peace to blanket around my body.

"Pull over," he softly says.

That's exactly what I do.

We sit a few mute seconds. I wait patiently for him to answer as he rakes his free hand through his glossy black hair, his other hand still clasped over mine.

"Okay," he starts, his eyes aglow and focused on me. "Let's go in order of your questions. And I know my answers will just add up to more questions, so I want you to listen carefully and let me talk – got it?"

"Yeah," I concede carefully. "Got it. You talk. I listen."

"Alright." He releases my hand, his eyes staying on mine. "Now, the reason everyone around you is acting strange is because a *glamour* has been cast by the enemy, surrounding these three individuals with sparkling beauty." Before I can ask what a *glamour* is, he raises a hand in the air and declares, "No, Clarity. No more questions until I've answered the others – that's the deal."

I roll my eyes, then nod at him to keep going.

"A *glamour*," he says, "is something the enemy uses to fool humans into thinking what they see is real, even when it's the exact opposite of what they should be seeing. With Livian's pawns, you see just regular teenagers, while your friends see two kings and a queen. You are not affected because God has lifted the veil from your eyes so you can see both the earthly realm and the spiritual realm. Your closest friends are drawn to them like ants to honey because they're being targeted by the enemy.

"Angels are appearing everywhere because they know Livian is here and they are protecting their Charges. Demons are here to create as much chaos as they can so Livian's plan can come to pass." He pauses, then adds, "A demon will always stay hooked to the possessed – that's self-explanatory. And the black circles on the possessed pawns mean they have been marked by a demon – that, too, is self-explanatory."

"So the black circles below their wrists are demon marks that Livian placed on them?" I ask.

"Exactly," he says.

"And I'm the only one who can see the marks?"

"Yes," he nods.

I stare at him, completely numb, as I take in this new bit of info and formulate it in my brain. Still a little miffed, I say, "So a *glamour* is something that makes things, or in this case, *people*, appear one way, though in reality they're another."

"Yes," he says again.

Tension lifts off my shoulders as comprehension emerges. "So while I see them as normal people, my friends see sparkles and glitter. That's why I'm not affected."

"Right," he says with a smile, quick to agree. "You're not entranced like the others, though you have a huge advantage. You see the world from two very different views – Terrestrial and Spiritual. Mortal and Immortal. You look through human eyes, but also through spiritual eyes. It's part of your gift.

"Let me be clear on one thing. You see, it's not just how Livian's pawns look, but it's their touch, their smell, their whole existence has been magnified greatly so that the enemy is able to trick your unsuspecting friends."

A shiver rushes through me. Promptly, I turn the heater to full blast.

"Okay," I say, blowing into my hands for warmth, "I understand the whole *glamour* thing, but why are my friends being targeted?"

His smile slowly fades as concern shadows his features. "They are being targeted because of you."

"Me?" I remark, confused. "But Livian has a problem with me. She was sent after *me*. My friends are innocent."

He frowns. "The enemy will stop at nothing to gain souls. Livian knows that whatever she gains, Satan gains. She knows your friends are at the very core of your weakness. It makes sense that she would target them to get to you."

I hate to say it, but every word he's speaking rings true in my soul. Hurting my friends, the ones I love and care for, is a huge weakness of mine. Though I'm still working on my daily walk with God, I know that my friends are painstakingly lost. That makes the situation even harder, knowing that Livian, a General in Satan's demonic army, has set her sights on them.

"This may be an unanswerable question, but..." I pause, taking a breath and releasing it slowly. "Does Danielle, Darren, and David know they are possessed?"

"No," Sam readily replies. "They are too brainwashed to know they're being used. They look to Livian as their mother figure."

I shake my head and stare out the windshield. "Livian is after me and using my friends to get to me."

"Yes and no," Sam says. My gaze shifts to him as he continues. "Livian is in the deceiving business and wants to win as many souls as possible, so as to please Satan. But yes, her assignment is to take you out, but she also has a more selfish reason for wanting to come to Garlandton."

"What's her selfish reason?"

"She wants to add to her family," he says, his blue eyes unblinking. "The three pawns look up to her because she took them in when nobody else would. They really believe she loves them." He grimaces. "They really believe that she's their mother, and if she sees a way to add to her clan, she'll do it. She'll swoop in and snatch them up, like a night owl catching its dinner."

"Wow," I whisper, leaning my head back and staring at the ceiling.

"Yeah," he whispers back.

Rolling my head to the side, my tired eyes stare at him. "What's Lara's problem? And why can't David, Danielle, and Darren's angels get rid of the demons?"

He looks away from me. "To answer that second question, you humans have freewill to choose whether to walk the path of life or death. There's only so much us Guardians can do for our Charges in that respect. Only word from the Throne Room can we intervene. As for Lara – she's a bit hard on herself. She thinks it's her fault that Danielle is going through this. That's why her attitude stinks. She feels like a failure."

"That's crazy!" I exclaim, perplexed. "I didn't know angels had such thoughts and feelings."

Still staring out the window, he says, "We feel a lot more than you think, Clarity." He turns his eyes on me. "You forget, we all have freewill … just like you humans."

Makes sense. A third of the angels rebelled against God and were thrown out of heaven, all thanks to the freewill He gave them.

"You've got to help them," he suddenly remarks.

"What are you saying?"

"They've been marked by darkness," he explains. "The only way they can be saved is to bring them back to the light."

Though I dread the answer, I ask, "And how does one get brought back to the light?"

Once again, he gazes out the window. "By letting go of darkness."

I sigh, perceiving that I'm not going to get a plain, straight answer. I've known from the very beginning that Sam can't give me too much information, because most of it I have to figure out on my own. Of course, I had one more question...

"How do I protect the ones I love?"

"By staying close to your enemies."

With that said, he disappears, taking away his lavender scent and leaving me to ponder his baffling words all the way home.

Kora

"So ... tell me more about the beautiful lady with white hair." I observe David, who's sitting across from me on the bed, and eagerly await his response.

He grins, with a blush coloring his pale cheeks. "Well, it's simple. She's my mother. She takes care of me and gives me everything I need and want."

It didn't take much to get David to come over. All I did was walk up to him in the school's parking lot. He'd been leaning back on the metal fence, casually smoking a cigarette. Somehow I'd found the nerve to go up and talk to him. We talked for a couple hours there, then, finding courage, I'd asked him to come over to the house. Of course, I had to sneak him in. I haven't lived with A.C. and Clarity long, but I know them, and they would not be happy about me bringing a strange new boy into their house. Though for some reason, I just don't care how they feel.

"Wow," I whisper. "She's really your mother. She's ... *real.*"

He nods, his dark eyes gleaming with delight.

"I thought she was just a figment of my imagination."

"She's really something," he tells me. "I mean, she took me in when everyone else had given up on me. She picked me up and turned my life completely around, just like she did with Danielle and Darren. I can't even remember my past or where I came from. She said that the past needs to stay there, and the future is where it's at."

I smile, taking in his extremely good looks. His look is so different from Kevin's rugged handsomeness, though his temperament is that of joy, sincerity, and respect. We've been talking for five hours, but I feel like I've known him my entire life.

"You're lucky to have someone who loves you," I say softly. "My mom is dead, and I never knew my dad."

David takes my hand in his. A shiver courses through my body. I gaze into his almost black eyes, feeling as light as a feather and as high as a kite. I feel like I could get lost in his penetrating gaze. What he speaks next causes me to altogether melt.

"Mother loves me so much," he whispers, "that she sent me to you." As he leans forward, his focus glued to my lips, I close my eyes, anticipating the kiss.

Suddenly a *rap-rap* sounds on my bedroom door. My eyes pop open at the noise, which causes my heart to do handsprings in my chest. In an instant, I pull David off the bed and drag him over to the closet, shutting the door. Then, as quick as I humanly can, I plop back down on the bed and flip my math textbook wide open.

Nonchalantly I call out, "Come in!"

A.C. opens the door, broadcasting a humongous smile. She must have just gotten home from work, because she's still wearing her hospital scrubs. For all I know she's planning to go back to the hospital. All she ever does is work.

"Hey guys! I wanted to share – " Her words cut off as her eyes grope the room. With her expression muddled, she says, "Oh, I thought Clarity was in here with you. I thought I heard you talking."

My heart continues to thud, jumping from my chest to my throat with every beat.

"I, uh," I stammer, "sometimes when I do homework I … read the problems out loud, especially the reading problems." I shrug my shoulders and giggle, hoping I don't sound guilty. "It's stupid, I know. But it helps me to understand – "

"You don't have to explain," she interjects. Still eyeing my room she remarks, "I love how you decorated the room. It's very … *you*."

I smile, admiring my work, as well. When I'd first moved into the guest room, I'd been deeply depressed. The off-white comforter, curtains – everything had been decorated so drab-like, which didn't help my spiraling emotions.

So I put my own touch to my little space of solitude. Instead of white curtains, black fabric covers the windows, with a sheer red overlay. The full-sized bed is now wrapped with black satin sheets, with red satin pillowcases and a matching red comforter. Red and black have always been my favorite colors – my hair has been both shades, though now it's back to its natural black.

"Thank you for noticing," I say, smiling wider. "So, what's up? I don't think I've ever seen you this happy."

"Well, I'm happy because…" She trails off, tilting her head to the side, then adds, "Clarity is here! Come downstairs and I'll tell my exciting news to both of you!"

Without another word, she swings around and tromps down the stairs. Quickly, I close the door, locking it. Behind me I hear my closet door creak open. Turning around, I almost laugh when I see David's amused and shocked face.

"What was *that*?" he wonders, his eyebrows raised.

Walking over and stopping just in front of him, I answer, "Caroline, Clarity's aunt. We call her A.C. for short." I pause, shrugging my shoulders. "She gets excitable sometimes. Kind of hyper."

"Oh."

We stare at each other a few quiet seconds, and I silently wish that he'll try to kiss me again.

"I better go," he says, his eyes still grazing my face.

"Oh, okay," I reply, not bothering to hide my disappointment. Then, forcing a smile, I tell him, "I've really enjoyed spending time together."

He grins. "I've enjoyed it, too. You've made me feel very welcomed." He tilts his head, his gaze unwavering. "And I foresee many afternoons like today in our near future."

Before I can offer a response, he pulls me into his arms, palming my face with his free hand, and kisses me. An electric jolt streaks through my veins, just by the touch of his lips. Tension and anxiety releases their hold on my body, leaving me like putty in his hands. When the kiss ends, he leans back so as to gaze into my eyes. His eyes, his beautiful dark eyes, have me completely and passionately enthralled.

"I also see many moments like this one in our future, too."

Spinning on his heel, he walks to the window and easily climbs out. I rush to the window to see how he's going to get down. I know there's not a tree nearby – he'd have to walk over to Clarity's window to climb down.

Surprisal hits me like a freight train when I find that he's disappeared completely.

Like he'd jumped out the window and vanished into thin air.

Chapter Twelve

Clarity

As I walk through the doors of the house, A.C. startles me by throwing her arms around my body, delivering the tightest bear hug I've ever received. She's still in her hospital scrubs, stinking of the nasty disinfectant they use constantly at the hospital, the scent assaulting my nose with a brutal vengeance.

Kora walks up behind A.C., wearing black pajama pants and a matching camisole. Her expression is bewildered; most likely I'm diffusing the very same look.

When she lets up on squeezing the life out of me, I inquire, "A.C., what *is* it?"

Finally, she releases me, taking a step back. Her face is flushed with burning excitement.

"Doug asked me to marry him!" she squeals, lifting her left hand and displaying a one-carat diamond nestled on a six-pronged platinum band.

"Wow," I express, "whoever he is, he has good taste ... and money."

"Clarity," she frowns. "I told you about him. His name is Doug Cox and he's a paramedic at the hospital."

"Did you?" I rack my brain, attempting to pull up the name "Doug Cox" in my filing system. In the end, my searching fails. "Sorry, I don't remember."

I honestly don't remember her mentioning she was dating someone. A.C. probably had mentioned him, but most likely I hadn't been listening. The past few months have been sort of a roller coaster ride of turmoil, stress and chaos.

"I told you – oh, never mind!" She sighs, throwing her hands in the air.

I laugh. "Sorry, A.C., really. Congratulations, though."

"Yeah," pipes in Kora. "Congratulations."

"Thanks girls." She smiles, holding her hand out and admiring her treasure.

We three walk to the kitchen and sit at the table. A.C. liberates her hair by releasing it from its clip, which allows her brown hair to flow freely to her shoulders.

"So, how did he do it?" asks Kora. "Did he get down on one knee?"

"He asked me at lunch today," she responds, wiping a happy tear from her face. "He was so sweet! We met for lunch in the hospital's cafeteria, like every other day, though I knew something was up when I saw all our friends there. He'd hired a photographer to capture the moment when he dropped to one knee and proposed. Then we ate cake!"

"That's so romantic!" I exclaim in a snarky tone. "I hope I get engaged in a nasty hospital lunchroom, too!"

Kora laughs, adding, "It's always been my dream to be proposed to in the theater's projection room." We both laugh, our sides splitting.

"Yeah, okay, that's enough." A.C. rolls her eyes, obviously picking up on our witty sarcasm. "Anyway, we're taking a little celebratory vacation to the beach. We're leaving this Thursday and coming back on Monday, so you guys are going to have to take care of each other."

"You mean you're leaving us *alone*?" I wonder in complete disbelief. I'm about to be eighteen (February fourteenth, Valentine's Day to be exact), but still, I'm shocked she's going out of town and leaving us by ourselves. Especially after what Kora did a couple weeks back.

Really, though, she's never home, thanks to her workaholic status.

Shock is evident all over Kora's face, too. She stares at A.C., with her famous *Do-Huh* feature. She glances at me with wide green eyes.

"I think you guys can handle it," she says. "Kora, you're doing tons better. You're feeling back to normal, right?"

Kora nods in an overzealous manner, replying, "Oh, yes! The new medicine keeps me happy and I feel great – er, well, normal."

A.C. grins, then looks to me from across the table. "See? You guys will be fine for a few days."

"We're not babies, A.C., jeez!" I remark dryly. "*Of course* we'll be fine."

"Good," she says, standing up. "Now, I know I have a couple of days, but I'm going to start packing tonight. It's been years since I've been to the beach!" She skips to the stairs – I have never seen her this happy!

Abruptly she stops, turning around and hanging on the banister. "Oh, and girls?"

"Yes?" both Kora and I say simultaneously.

She knits her eyebrows together. "No parties." And with that out, she hops up the stairs and into her bedroom, slamming the door behind her.

I love seeing A.C. so happy – all upbeat and giddy. I haven't seen her like this in a long while. She's been taking care of me since I was thirteen. It's about time she gets a life of her own. And knowing that my graduation is coming up in a few months should relieve some of her tension and stress. She can plan a wedding, pop out a couple of kids, and move forward in life.

Just like I'm planning to do, minus the whole *kids* thing.

"Wow," I say to Kora, still reeling from the engagement news. I stand up and walk to the fridge, snatching a soda. Popping it open and taking a swig, I add, "I can't believe A.C. is going to settle down."

"Me neither," Kora agrees, her elbows resting atop the

table. "You know what else I can't believe?"

"What's that?" I ask, plopping back down in the chair and taking a huge gulp of cola.

She wriggles her brows up and down as she answers, "That she's leaving us alone on a Saturday night - a perfect night to host a party at the Miller house."

I choke, almost spewing the dark liquid out of my nose.

"Kora!" I whisper harshly, grabbing a paper towel and wiping at the sticky mess on my chin. "You heard what A.C. said – no *parties*."

"Oh, *puh-lease!*" she jeers, her lips curling into a cynical grin. "Seriously, when did you turn into a wuss?"

I gawk at her, replying, "I am not a wuss!"

"Oh, yes you are."

"Where were you one minute ago when A.C. said 'No parties'?" I reach across the table and tap her forehead. "Hello? Anyone in there?"

She hastily slaps my hand away. "C'mon, Clare. I need a party. *You* need a party."

I lean forward and glare at her. "The only thing you need

is another *Xanax*. And the only thing I need is my warm, comfy bed." I lift to my feet, suddenly feeling the need to crash for the night. Kora wears me out with her silly, immature antics.

Kora also stands, blocking my exit from the kitchen.

"Please, Clare, please!" she begs, her hands clasped as if in prayer. "The last few months have been rough. I lost Kevin, I lost my mom, I had to move in here and be a burden to you and your aunt – "

"Whoa, Kora," I interrupt. "You are not a burden. And I really don't appreciate you trying to manipulate me."

"I'm not trying to manipulate you!" she gasps, her expression shocked. "For the longest time I used my body to take away my pain, but I've stopped all that. I'm never going down that road again. I want to get on with my life, and I think we should celebrate moving on by inviting a few friends over – oh, and a keg."

Oh, she is so manipulative and sneaky! Though, observing her wide green eyes and her imploring countenance, I feel my guard slipping away.

Crossing my arms I ask, "How many is a few?"

"Ten, fifteen tops," she responds quickly.

I ponder this a moment, still not knowing what to do, and the guilt trip she's laying on me is totally unfair.

True, Kora has had a rough few months, and true, she is doing loads better, but A.C. had laid down the law. No parties. Could I really disobey the person that took me in when I'd become an orphan? Not only that, but taking my best friend in? I mean, I have disobeyed her in the past, but...

Is it in me, after all I've gone through, to be so deceitful?

I sigh. "Kora, I'm not sure if we should..."

"Caroline will never find out!" she insists. "We'll have the whole next day to clean up the house – A.C. will never find out, I swear!"

"Kora – "

"*Please!*" she whines, poking her bottom lip out and staring at me with her supplicating gaze.

I close my eyes, pinching the bridge of my nose. I can feel a headache limping across my brain as I attempt to do the right thing, which involves telling Kora no. That manipulating me into having a party is not going to work. But when I open my eyes and see the most pitiful look I've ever witnessed, I turn my back on what's right, doing the exact opposite of what I should.

In other words, I'm caving – *big* time.

"Fine," I say, fully giving in and dismissing every moral fiber in my heart. "As long as there's no more that fifteen people, we'll have the dumb 'ol party."

She breaks into a winner-sized grin. "Oh, thank you, thank you, thank you!" Grabbing me, she embraces my body in her arms tightly – she's super strong for such a tiny girl.

When she lets me go, I emphasize, "Just remember that the *both* of us will clean the house afterward, and also make sure it's not trashed, understand?"

"Totally." She loops her pinky with mine and adds, "Pinky promise! This house will be spotless before Caroline comes home."

Walking up the stairs to my room, I can't stop the feeling of dread encompassing my body. The realization that I've made a terrible mistake sinks like a stone in my stomach. Can't help but think something terrible will come from allowing this unsupervised party.

That night I toss and turn in bed, feeling lowdown, dirty, and weak. A.C. trusts Kora and I, and how are we going to repay her for the confidence in us? By throwing a party behind her back, that's how. Betraying A.C. leaves me feeling like a piece of dirt lodged way under someone's dirty fingernail.

Wait a minute … it's just a stupid party! Just a few friends over, with some music and beer. What's the worst that could happen?

As Friday arrives, I receive part of that question.

Tuesday night had been the night Kora talked me into throwing the party. The list of fifteen party guests has grown to a whopping sixty-five. A very talented DJ has offered to provide music, promising to bring everything we need for an "awesome, mind-blowing experience" – his words, not mine.

From all the talk infecting the Garlandton High halls, I'm gathering that the party at my house will be the party of the year, which is crazy because it was only supposed to be a few of us. However, what bothers me the most is that my partner in crime has yet to come clean and inform me on how the whole senior class has been invited to our so-called small shindig. So when the bell for lunch rings, I run right to Kora and grill her for information.

"Kora, what's going on?" I wonder, completely exasperated.

"What are you talking about?" she inquires innocently.

I glare at her furiously, trying to keep my anger in check. "You know exactly what I'm talking about! What happened to the fifteen people we agreed on, huh? Why is the entire senior class talking about this being the party of the year, HUH?!"

She shrugs her delicate shoulders, avoiding my eyes. "I guess good news travels fast."

"Kora," I say through a clenched jaw.

"It will be okay, Clare," Brenton walks up, breaking into our discussion. He places his arm around my waist and pulls me close. "I'll be there the whole time, making sure people behave and don't break stuff. I'll even stay over and help y'all clean."

"See?" Kora reacts, slinging a rankled look my direction. "You're own beau thinks it's a good idea to get our party on!"

I icily glare at Brenton. He laughs in return.

"Yeah, Clarity, I think a party will do us good – all of us." He smiles his dimpled smile, and my anger melts instantly.

I sigh, clearly outnumbered and defeated. "I hope the both of you are right."

"We are," insists Kora. "You can trust us!"

Boy, I sure hope so.

With Kora and Brenton blabbing back and forth about the party, I work on blocking them out. My eyes scan the cafeteria. Just like people are clustered in their little groups and cliques, the same can be said for angels and demons. Yes, they are still around ... and it seems that it's going to stay that way.

It may seem crazy, but I've become accustomed to seeing supernatural beings all the time, even though they had shown up only a few days ago – the day the new kids dropped into school. Classrooms, library, lunchroom, gym ... everywhere I turn, angels are there, watching over and guarding their humans. The demons, however, are staying far away from the Guardians, using their claws and feet to hang onto the ceilings and corners. I'm unfazed by it all ... to a certain extent. What comforts me is knowing the angels have mine and everyone's backs.

Still, though, I feel the change in the air, all weird and electrically charged, like the air before a massive storm. An unearthly feeling, one that is too elusive to describe. And there's the smell that comes with it, like mixing a perfume department with a cesspit. That's the aroma clinging to the air. An aroma I call *Floral Poo*.

A sudden chill skitters down my spine. My gaze finds Sam. He nods his head in perfect understanding. Livian is here, there's no doubt about that. Her army is all over the place.

The problem is ... I don't know where exactly *she* is.

Livian

My David has become smitten with this broken-souled Kora. He's been over every night since they met, staying over until the wee hours of the morning. And it appears that Kora finds him equally attractive. I delight in watching them roll around, barely clothed, in her bed, allowing their fleshly desires to take place. The sin energizes me, surging through my existence at a ferocious pace. So many things can come out of this one coupling. So many situations...

"Hello, Livian."

I don't let the angel's sudden appearance deter me from my observation of the two human's sinful natures happening right before my eyes. I don't let his celestial presence take over my feelings of elation at the unholy debacle set in motion.

"Hello, Sam," I say as I tilt my head to the side. "To what do I owe the pleasure of your visit?"

He walks over, standing in between the humans and I. "I wanted to let you know that this will not end well for you."

"Oh, little angel," I smile, gazing sweetly into his eyes. "You know nothing of what I can do. I will not stop until I succeed. And besides, there is nothing you can do to stop me. Kora's freewill is in place. She has invited sin into this house. You can't touch me, and it's *killing* you." His blue eyes blaze up with fury as I continue. "You want to touch me, destroy me, but thanks to your Father's rules, you can't. If humans choose to sin, choose to follow the path of darkness, The Light cannot interfere. Only when a human cries out for help, cries out for The Light – that's the moment you can intervene."

With his eyes glowing brighter, his fists clenched at his sides, he snarls, "I'm going to enjoy sending you back to Hell."

I cackle, enjoying his remark. "You know, Sam, you're right. One day you may get that chance, but for now..." I narrow my eyes and growl, "Darkness reigns in this house."

Chapter Thirteen

Clarity

Music pounds in my ears. My living room has been transformed into a dance floor full of sweaty bodies bumping to an erratic rhythm. A strobe light blinks on and off, causing a wooziness that usually comes from too much alcohol. The mood is chill and everyone is having a good time. Knowing that the party has become a huge success, a sense of relief causes my spirit to soar.

Brenton grabs my hand, charging us into the crowd. We laugh madly, we dance wildly, and kiss – dance and kiss, kiss and dance – I'm safe and secure in his arms. I never want this night to end.

But in a split second, reality crashes the party. The music stops, the dance moves pause. All actions have been halted, except for the frenzied flash of the strobe light.

I stare in fascination and horror at Brenton, whose body is frozen in the middle of a dance move. His lips are twisted into his smooth, easy-going grin. In fact, everyone is frozen in place, as if someone has swiped a freeze gun and zapped all my friends. Now I'm left wondering ... why?

The air is coated with a thickness so heavy that it's hard to breath. I try to move, but find my legs have turned mushy, all flimsy and loose. Thoughts run laps in my skull, that dense foreboding feeling rushing through my veins.

"Clarity ... Clarity..." a sing-song voice calls over and over again.

What? I respond in my mind, thanks to my will to speak being stripped away.

A shape materializes in front of me, hovering a few feet off the ground. I would have gasped if it were possible to make a sound. Standing before me is a seductive, beautiful woman. Her hair and skin are white as snow, just like her eyes. She wears a long, lacy white dress, and her hair falls in loose curls down her back. She has cherry red lips, and a voice that sounds like a chorus of angels. I stare in quiet awe at her raw resplendence, entranced by her fabled beauty. When my hands catch on fire and glow a bright red, I shake out of my muddled stupor.

Recognition slaps me across the face. I narrow my eyes and squeeze my hands into tight fists. I know exactly who this creature is.

Livian.

"Yes, my child, we finally meet." She gives me a breathtaking smile, regarding me with her creepy white eyes.

What are you doing here? I inquire, with fear and anger choking my heart.

"I've come for someone special," she answers in an angelic voice, though I know there's absolutely no holiness underneath her pale skin. *"Mostly I've come for you, my little Ra'ah."*

My eyebrows furrow and I curl my lip, trying to appear as menacing as possible.

I don't want to hear anything you have to say. Get out of here and leave this town alone!

I can see by her reaction that I'm not as scary as I think.

Throwing her head back, she laughs the most bitter laugh I've ever heard. I watch in silent angst as her form completely alters. Glossy black feathers spread all over her body, covering every inch of her skin. She grows taller and taller, and if I had to guess I'd say she's grown to at least twelve feet tall.

Making eye contact, she glares at me through glowing yellow eyes. Long sharp fangs hang out of her mouth, resting just below her *blood red lips. She's transformed into some kind of crow/vampire creature, though those don't exist. However, demons do exist.*

"My little Ra'ah," she sneers, her voice deeper, "soon you will know the answers you seek, but for now..." Her words trail off as she lifts her head to the ceiling. Black wings pop from her back. I flinch as she charges toward me, her shrill scream bouncing off the walls of my skull...

I wake with a start, throwing the covers off and jumping out of bed. I'm in a defensive stance, with my fists up and legs crouched. When my eyes become acquainted with the dark, I find Sam sitting on the window ledge, his blue eyes glowing fiercely. Upon seeing him, my body relaxes. I stand up straight and lay back down. On my side, I stare back, waiting on him to say something. The dream I'd just had hits too close for comfort, and I know he has the meaning to it. When he doesn't speak, I deliver my own reaction.

"Livian will be here tomorrow, won't she?" I inquire, already knowing the answer. "She's coming with her little army of *Tsipors* and they're going to terrorize my friends ... and me."

With an expressionless look, he says, "Livian has already been invited into this house."

Before I can inquire of what exactly that means, he

vanishes.

Rolling onto my back, I sigh in defeat, staring up at the ceiling. A deep, churning ball of disquiet becomes settled in my soul. Livian had been in my nightmare, and the nightmare had been inside my house. And according to Sam, Livian has already been invited into the house. He'd disappeared before I could ask what that meant.

With that feeling of unease still reeling around in my soul, I realize that I'll be getting the answer I seek sooner than later.

***

After Sam had left, I'd tossed and turned a thousand times before settling into a restless slumber. I awoke around two in the afternoon, thanks to Kora's banging and yelling for me to get my "big butt" out of bed. I'd been too tired to assault her with a comeback. I'd rolled out of bed, my body up, but it took awhile for my brain to fully charge.

All afternoon we prepared for the party, moving furniture around and setting up tables for food and drinks. We'd decided that the kitchen would be the perfect space for the bar, and instead of risking all of our breakable glasses, we bought some bright red plastic cups. Not one, but *two* kegs were delivered, per Casey Anderson's *totally wicked* connections, along with a variety of liquors. Just gazing at all the vodka, tequila, sour mixes, and juices makes my mouth water, but I don't touch any of it, and I never will. I'd made a decision, a good one, and I'm sticking to it.

Truthfully, I'm battling a feeling of strong conviction. I comprehend the fact that drinking is wrong, especially underage drinking, but how can I tell someone not to drink when I'm allowing the stuff in my house?

If I was to tell someone that they shouldn't drink, while at the same time I'm holding a party with a full bar, what does that make me?

The answer to that question is *hypocrite*. Not something I want to be perceived as.

The DJ arrived around five to set up all his equipment – amps, mixing board, PA system – and other stuff I'd never seen before. He'd brought a wide range of music, from country to rap, contemporary to metal, and everything else in between. I figure once everyone ingests some alcohol, they won't care a bit what's blasting through the huge speakers in the living room.

Now, as the clock strikes seven, my stomach starts twisting into itself with a nervousness so profound that I'm fighting not to puke. The party guests are beginning to show, and one thought is revolving inside my brain. What if A.C. comes back early and walks into a raging party full of drunken teens and dirty dancing? What would we do then?

Well...

Too late now.

As people begin arriving in droves, I force that thought from my brain. I still feel like a lowdown scuzz for disobeying A.C., but the time to cancel this shindig has passed. Kora had manipulated me, I'd caved, and now we're in the middle of a wild party.

Seriously, it's a good thing I don't have any neighbors, because the music was shaking the whole house.

"Take a shot!" Kora yells over the music, trying to hand me a bottle of tequila. "It'll loosen you up a bit."

I shake my head. "No thanks."

"Come on, Clare!" she urges, still pushing the bottle in my face. "You look as tight as a wound-up yo-yo. You need to chill!"

Gently, I push her hand away and glare into her already glazed eyes. "I told you, Kora. I'm not drinking anymore."

"I'll take that!" Casey swoops in, snatching the bottle from Kora. He quickly knocks it back, taking a few gulps, and runs into the living room making a *woot-woot* noise.

Casey was one of the first to walk through the doors, along with some sophomores I didn't know. Letting my eyes graze over the house it becomes clear that underclassmen also heard about the party. My house is a decent size, though it has shrunk with almost half the school in and around it. The original head count of fifteen has grown to eighty, and people are still pulling up.

Around eight o'clock, Daria and her crew make an appearance, all glamored up and beautified. I'm shocked that she's here. Never thought my house would be good enough for her to grace with her uppity presence. What shocks me even more is that she's headed my way with a smile on her face.

"Hey, Clarity, cool party!" she yells over the music.

Perplexed, and a bit skeptical, I reply, "Uh, thanks!"

She leans closer and whispers in my ear, "I never told you how much I appreciated your visit to my house."

"What?" I wonder, my confusion growing.

"You know." Her grin fades, her expression switching to serious mode. "After all that happened at the dance ... I'm pretty sure you saved my life." She gives my arm a squeeze, then spins around and heads into the dancing crowd.

I stand there, mouth agape, completely stunned. Didn't expect that. Not at all. Not in a million years had I expected Daria Phipps to speak anything to me unless it was an insult.

A voice calls my name from the kitchen, instantly slinging me down to the present.

Janey and another fellow senior, Tasha, are acting as bartenders, and they've been super busy. By their laughter I can tell they're enjoying every second of it.

Janey had showed not long after Casey, and I'd expected a huge blow-up between the two. Surprisingly they had ignored one another, keeping as much distance as they could between them. I'd noticed Casey staring at Janey with a look of longing painted all over his face. That's when he'd grabbed a bottle of alcohol. After taking a few swigs, his emotions became numb, and his feeling to care had diminished.

"Yo, Clarity!" Janey calls, waving her hand to get my

attention. As I walk up to the "bar area", she asks, "What's your poison?"

Tasha snorts, arching a thin eyebrow. "That's got to be the lamest phrase in the book."

"Nuh-uh," Janey counters. "All the greatest bartenders of all time say it."

"Like who?" Tasha challenges.

"I don't know," Janey shoots back, shrugging her shoulders. "I heard it in some cowboy movie."

Tasha guffaws, her dreadlocks swinging from side-to-side with her head's shaking. "Girl, sometimes you just too weird."

Not only are Janey and Tasha acting like bartenders, but they've also been participating in the guzzling of alcoholic beverages.

"You guys better slow down," I warn, wagging a finger at them. "If you drink too much you'll be face down on the floor. Think of all the brain cells you're killing right now."

Janey's face scrunches up. "I miss the old you, Clarity. The one who never worried about falling on the floor drunk or killing brain cells. You've turned into a prude, Clare. What is *up* with you?"

Surprised by her critical words, I'm about to reply when Tasha releases an abrasive groan.

"What? What is it?" I ask, observing the evident shock on her dark face.

With wide eyes, she gazes and points directly behind me. "Look what the cat drug in!"

"What are you..."

As I turn around, every muscle in my body becomes rigid and a frosts covers my skin.

Yep, this night was about to take a turn for the worst.

Chapter Fourteen

Clarity

All eyes are on David, Darren, and Danielle as they walk into the house. My body stiffens at the sight of demons sitting on their shoulders, their yellow orbs glaring maliciously at the crowd. The music is the only background noise, because all conversations have ceased. Everyone is staring at the newcomers, with mouths hanging open and eyes bugging from their sockets.

Seriously, this is getting old! When is everyone going to get over these new kids?

With a sudden burst of light, many angels appear around the room, along with a multitude of various demons. The demonic beings range in size from twelve inches to twelve feet. Some have hair covering their bodies, reminding me of the fabled Sasquatch, while others look just plain … *nasty*. I decide right then and their not to focus on the demons, though the

Tsipor's are harder to ignore – they're crawling all over the ceiling, some dropping and landing on the shoulders of my guests.

The smell is atrocious. It's a dense aroma that's worse than any perfume, and mixing it with the demon's roadkill scent doesn't help a thing. How am I supposed to overlook the whole angel/demon grouping in my living room?

I don't recognize any of the Guardians here, though they all harbor the same celestial blue eyes. Tonight those eyes are glowing vividly, and all are glued on the new party arrivals.

Kora breaks the silence by squealing and jumping into David's arms – wait, what? Why is she jumping into his arms, and why is he catching her? And ... why are they *kissing*?!

Whispering follows as the crowd is forced to watch this awkward make-out session in the middle of the living room. As much as I want to yank Kora away from David and slap her silly, I don't move. A scene would only cause a problem. Thanks to my spiritual eyes, I see that there's already *many* problems in this house.

When the twosome break apart, talking and dancing resumes all around the room. Darren finds Brenton with a group of guys and starts gabbing up a storm, and Danielle ... is walking directly at me, with a fake smile plastered on her lovely pale face. Her blonde hair flows down her back in waves, and her lips are painted blood red. The short black dress she wears leaves little to the imagination. I feel a bit overdressed in my red sweater and skinny jeans, though compared to Danielle every girl at this party is overdressed.

"Hello, Clarity, I love your house!" she gushes excitedly. She turns to Janey and Tasha. "Hey, y'all the bartenders? How about us doing a few shots, uh?"

Danielle wags her eyebrows up and down. I cringe at the *Tsipor* demon on her shoulder as it grins. Thick saliva drips from its fangs, dropping on her skin. Her skin absorbs the wetness – *gross*. I can't stop the shiver that flies through my body.

Danielle notices my body convulse and wonders, "What's wrong, Clarity? You seem a little … *edgy*." She winks, then switches her attention back to Janey and Tasha. "So, about those shots..."

Tasha's bewildered expression shifts into a huge grin. "Yeah, sounds like a plan!"

As Tasha and Janey introduce themselves, I use that as an opportunity to escape. I've got to find Kora, and fast. I've got to get her away from David and –

What's happening on the dance floor causes my feet to stutter.

Kora and David are dirty dancing, sickeningly all over each other. People around them are pointing and laughing at the two. After all she's gone through, now this. It's embarrassing.

Mustering up my courage I march over to the gruesome twosome and clamp a hand hard on her shoulder.

"Clarity!" Kora reacts with surprise. "What do you think you're doing?"

"Can I talk to you a minute?" I inquire, my eyes narrowing.

"Sure, okay." To David she says, "Go on up to my room – I'll be up there in a minute."

"No!" I exclaim, looking to David. "Do *not* go up to her room." Then at Kora I say, "Kora – "

"You're not my boss, Clarity," she sneers. Without looking at him she orders, "Go to my room, David. *Now.*"

David laughs. "Sure, babe. Don't worry, Clarity," his dark eyes roam my way, "I know exactly where her *bedroom* is." He spins on his heel and sprints up the staircase, laughing the whole way.

With my mouth agape, I question, "Kora, how does David know where your room is?"

"He's been over before," she woodenly expresses, crossing her arms at her chest. "And I don't appreciate you trying to embarrass me in front of him."

Appalled by her stressful admission, I exclaim, "He's been over before?! When? How did I not know?"

"You never asked," she says tonelessly, her arms still crossed.

I want to scream at her. Grab her by the shoulders and shake some sense into her, but I'm able to restrain myself.

Taking a deep breath, releasing it slowly, I say, "Kora, you know nothing about this guy. He hasn't even been in town a week and you're letting him grope you. And for some odd reason, you sent him to your bedroom – "

"Leave me alone!" screams Kora, shoving me in the chest. I'm knocked back a couple of steps, but keep my balance. Taking a quick glance around the room, I'm grateful that no one is watching this terrible altercation.

Shocked, I say, "Kora – "

"No," she interjects, throwing one of her hands in the air. "This is my life. I like David and he likes me. If I want to be alone with him in *my* bedroom, then I will." Then, glaring viciously at me, she adds, "And there's nothing you can do about it."

Kora spirals around and walks to the stairs, stomping up them. I'm left alone, stunned and discombobulated. I can't believe Kora put her hands on me like that, and yelled at me! All because I was trying to talk some sense into her.

I have to stop her from making a mistake. I have to stop whatever it is that's about to happen in her bedroom. I –

An arm slithers around my waist, while a voice speaks right in my ear.

"Hey, Clare-aby, wha's happnin'?" Brenton's breath is hot on my cheek and reeking of alcohol.

I twist around in his arms and reply, "Well, Kora just pushed me and invited a guy to her bedroom – hey, what a minute ... are you *drunk*?"

Brenton's clearly wasted. I know he is, and I'm totally dumbfounded by it. He hates how alcohol causes you to lose control, not to mention that people's IQ's drop low after a few shots.

"Nah," he says, pulling me closer. "Jus happy to 'ave ya in ma arms, is all."

Yep, he's drunk. I can tell by the incomplete words he speaks. Totally not my Brenton.

"Brenton – " I attempt to pull away from him, but he won't let me. His grip is strong as steel.

"Come on, 'lare baby, give me a 'iss." He leans in for a kiss, and at the last second I turn my head. His wet, slobbery mouth lands on my cheek.

"Brenton," I say, pushing at his chest, "this isn't a good time. And you're drunk. You're not acting like yourself."

A look of anger crosses his face, erasing the jovial grin he'd had a moment before. His cheeks burn red with fury as he releases his hold on my waist. There's a haziness in his brown eyes, a sure sign that he's downed too many illicit drinks.

"What is your problem?" he wonders, his tone dark. He speaks slower, the words making more sense.

Immediately I say, "I don't have a problem – "

"Yes you do!" he yells over the music, his voice causing my body to jerk.

Backing away a couple of steps, I say, "Brenton, listen, I –"

"Shut-up!" He lurches forward, and I cower, thinking he may lay a hand on me, but thankfully he doesn't. Instead he backs away, then in one quick motion he shifts around and sprints out the front door, leaving me alone amongst the wild party participants.

Again, I have a weird confounded feeling wrapping around my existence like a rope, which is pulling tight and squeezing the life out of me. Two friends, two of the people I love most in the world, have attacked me tonight. Within five minutes of each other.

What has happened? Was it just me, or did Brenton act like he wanted to hit me? Kora *did* place hands on me, but why? Why is this happening?

How can I fix all of this? Or better yet...

Is all this fixable?

Livian

The Seer's boyfriend storms out of the house in an obvious rage. His face is red, his heart is pounding like a vicious drum in his chest – now is the perfect time to destroy his life.

I follow as he walks to his truck. Opening a mini-cooler located in its cab, he pulls out an amber bottle, unscrews the top, and drinks it down in a few gulps. He leans against the truck and stares at the sky. I sidle up next to him, flush with his body. He can't see or feel me, but he'll be able to hear me as I speak. Sure, he'll think the thoughts are his, but he has no idea...

None at all.

"Oh, Brenton, why does she do this to you?" I wonder in a pitying tone. "Why does she push you away when you're only trying to get closer to her?"

He groans, then throws the bottle at a nearby tree. It explodes on impact, raining down little glittery bits of glass. I smile at his anger, revel in his pain, breathe in the rejection he's suffering. The alcohol has dulled his senses, numbed his brain – *weakened* his flesh.

"I know someone," I whisper in his ear. "She's beautiful, and will do anything you want."

"No," he growls, raking a hand through his hair.

"Yes," I persist. "Clarity doesn't love you. If she did, she wouldn't push you away." Getting closer, my lips almost touching his ear, I add, "Hurt her – make her pay for not loving you the way she should."

At that moment, my lovely little Danielle arrives.

"Hey, my name's Danielle," she greets. She walks up to him and places a hand on his chest. Smiling flirtatiously, she whispers, "And you're about the yummiest thing I've ever seen."

Brenton looks down at her and grins. Danielle kisses him, soft at first, then harder, wrapping her arms around his neck. He doesn't pull away, he doesn't resist. In the end, he pulls her closer to him and returns the fiery kisses. What happens next pleases me greatly.

"Brenton, what are you *doing*?"

Brenton and Danielle act as if they don't hear her.

These retched humans are too easy.

Chapter Fifteen

Clarity

The reality of my little world starts to dissolve right before my eyes. My mind just can't process what it's witnessing.

Standing next to Brenton's truck is Brenton himself, with Danielle hanging onto him ... *kissing*.

At that precise moment my entire life becomes undone, unraveling and falling helplessly to the ground. My heart is tearing into a million little pieces, each piece a painful jab to my chest. Bile rises in the back of my throat, and a cold chill stabs through me like a knife.

Though somehow, with all the confusion, the hurt, the unrelenting *pain* that's attacking my heart, I find my legs are moving, pulling me toward the pair. Dragging me towards betrayal. Anger boils red-hot in my blood, and embarrassment floods my veins as people start pouring out the doors of the house. Whispers and giggles fill the air. Everyone is anticipating a good fight right about now.

Who does Brenton think he is? God's gift to women? Well, I'll show him.

Lifting a heavy arm, I tap Brenton roughly on the shoulder. They instantly break apart, becoming two separate individuals. Brenton's gaze finds mine, his drunken eyes overflowing with confusion. He's shocked, and for good reason. I have to stop myself from pounding his face in!

Danielle's expression tells a different story. Instead of surprisal, she has a tempestuous gleam in her eyes, like I've upset her by interrupting her make-out party with my boyfriend ... *my* boyfriend!

Yes, the urge to scratch her eyeballs out weighs heavily in my clenched fists, but I decide to pay her no mind. All my energy is focused on Brenton. I'll have time to deal with *her* later.

"Brenton ... why?" I ask, appalled, mad and crushed at the same time.

Rigidly he answers, "I ... I don't k-know." He steps away from Danielle, steps closer to me. I back away, shaking my head. His eyes shift to his feet, while he nervously runs a hand through his disheveled hair.

"Oh, he knows," Danielle sneers. Walking by, she pauses and brushes shoulders with me. In a whisper she adds, "If you won't give him what he wants, I will."

Chill bumps crust over my flesh. I'm horrified at the cold, malicious words that sail through her lips. Daring a look into her eyes, my heart halts a couple of beats. For a split second her blue orbs are completely white, with her lips twisted into an evil leer.

When I'm about to retort, something big and fast flies between us, hooking Brenton around the waist and tackling him to the gravel drive. Evidently Casey had heard about the pair kissing. He seems as unhappy as I am, his jealousy getting the best of him. Danielle cackles, obviously enjoying this fiasco. She wears a pleased expression, overtly loving the fact that two boys are fighting because of her.

Incredulously, I watch a fight between good friends unfold in my driveway. They're on their feet now, circling one another with fists up and ready to swing.

"You got a girl, Sparks! Why you gotta go after mine?" Casey punches Brenton in the jaw.

Brenton returns Casey's punch with a knee to the

stomach. "She came onto me, man! I didn't do nothing!"

A tight band of people has circled around the dueling friends. I'm pushed to the side as the crowd chants, in unison, a rowdy *fight fight fight*.

Demons are appearing everywhere, their scratchy voices joining in with the chanting. Just like the humans, they raise their arms and pump their fists in the air with each word. A cloud of black and gray smoke hovers above the fight, holding little *Tsipor* demons. They poke their heads out of the mist, grinning at the sight below them. They appear pleased by the unfortunate disaster.

Angels are everywhere, though they don't join in with the rest. They watch the fight in silence, their expressions sad and forlorn. My eyes fall on the angel that had stood next to Brenton in the classroom the day David had walked in. Her blue eyes are wide and anxious. She wants to interfere, to separate the two, but she can't. There's tears in her eyes – she's feeling every emotion Brenton is at this moment.

Yes, his Guardian wants to break up this fight, but freewill is in play. Brenton chose to drink, chose to kiss Danielle, which essentially pushed him into choosing this fight.

I am lost, so washed-up with complete disbelief. When

I'd gone after Brenton to make sure he was okay, the last thing I thought I would find was him kissing Danielle. I never thought I'd see the day when Casey and Brenton would come to blows. Boy, the rumor train will be chugging like crazy when Monday morning rolls around.

Could this night get any worse?

After a few tense seconds of name calling and shoving, a couple of burly football players force their way in, snatching Casey and Brenton by their shirts and separating them. After that, the crowd disperses. Now that the fight is over, they push their focus back on all the festivities in the house. The party-goers start up dancing and drinking as if nothing had happened.

Though something had happened. Something big. Something that has me feeling like I'm trapped in the middle of a nightmare, with no way of ever waking up.

Staring down at Brenton, who is sitting on the ground, I find that he's staring back at me pitifully. He's just now recognizing what he's done, that he's messed up – big time.

Casey, on the other hand, appears to be in better shape. He's back in Danielle's arms, allowing her to pamper and kiss his wounds.

Janey has walked up beside me, her expression explaining all she's going through. She's conflicted, hurt by seeing her ex-boyfriend in another girl's arms. Not only had Danielle replaced Janey at Baker's, she'd also taken over being Casey's girlfriend.

"Janey," I say, but I can tell by her countenance that any efforts to console her will be proven useless. She doesn't look at me or speak. Shaking her head, she runs back inside the house, attempting to hide her sorrow.

"C-Clarity."

Brenton is now standing to his feet and gliding toward me in a drunken stagger. That's when I twirl around and sprint to the house, through the doors, and up the stairs. A million emotions are sloshing around in my brain. I'm bereaved by what Brenton has done; mad that I may not be able to trust him again. Scared that there may not be a future for us after this.

Making it to my room, I slam the door and throw the lock. Turning around, I lean my back against the door, sliding all the way down to the floor. Tears that had been threatening to burst have made their escape, the overwhelming agony pouring down my face. Racking sobs attack, so hard that it's painful. I want this night to be over. Over and done with. Just like Brenton and I ... over and done.

"God, please," I say softly, lifting my eyes to the ceiling. "Take away this pain. I can't do this. I can't handle it."

"Clarity!" Brenton shouts, his fist pounding on the door. "Clarity, please let me in!"

His presence causes me to flinch. I wipe at the tears wetting my skin. Pressing a hand against the wooden surface, I lean my forehead against the door. I know he's doing the same thing.

"Clare-Baby, *please*! I'm so sorry! I-I don't know how it all started! One minute I'm staring up at the sky and the next..." He pauses, and my heart caves in at the sound of his sobs.

I want so badly to swing the door open and console him, but the mental picture of him kissing Danielle flashes behind my eyes, taunting me over and over again. The harsh realization of betrayal digs in my heart, hollowing out the place where Brenton once resided.

"It doesn't change what you did," I whisper.

"Clarity, *please*! Open the door." His voice is in my ear, flowing through the cracks of the door. "I love you more than life. If I don't have you I'm ... I'm *nothing*."

I can't take it anymore. Standing to my feet, I cross the room and open the window wide. About to climb out, I'm halted when lavender fills the room.

Sam has appeared beside me, touching my shoulder with his hand. His blue eyes shine with intensity, his countenance that of seriousness. My palms burn with celestial heat, the temperature shooting up a couple of degrees. A calm sensation tries to burrow its way through my veins, but I stop it from happening.

"What are you doing?" he inquires.

I grimace, the sadness in my chest cultivating and spreading. "Getting out of here."

"You can't run away from your problems."

"I just need a moment to think." I gaze into his heavenly orbs. "Please, Sam. Take me away from here. If only for a little while..."

He remains quiet, his stare strict and unyielding. Brenton is still pounding on the door, wailing my name.

"Please, Sam," I whimper. "My heart is broken."

"You don't like to fly."

I counter with, "I also don't like betrayal."

He stares at me a few seconds longer, then relents. Welcoming me into his strong, safe arms, I allow his warm calmness in. I let all my emotions rise to the surface, let loose all my fears and frustrations. He lifts me up and out the window we go, flying off into the dark, moonless sky.

Sam

Clarity is still in my arms, unmoving and lightly sobbing. It pains me deeply that she's going through this, though I know that in the end God will turn it around for her good – as long as she is faithful to The Father and the gift He blessed her with.

All that's happened tonight, all the confusion, anger, bitterness – it was all orchestrated by the enemy. Her thoughts are screaming negativity about Brenton, Kora, and her life. I have to help Clarity get through this, help her see that this isn't the end of friendships or relationships. I've got to show her that no matter how hopeless a situation is, right now is not the time to give up.

There's no such thing as giving up.

Landing in front of our destination, I keep her in my arms and walk up the stairs to the little building that Brenton and Clarity call their hideout. Kicking the door open, I tell her, "Clarity, I'm letting you down now."

She mumbles, "No."

I sigh. "Well, I'm doing it anyway. It's up to you whether or not you fall on your head."

"Sam, *jeez*," she groans. "Haven't I been through enough junk tonight?"

"Yes, you've been through it tonight, but trust me – there's more coming. You might as well realize that you can't hide from reality. No matter how hard you want to."

"Fine," she says, opening her eyes.

Gently, I permit her feet to touch the floor. I keep a hand on her lower back until she's able to steady herself. She takes in a sharp breath when she realizes where I've brought her.

"Why did you bring me here?" she inquires softly.

A flash of memories shoot across her mind. Happy childhood memories of her and Brenton playing, and family cookouts. Before the memories go dark, retreating to the back of her mind, an image of the two the night of the Thanksgiving dance flies by, leaving a trail of sadness and tragedy.

This hideout used to be a cheerful place, though now it's blanketed in dust, cobwebs and despair. I observe her as she views the filthy clothes strewn all over the floor, and the dirty dishes inhabiting the small table. I follow as she walks over to the couch in the corner by the window. A pillow and white quilt covers the couch, rumpled and displaced.

"Is Brenton … *sleeping* here?"

"Yes, most nights," I reply.

"Why did you bring me here?" she questions again, with an angry gleam in her brown eyes. "I told you I wanted to get away. Instead you have brought me to the heart of all my problems."

"Brenton is not the cause of your problems," I tell her calmly.

"Isn't he?" she shoots back. "Sam, he got upset with me because I pushed him back when I saw he was drunk. After that, I find him kissing Danielle – "

"Who just happens to be possessed by Livian," I point out. "Livian orchestrated the whole thing, Clarity. And with

Brenton's mind a little fuzzy, he bought the lies she whispered."

"That doesn't matter!" she shouts. "The fact that he did what he did in front of half the school, and Kora..." Her words trail off. A sorrowful look crosses her face. "I'm losing the battle, Sam. Plain and simple."

She plops onto the couch, her eyes spying the pictures scattered on the floor. Leaning over, she picks them up and starts rifling through them. Tears streak down her face with every picture she glances over.

Sitting down next to her, I look at the pictures, as well. Some are pictures of Clarity and Brenton when they were younger, while some are more recent. There's a picture of the two of them at the Thanksgiving dance. It portrays a worn and withered look, as if someone has looked it over many, many times.

One in particular has her captivated at the moment. Janey, Casey, Kora, Brenton, Kevin and Clarity are in this one, with their arms around each others necks. All harbor bright smiles on their faces, unknowing of the fact that one of them would be gone a couple of months later. I remember that this was the night of the barn party, just a few days before she met me.

"Life has changed so much," she despairingly notes, dropping the photo to the floor. It's too much for her to handle at the moment.

"Clarity," I say, clasping her hand, "life is a continuous wheel of change. Sometimes change is great, sometimes not so great. The life you knew before is gone, and it's time for you to move forward."

She gazes at me with tears brimming her eyes. "How do I move forward?"

"You must have a forgiving heart. I know what happened has hurt you deeply, but you've got to remember that the enemy is at work. I told you that Satan aims for your weaknesses, and your weaknesses are the ones you love. Livian knows all about this, and she's targeting *you*, Clarity. You are her mission. She knows what you're capable of, and she wants to bring you down. Danielle, David, Darren – she has them fooled. They are willing to do anything she tells them."

I breathe out a sigh before adding, "Clarity, you're stronger than you realize, and the day is coming where you will have to fight."

"Sam, how am I supposed to fight the supernatural?"

"You don't get it!" I exclaim, surprising her. "Haven't I explained enough? Haven't I been here for you, showing you things and ministering to you? You, Clarity Miller, are a part of the unseen world! God gifted you to fight in The Light's army!" I let out an aggravating groan, then hug her close. "You've got to defeat this urge of giving in and giving up. Because if you don't, darkness is going to drain out every bit of light within you."

Clarity doesn't say anything, so I hold onto her even tighter. She's needing to feel loved and protected right now, though a time is coming that she's going to have to take a stand and face the demons head on. As of right now, she's not strong enough. She doesn't have the confidence it takes to defeat the enemy; she doesn't have the full amount of faith needed to succeed.

"Sam?"

"Yes, Clarity?" The next words she speaks showers me with soaring hope.

"Please pray for me," she whispers.

"I will," I promise.

If there's anything she needs right now, it's prayer, so I prayed with a loving, sincere and faithful heart.

I'm expecting miracles.

Soon.

Chapter Sixteen

Clarity

Waves crash onto the white sand as the dark sky rumbles above. The tempestuous winds attack my body, forcing my clothes to cling tightly to my skin. Lightning strikes over the ocean, the ground shakes beneath my bare feet. Sea Gulls call out to each other, flying in all directions. This island is bleak and desolate, and about to be hit head-on by a major storm.

Why am I here? What's the purpose?

Suddenly, a light shines to the right of me. Turning my gaze toward the brightness, it takes a few seconds for my focus to clear. Two figures materialize a few feet away. Somehow their side of the island is bright and sunny, while my side is stormy and bruised.

"Hello!" I call out as I begin to trek over to the calm side of the island.

I can't move too far, thanks to an unseen barrier blocking my way. Lifting my hand in front of me, I feel the barrier – it's like an invisible wall has been constructed between the two people and I. Opening my mouth to call out to them, the words become stuck on the tip of my tongue. The two come into view, and fear snakes through my ribcage. One is small with dark hair, while the other is tall with long white hair.

Kora is there, being held close by Livian.

"No!" I shout, banging on the invisible wall, hoping to break through. I stop when Livian's white eyes lift to mine. My heart stutters as she speaks in her lyrical voice.

"Mine! All mine!" She leans her head back and cackles.

A raging wind blows, lifting me off my feet. I'm flying in the air with the Sea Gulls, yet they are no longer Sea Gulls. Nope. Tsipor demons have taken their place in the dark, growling sky.

I start to fall. The huge waves reach for my feet. I scream as I'm dropped into the angry sea. The cold depths pull me under, all the way to the bottom. There's no light at the bottom of the ocean. No light at all.

I'm crying out for help, my hands reaching upward; I'm praying for God's hand to save my life and pull me out of the dark waters.

Nothing happens. Nothing but my lungs filling with water. Instead of the helping hand I so desperately need, I'm pinned to the bottom, the ocean swallowing my body and stealing my breath...

Stealing my life.

Immediately I wake, sitting straight up. Unable to breathe, I'm choking, gasping for air. My lungs actually feel like they're full of water. I cough and cough, my fist beating at my chest. I can still smell the briny, salty air. I can still hear the waves crashing upon the shore; I can still hear Livian's abrasive, evil laughter. A sound that I'll never be able to forget.

"Kora," I whisper aloud.

Jumping to my feet, I open the door and cross the hallway to Kora's bedroom. Gently, I crack her door open and take a peek inside. She's sound asleep, quiet and still, underneath her covers. From my vantage point, I spot a peaceful look on her face.

"Livian has her fooled."

Christopher has materialized next to me, the glow of his eyes lighting the hallway. Slowly I close her door, then turn to him.

"Livian is using her dreams to snag her, right?" I inquire.

He nods. "Yes, and unfortunately it's working. Livian has told Kora that she's her savior, and that David is a gift. What Kora doesn't realize is that it's a ploy to pull her into her devious game." He pauses, his eyes narrowing. "You've got to help her."

"I already know that, but what can I do?" I ask. "I want to help her, but I don't know how."

"There's only one thing you can do for now. One simple thing that can produce great results. You can't imagine how great the results."

"What?"

His face softens as he replies, "Pray."

Prayer has always been hard for me, only because I never know what to say. For years I didn't talk to God at all, though lately, little by little, I'd been seeking Him. More and more, everyday, I try reaching out to Him. The thing is, I wonder if He's still listening. With all the negative stuff happening, I'm always questioning if He's there, which I know He is. Sometimes, in my humanness, I feel like He's abandoned me, even though that is contradictory to His Word.

Walking back to my room, I drop to my knees by the bed. I push all negativity from my mind, from Brenton all the way to Livian. My energy becomes focused on God, and in no time I know exactly what needs to be prayed, which shocks me. I've always found it hard to pray, but not this time. It just hits me, like rain falling from the sky. As if God is pouring life into my soul and I'm speaking it. I don't even have to think – the words just come out.

"God..." I begin.

From that moment I prayed until sunrise, believing a miracle was on the way.

***

The next few weeks fly by in a hazy rush. Each day holds its own strength of despondency and bleakness. Garlandton High students walk around like zombies, as if they've given up all their internal lights. A dark gloomy cloud of sorrow hovers over the small town, raining its lamentable spores onto every soul within the town's limits.

My whole reality has been turned upside down, inside out, and trampled beyond recognition. Nothing feels complete anymore, nothing fits right. The pieces of my life's puzzle wanders aimlessly in the chaotic winds of disarray – my ongoing nightmare.

Kora and I live under the same roof, but we have become strangers. We have no choice but to be cordial, since our bedrooms are across the hall from each other. As far as I know, David is still around, most likely in her room every night. I can't be too sure, because she never talks to me. She has shut me out of her life completely, locking my existence behind a door of resentment.

Brenton calls my cell phone nearly every hour of the day, but I don't answer. He attempts to speak to me in class, in the halls, at work – I never say a word, giving him the same treatment Kora is giving me. I'm not ready to talk about what happened. The hurt is still strong and bitter – I need more time to heal.

Two holes reside in my heart, the aches resulting in constant pains.

Danielle acts like nothing happened, never apologizing for kissing my boyfriend in front of half the school. She chitchats about this and that, never noticing my disinterested expression, or the fact that I never say a word.

Casey seems to have forgotten that night, as well. At work he and Danielle spend a lot of time together, leaving me to cashier the store alone, which I'm totally okay with. The less time around her the better.

A.C. came back from her beach getaway with Doug a renewed woman. She's still flying high on cloud nine with their engagement. Thanks to her focus on an upcoming wedding, she has failed to notice that Kora and I are not on good terms. In front of A.C., we act like the best of friends, but once upstairs we go our separate ways; Kora to her room, and I to mine.

Also, A.C. has no idea that we had a party behind her back. I still feel like a piece of dirt for having it.

With all the drama and confusion in my life, I'm attempting to understand all that's happening. I also know that no matter the situation, life and everything that follows continues to spin on. Like right now, it's two in the morning and I'm sitting at my desk, listening to the rain batter the roof. A math book is opened, a pencil is in my hand, and I'm staring down at a blank piece of paper. Try as I might, I can't concentrate on this Trig problem.

In a few hours I'll be leaving out for school, and it will be a tough one. After all, today is Valentine's Day. To most people this day is special, since it's a day dedicated to love and being with the one you love and *blah blah blah...*

For me this day marks a new milestone – my birthday.

My *eighteenth* birthday. And what are my plans for this super special day?

A mental list forms in my brain of how the day will commence.

I'll go to school with the rest of my dopey friends, sit in classrooms all day and learn crap that will never be used in the real world. I will avoid Brenton like the plague, even as he begs for forgiveness for groping the new girl, while Kora hangs all over David, who just happens to be possessed by a General in Satan's army. A demon I have yet to meet – I don't count the dream as a meeting.

I'll be ignored by my best friend, then after school go to my sucky cashier's job where I will work behind a register, while Casey and Danielle smooch in the stockroom.

My heart will continue to be broken. My existence will continue to be marred.

Happy Birthday to *me*.

A loud knock on my window jars me from my woeful thoughts. The sudden sound causes my heart to leap to my throat as my mind conceives the fearsome idea that Livian is knocking on the window, with her army following behind.

When a familiar face appears, peeking through the rain-soaked window, relief caresses my nerves. My heart falls back into place, though it's thrumming hard against my ribs at the sight of him.

Brenton.

Rushing over, I lift the window. Cold wind and rain buffets my bare flesh in return.

Without a word he climbs in, drenched from head to toe. He looks me over with amusement dancing in his brown eyes, and his lips stretch into a grin. A blush creeps across his face as his gaze drops to the floor. Clearly something is funny to him, and I'm about to ask him what it is when I remember the sleepwear I'm in.

Red boxers and a black camisole. No bra.

Quickly, I grab my robe off my desk chair and tie it around me, my face burning with abashment.

"Thanks for letting me in," he says, taking his leather jacket off and laying it across the back of the desk chair. His hair is in short ringlets, with rainwater dripping like teardrops onto the carpet. Taking a look at him, I see that his face is paler than usual, and he appears to have lost some weight.

"You're soaked," I mutter. Picking a towel up from the floor, I throw it in his direction.

He catches it, giving me a grateful smile. "Thanks."

Biting my lip, I don't offer a reply. I watch as he dries off the best he can, which isn't too good. When he's done, he plops down in the chair, his gaze falling on me. I regard him with mute detachment, standing a few feet away with my arms at my sides.

After a few weird and silent seconds, he says, "I miss you."

I cross my arms at my chest, not allowing him to get to me. Willing myself to be unmoved, I reply with, "Wow, you miss me? Huh, maybe you should have thought about that before you made-out with a total stranger!"

His eyes pop wide open, and I can tell my biting words are crawling underneath his skin. A miserable grimace leaps across his face. He's hurting as much as I am right now.

Good.

"What are you doing here?" I ask tonelessly.

"I had to see you," he replies. "I couldn't go one more

day without telling you how sorry I am."

I scowl. "You couldn't have waited until school tomorrow?"

"I've tried that!" he mournfully cries. "I've tried and tried, and tried some more to get you to talk to me, but … Clarity, you've shut me completely out of your life and it's killing me! I-I'm miserable without you." He leans forward in the chair, his elbows resting atop his legs and his head dropping into his hands.

An ache begins quivering to life in my heart. I plop down on the bed, facing him as I say, "Tell me how I'm supposed to feel. Tell me how I'm supposed to react. Should I feel bad? Good?" I release a shaky breath, then ask, "Do you think it's been easy cutting you out of my life?"

He lifts his head, raises his eyes sharply to mine, and responds, "By the way you've been ignoring me, I figured it hadn't been too hard on you at all."

"*What*?!" I shout, with anger igniting fresh in my bloodstream. "Are you serious? Brenton, you're the one who ripped my heart to shreds. You, of all people … I never thought you'd do that to me, but..." My words suddenly become stanched, thanks to the daunting sob that's threatening to bust wide open. I stand up, my back to him, not wanting to show how weak and frail I am.

"Clare-Baby, I'm sorry. You'll never know how sorry I am. I feel like the biggest scumbag to ever walk the earth. And I know you deserve so much better than me." I hear the chair creak as he stands to his feet. "What I did – I can't even remember most of that night. I don't even know what I was angry about. But what I do know is that I hurt you, embarrassed you, and ... I'll never hurt you again, Clarity."

Shifting around to face him, I'm surprised that he's only a couple of steps away. There is a pleading set in his eyes, one full of hope and yearning. His body holds a defeated edge, his arms dangle loosely at his sides. I've never seen him so discomfited.

"Please, Clarity," he speaks softly, "forgive me. Please give me another chance."

Tears burn my eyes as his words soak in. My guard is slipping away fast ... and I hate it. The more I tell myself that I don't need him in my life, the more I realize that statement is untrue. I do need him. Not only that, but I *want* him in my life, and that scares me.

The problem is (and this is a biggie) I don't know if I'll ever be able to fully trust him again. If we were to get back together, and that trust never truly recover, would that be fair to him?

When I don't respond he says, "I love you. I need you. I want to spend the rest of my life with you." Reaching into his back pocket, he pulls out a small black box. My stomach drops to my knees, my body trembling with restrained emotion.

"Brenton, what is – " My voices snags in my throat when he gets down to one knee and pops open the box. A very delicate white gold band is nestled inside, with a small round diamond resting on four prongs. Placing a hand to my chest, my mouth hangs open in surprise, while my heart thumps triple its usual time.

"I've had this planned a long time," he begins in a quivering voice. "I was going to give this to you the night of the party, but I screwed it all up."

What's happening? Oh, what's happening?!

Thoughts are swirling round and round like a cyclone in my brain. Numbness attacks my body as it prepares for what's coming next. Wait, what is coming next? Surely not what I'm thinking. Surely not...

He clears his throat and continues. "Like I said, you

deserve so much better than me, but I can't go on without you. I know you're the one, and while you may be skeptical, this isn't an engagement ring – I plan a much bigger diamond for that occasion. This ring is a promise, from me to you."

"Oh, Brenton," I whisper, struggling to steady the ebullient beat of my heart.

"I promise you, Clarity," he says, "to love you with all of my heart. I'll never again hurt you no matter what happens. This ring is a gift for you to keep forever. It represents my heart, and whatever you decide, always know that my heart belongs to you."

He eagerly awaits my response, but I'm too stunned to speak. When I'd imagined this moment I'd planned to say so many things, but those words are lost in the hurricane winds of surprise.

"I don't know ... what to say." Seriously, I don't.

"I love you, Clarity Elise Miller," he declares, taking my left hand. "I always have and I always will. No matter what the future holds, my heart is yours, always and forever."

I clear my throat, the inside of my mouth as dry as sand paper. "Don't make any promises you don't intend to keep."

A pained look shadows his features. "Don't you know me better than that?"

"I thought I did," I counter softly. "How can I trust you, Brenton? Please tell me how."

He closes his eyes and answers, "I don't have that answer." Opening his eyes and staring intensely into mine, he adds, "But I can tell you that I'm done drinking alcohol. *Done*. It made me something I wasn't, something I didn't recognize. All I can do from here on out is be loyal to you, and love you forever."

"Forever's a long time, Brenton."

He smiles. "Yes, it is."

Taking my hand out of his, I walk over to the window, the storm still raging. He walks over as well, staring out the window alongside me. Then, in a sudden movement, he turns me around in his arms, pulling my body close.

"I know you'll never forget what I did," he says, placing an unruly strand of hair behind my ear. "I can't take it back, but I can make sure it never happens again."

Despite my anger and hurt, I believe him.

With lovelorn tears stinging my eyes, I whisper, "Promise?"

"Promise," he replies. "Will you forgive me?"

I nod and say, "Yes, I forgive you."

Smiling, he takes my left hand and places the ring on my finger.

A perfect fit.

"I've missed you so much," I confess, gazing into his eyes.

"I've missed you, too." Then, in a soft tone, he says, "Happy Birthday, Clare-Baby."

We stand there in a tight embrace as the storm outside begins to cease. Joy flows through my veins, captivating my soul. For the first time in months, I'm at peace (excluding all the times Sam has forced it on me).

No, this peace is a different kind, one that happens on its own.

Though one single thought has me on edge. The words Brenton spoke "no matter what the future holds" has me stumped, because one day, if we are to be married, he'll need to hear the truth. He'll need to know the gifts God has bestowed on me – the gifts of a Seer. That leads me to wonder...

Will Brenton be able to handle it?

Chapter Seventeen

Sam

I lean back on the window, observing my Charge as she sleeps. She's finally at peace, thanks to Brenton coming over with a humble heart and admitting he had been wrong. In return she'd forgiven him, and now they are back together, stronger than ever before.

A flash of lightning draws my attention to the outside world. The storm has passed, though another is on the way. Clarity's moment of peace will not last long. Not with the enemy still reaching for her heels in hopes of snatching and dragging her down.

"It won't be long now," says Christopher, who has appeared next to me.

"I know," I reply in agreement, knowing the truth of the matter. "How's Kora?"

"Good," he answers. "She's asleep and having a heavenly visitor in her dreams."

I glance at him. "You think she will see the light?"

He sighs and says, "I hope so. Boy, do I hope so."

Kora

I stretch out on the sand, with hands locked together behind my head. My eyes are closed as I listen to the waves crashing and receding, over and over again. A soft breeze ruffles my hair, the salty air cleanses my senses – I am at total peace.

"Kora."

Immediately, I open my eyes, the sudden voice sending my body to a sitting position. Who the voice belongs to causes a violent tremor to attack my system, one that starts at the top of my head and ends at the tips of my toes. I grasp at comprehension, but my mind just won't let it compute. I never thought I'd see this person again.

"Kevin!"

Kevin is here. On my private island. Sitting on a huge rock underneath a palm tree. He stands to his feet and smiles. The clothes he's wearing are very simple, consisting of t-shirt, jeans, and a baseball cap. Exactly what he wore when he was alive.

Wait ... how can this be? How can Kevin be standing before me?

Surging to my feet, I close the space between us and wrap my arms around his neck. He smells like he always did – clean, fresh, with a hint of summer. His arms wrap around my waist and another shiver courses through my body. I know my mind has made up this island, but this embrace feels real. Even more so than the slight breeze off the ocean and the hint of salt in the air.

A few peaceful moments pass before we break apart. I stare into his blue/green eyes, marveling at the fact that he's standing in front of me, wearing his shy smile. I have so much to ask him, so many things to say, I don't know where to begin.

Eventually, he takes my hand in his and says, "Come. Sit down with me."

I oblige, allowing him to lead me over to the rock. We sit down, staring into each others eyes. Three months have passed since his death. Three months since I've seen his face. I'd almost forgotten what he'd looked like, even after that short period of time. Crazy how the mind works.

"How are you here with me?" I wonder, keeping my eyes on his. "You died three months ago. You're dead."

He grins. "Yes, my body died. But I'm more alive than ever. More alive than you can comprehend in your flesh."

His words confuse me, though I choose not to point that out. "You look the same as you did before. How is this possible?"

"Kora, I don't have much time to talk. I must hurry and get out all I have to say." There's a distinct urgency in his voice, one that can't be ignored.

"What is it?" I inquire, studying his features.

"You're being deceived by the devil," he declares, his eyes falling to our hands. "This place, this utopia ... it's not real. This isn't reality."

I laugh. "I know that, silly. I've made this whole place up in my mind. The lady with white hair already told me that."

His eyes slowly raise up. "She is the devil I'm talking about."

"What?" My eyebrows shoot to double arches, his disturbing words a shock.

"She's not to be trusted," he continues. "She's a liar, a deceiver, a General in Satan's army. And she wants to destroy you."

"That's not ... can't be true!" Jerking my hand from his, I rise to my feet. "She's not evil. She loves me!"

"No, she doesn't." He stands up, placing his hands in his pockets. "She doesn't know how to love. She can't love."

"You're lying!" I shout, backing up a couple of steps. "She's been there for me! She sent me David –"

"Who is a worker of iniquity," he interjects.

I push onward, ignoring his statement. "She takes care of me, she's ... she's my savior!"

"There is only one Savior," he says, "and His name is Jesus."

I open my mouth to object, but instantly snap it shut. With his last remark, I'm left speechless. There is no argument I can give, no rebuttal that can dismiss what he's just spoken. He takes a couple steps forward, then palms my cheek. I lean into his hand – it feels so real.

"You are right," I say as an overflow of comprehension pours over me. "I can't believe how blind I've been. I guess since losing you and mama, I've been searching for what I've lost."

"You've been through the fire, and the devil sensed your weakness."

"I-I just wanted something to believe in, and someone to love

me."

"No one and nothing supersedes the love Jesus Christ has for you." He smiles. "Get back to church, girl."

I laugh as I reply, "Definitely. My eyes have been o – "

"Who are you talking to?" a stern voice inquires directly behind me.

Spinning around, I find the lady with white hair hovering slightly above the ground, though something is different. Anger is etched across her face, replacing her peaceful smile and loving demeanor.

"I'm just talking to Kevin," I respond. Her eyes narrow, and her lips stitch together in a tight line.

"She can't see me," Kevin informs.

"What?" I wonder, turning back to him.

He's frowning as he says, "Heaven's Army has me surrounded. I'm protected from the demonic."

"Demonic? What – "

Before I can finish my thought, a hand seizes my shoulder and wrenches me back. I lose my footing as I'm pulled farther and farther away from Kevin. Panic weaves through my limbs, sending my heart into contractions.

"Kevin!" I scream, reaching out for him.

"Kora, get away from David!" His voice is getting fainter and fainter. "Get away from them all!"

Suddenly I'm thrown to the ground, face first. Rolling onto my back, I stare up into the eyes of the beautiful lady, the one who said she was my savior. Only now she doesn't look as beautiful. Her eyes are now black, like bottomless wells, and her face has contorted into rage.

The sky above darkens as lightning starts flashing all around the island. The wind has picked up, sending sand into the air, stinging my eyes. The island starts to shake, the waves grow higher and higher. I'm paralyzed with fear, my eyes still caught in the woman's glare.

"You ungrateful piece of garbage!" she yells. I scream when long fangs grow out of her mouth, touching her bottom lip. Sneering, she adds, "You are not worthy of my love – you are not worthy of any love! You are DEAD to me!"

She reaches out a hand, which now has long black talons on each finger. As she does this, the air in my lungs become constricted. I grab at my neck, disbelieving what is happening. It feels so real, too real to be a dream. I can't breathe. I can't …

I'm dying.

Clarity

Something stirs me from my slumber. A choking noise. A loud, horrible choking noise. And it's coming from across the hall.

"Kora," I whisper.

Becoming fully awake, I spring from the bed, sprinting across the hall to Kora's room. I don't think about our problems, about her being upset with me. None of that matters. What matters is that she's in her room, choking, and I've got to help her.

Throwing the door open, banging it hard against the wall, I freeze at the sight before me. A large *Tsipor* demon sits on her chest, and by the size of it I'd say he was close to crushing her little body. My palms burn with a fierce passion, shining a bright red. Not sure of what to do, I start charging forward, my hand lifted in front of me. That posture just seemed right.

The demon turns its head, its yellow eyes growing wide. I'm unafraid as I jump on the bed next to her. However, the demon is fast. It makes an annoying squawk sound, then flies out the open window.

With the demon gone, Kora sits up, seemingly awake. She's coughing her head off, attempting to suck in the air her lungs desperately long for. I sit down beside her, placing an arm around her shoulders. Once her breath has been caught and her heart a steady beat, she looks up at me. A tinge of fear is set in her green eyes, telling me all I need to know – she'd been dreaming, and she's scared.

"You're okay, Kora," I say, hoping to soothe her overwhelming fear.

She shakes her head. "No, Clare, I'm not. I'm *not* okay."

"You want to talk about it?" I ask, giving her shoulder a squeeze.

"It was horrible," she starts. Her body trembles. "I've never – not ever had a nightmare like that one. It felt so ... so *real*. All of it. And there's a part of me that wants to believe that it was, in fact, real."

"What happened?" I wonder, releasing my hold from her shoulders.

"There's this lady in white..."

A shiver forces its way through my system, though I'm able to hide it. I know exactly who she's speaking of...

Livian.

"She told me," she continues, "that she was my savior. That she loved me and would take care of me. She said that David was a gift, and that should prove her love." A tear slides down her pale face. "I believed her, Clarity! I believed every single thing she'd ever said to me, but then..."

When she hesitates, I push, "Then what?"

Another tear slides down her cheek as she replies, "Kevin showed up and reminded me that there's only one Savior, and that's Jesus."

"Wait, Kevin spoke to you in your dream?" I'm beyond shocked, though I've learned to believe the unbelievable.

She nods. "Yes. And Clare, he looked the same as he always did. Seeing him and talking with him helped me to remember the way it was before, and all the times we went to church together. I believe ... God sent him to wake me up.

"In the dream, Kevin warned me about the lady with white hair. He said she's a devil, and that David is a worker of iniquity. I-I didn't believe him at first, not until the lady who I

thought was my savior turned into some kind of rage machine."
She laughs out loud, then whispers, "I sound crazy, don't I?"

I smile. "Actually, no. You don't sound crazy at all."

"I've got to break up with David," she whispers
suddenly.

The proclamation that leaves her mouth soars right
through me. My legs want to leap up and jump for joy, but I'm
able to hold it together. Kora has taken the first step to freedom,
and that first step is separating herself from the enemy.

"I'm so sorry, Clarity."

Again, shock touches every single synapse my body
holds.

"Kora, it's okay – "

"No, it isn't," she strongly interjects. "You've been
nothing but a good friend, and all I've been is ugly to you. Will
you forgive me?"

Staring into her eyes, I can see the sincerity there.
Wrapping my arms around her, I say, "Of course I do."

For the first time in my life I realize that prayer produces
miracles, and that's a true faith builder. When I'd prayed for

Kora and given all my hurts to the Lord, He went ahead and orchestrated a wondrous work, not only in Kora, but inside of me. Even after God's hand lifted me from the dark depths of the cold river, my faith had remained weak. However, now I can feel the actual hand of God holding my life.

"Told you."

Christopher appears behind Kora, his smile broad and his eyes aglow. His fresh cut grass scent fills the air, reminding me of a lazy summer day.

"I told you," he continues, "that prayer can produce great results."

Boy, it sure does.

Chapter Eighteen

Clarity

The rest of the week goes by splendidly, a few of the wayward puzzle pieces of reality fitting back into place. Brenton and I are back to be the loving couple we once were – I wear my promise ring proudly. The ring is small, but to me it's the best promise I could get on this earth.

After dumping David, Kora is back to her easy-going, joyful self. She's anticipating this upcoming Sunday. We're going to the church Kevin had gone to, and she's beyond excited. I haven't seen her this joyous in a long while.

Janey is in higher spirits, though the reasoning behind her joy is most likely due to the fact that Danielle hasn't been in school for the past three days. With Danielle's absence, Casey wanders the halls alone, like a mangy lost puppy searching for someone to love.

Actually, all three of Livian's pawns have been no-shows the last three days of the school week. The day Kora broke it off with David was the last day they had been in school. I wasn't there when the breakup occurred, though I've caught bits and pieces from the gossip pool spilling out every which way in the Garlandton halls.

Apparently David had taken the news pretty well, showing absolutely no emotion whatsoever. He had walked out of the school without saying a word. The craziest part of it all was Darren and Danielle. They'd shown up beside him right after Kora walked away from him, and followed him out like programmed robots.

Some are saying that they're so close they can feel each others emotions. Sort of like what twins feel for each other when one is sad or in trouble. However, I know better than to believe that. I have the real truth.

The reason they came together is because they're possessed by a demon. Plain and simple.

Since their absence I've noticed that every single demon has left the school, along with all Guardians. The last few days I haven't suffered headaches that come with all the demon and angel smells in the air. Okay, so no one besides myself knows

228

this substantial information, but still, it's an important factor.

Friday night has arrived, and I'm at Baker's working my menial cashier job. Thankfully it's a slow one, especially since Casey called in sick and Danielle disappeared, along with her two "brothers". In the back of my mind a tiny thought breezes between my ears, saying maybe, just *maybe*, Livian decided to leave this town alone; that maybe she's giving up.

I know that's a big heap of nonsense.

I try not to dwell on the negative, and trust me, there is a lot of junk I could harp on. Rather, I attempt to stay positive, enjoying the peace that has settled around my friends and I. That peace, at any given moment, could be yanked out from under us, with Hell breaking loose with its absence.

The bell at Baker's makes its *ding-ding* sound, indicating new customers coming in. A sinking feeling punches my stomach with strong anxiety. My palms blaze red hot, igniting that way too familiar heat.

Slowly, I lift my eyes and catch sight of the customers. David, Danielle, and Darren stand side by side, expressionless and eyes milky white. I know, without a shadow of a doubt, that Hell will be making its presence known in Garlandton.

I stare at them in wonder, with fear permeating deep in my bones. They're clothes are dirty and rumpled, and their hair is tangled and bushy. No expressions paint their faces. Their statures are stiff and rigid – the perfect picture of possession.

Mr. Baker is holed-up in is office behind a locked door. I try calling out to him, but I find that my tongue is immobile, like it's been glued to the roof of my mouth. An icy blanket covers my skin, my legs going numb. This feeling – I've experienced it before. I know it all too well, a sort of premonition; a heavy sense of foreboding.

My body jerks involuntarily as the three pawns speak at the same time, their voices robotic and toneless.

"Our mother wants to talk to you."

I shiver, the chill freezing the blood within in my veins.

"Why?" I croak out, thankful my tongue is working again.

They don't answer. All they do is maliciously grin.

"She wants to barter with you," Sam softly speaks. Lavender explodes through the air, the scent instantly calming my nerves.

Not at all surprised by his abrupt presence, I shift my gaze to his and wonder, "Barter *what*?"

"You are not allowed, Guardian," they tell Sam. Hatred oozes through their voices, their eyes narrowing. Smiles no longer have hold of their lips.

"They can see you?" I inquire, dumbfounded.

He nods. "Only because she's in their bodies, controlling them." He keeps his gaze on the three possessed teens. "They are simply vessels, her puppets. She's using them to get to you."

That's right, Livian's sickeningly sweet voice echoes in my head, sending a shudder to course through me. My palms warm up tremendously by the sound of her voice. A sudden pain jabs at my skull. *Now be a good little Ra'ah and come to me.*

As if on some supernatural cue, the pawns start speaking in their machine-like tones.

"Come to the old gym at school. Be there at ten. We will be waiting for you." Simultaneously, in a group, they turn toward the door. Before they leave they tell Sam in cryptic voices, "Your kind is *not* welcomed."

I'm stunned. Entirely and altogether dismayed. All I can

do is watch in silence as they march out the doors and into the blackened night. The ringing of the bell snaps me from my incredulous state.

"Sam." My legs give out. I start to plummet to the floor. Sam keeps me from falling flat on my face. Fear clings to my bones, depleting me of all energy.

"You're alright, Clarity," he murmurs, his touch warming my skin.

"What do I do?" I ask of my Guardian. His response is confusing.

"You can't go."

"What?!" I wrench myself from his grasp. "What do you mean I can't go? How can I *not* go?"

His expression displays concern. "You are not ready."

I shake my head. "I can't believe you're saying this. You're always telling me that one day I will have to fight. What if this is that day?"

"Your faith is growing, and your knowledge of the Word has grown, but you still doubt yourself." He grimaces and continues. "After all you've seen and been through, you still don't see yourself as a threat to the enemy. It's hard for you to grasp that God thought so much of you that He gave you a powerful gift that can help the lost and crush the head of the serpent.

"When you go into battle, you must put on the Full Armor of God. Not only that, but you must believe in its power. You, Clarity, have that power running through your veins. The problem is, you don't know how to use it."

Sam's words bite – extremely hard. But they ring true. I do doubt myself when it comes to my Seer gifts, only because I've never been taught how to use them correctly.

"The Holy Spirit will teach you to use them correctly," he informs, obviously busy reading my thoughts. "The thing is, you won't let Him."

"I don't know how," I confess, becoming teary-eyed.

Narrowing his eyes, he says, "You need to realize that you aren't in control – He is. Once you let go of yourself, He will instruct you on what to do."

I gaze into the eyes of my Guardian, swallowing his *hard-to-digest* words. I realize he is right. The hardest part is letting go of self, and I'm a stickler for being in control of my actions. Well, except for the times I was drunk, but I'm not that person anymore. I'm changed, though I'm still learning.

"Sam," I say, lifting my chin high, "I know I've got much to learn, but I can't dismiss this meeting with Livian. If she wants to meet, we'll meet. I'm not going to run away – I've ran too many times in my life."

"Clarity – "

"My mind is made up," I inject. "There's nothing you can say or do to stop me. All I ask is that you go with me, and pray for me." I step closer, staring into his glowing blue eyes. "Will you do that, Sam? Will you stand with me and pray?"

There's a battle happening in my angel right now. It is broadcast all over his face. He doesn't want me to go, but he also knows he can't stop me.

Sam blows out a sigh and replies, "Yes, Clarity, I will. But you need to know that there's only so much I can help with. I can't interfere until the Throne Room says I can."

"That's a chance I'm willing to take," I boldly state.

"Well," he says, "your mind is made up. I'm going to leave you alone to pray, so..." He forces a smile. "Start praying."

Sam

Clarity has been praying for almost an hour now. She's in her car, and I'm guarding over it. As much as I want her to wait a little while longer, cognizant of the fact that she still needs to work on herself and her gift, I know that I can't stop her. She's too stubborn. She always has been.

Thunder sounds in the distance, one of the supernatural kind. Livian is getting ready to attack. Her plans to destroy Clarity's relationships have failed miserably, and she doesn't take failure lightly. Since then, she's been waiting for the perfect opportunity to meet with Clarity. With the recent breakup between Kora and David, this was the time to face her adversary – my Charge, Clarity.

I'm not happy that Clarity won't listen to a single word of reason. If she can't listen to rationality, there's nothing I can do. Nothing but watch as the meeting takes place.

"Why do you want to stop Clarity?" Gabriel inquires. He's materialized beside me, his gaze pointed toward her.

Turning to him I reply, "Because she's not ready."

"When is the right time for her to be ready?" he counters.

"When she stops doubting herself."

Taking a step in front of me, blocking Clarity from sight, he stares right in my eyes and says, "Maybe it's not that Clarity is doubting herself, but that you are doubting Clarity."

With an understanding expression, he vanishes, leaving me to ponder his words.

Chapter Nineteen

Clarity

The old gym is located on the abandoned side of the school. It is an ancient and broken down building, emaciated on the outside *and* the inside. The school uses it as a storage locker for all sorts of junk – extra band and athletic equipment, beat up furniture, and other miscellaneous artifacts that are useless. Dirty windows line the top of the gymnasium, their surfaces caked with dust and grime.

Walking up to the entrance, I notice a chain and padlock laying on the ground. Taking a closer look I come to the conclusion that the lock had come in contact with something heavy, possibly something sharp and medieval. A rock props the door open, keeping the weighty door from closing all the way.

A moldering smell travels up my nose as I enter the debilitated building. The dust of the last fifty years or so burns my eyes, tickling the back of my throat. A loud *click* sounds as the door shuts behind me.

My eyes travel over the retched scenery. The walls have rotted wood and mold cultivating on their surfaces. In one corner, a pile of desks are crammed one on top of the other, tossed away and forgotten.

A cold sheet of fear suddenly fastens around me. I'm no longer alone.

Shifting my gaze to the right, my heart leaps to my mouth. Standing a few feet away are Livian's pawns – David, Darren, and Danielle. They stand side by side, as still as statues. The darkness in the gym cloaks the atmosphere thickly, the orange glow from the lampposts outside the only lights available. The gym is a gloomy edifice, but even with the dim setting I see their eyes are clouded over with whiteness, a definite sign that Livian holds them on a very short leash.

Tentatively, I walk toward them, using extreme caution. I know that Sam is near, though he is invisible at the moment. I should be less nervous knowing my Guardian is here, but the waver in my heart and the sick feel in my stomach causes my fear to grow stronger. Sometimes it's hard to have faith in something ... or someone you can't see.

Halting my steps, I stand a couple feet away from the three pawns. I can't tell if they're looking at me or even aware that I'm here. Their expressions are stone-cold – comatose, like the mentally ill patients at the hospital after taking their daily concoction of pills. They look empty and lost, with no hope or reason.

"Well, I'm here," I announce, my voice breaking the restless silence. The sound reverberates off the walls of the dying gym. "So, where's your big bad mother?"

They remain unresponsive, their impassive faces staying chill and numb. I'm about to yell for them to snap out of it, but before I can, changes begin taking place in the gym.

First, all the windows frost over with ice. Second, the air becomes heavy and dense, making it hard to breathe. Third, a nasty smell overtakes the building's moldy odor. And finally, the hot and blistering feeling drilling my palms.

Wow. Nothing like a heavy dose of déjà vu.

My mind journeys back to the night I'd met Lukus and his gang, but this time it's different. This evil feels immense, unrelenting and venomous. The sudden itch to twist around and dart from this hazardous danger shouts at my synapses. I want to break away from the horror that wants to tear me apart, limb by limb. Instead, I fight back that impulse, squashing it like a bug. No way do I want to appear weak and frail. No. *Way.*

Since I've been chosen by God to be part of this supernatural war, I can't let Him down by running away. Though I haven't been around other Seers, I'm pretty sure that they wouldn't run away with their tails between their legs. Besides, what do I have to fear? It's not like I'm alone to fend for myself ... right?

The flapping of wings invade my eardrums, and a strong wind derives from an unknown place. My blood coagulates in my body as I catch sight of a creature so beautiful, yet so terrifying at the same time.

Right away I know this creature is Livian.

The dream I'd recently seen her in had given me a vague look at her appearance. Just as Christopher had described, she has pale white skin and eyes, with platinum white hair cascading down to her waist. She's wearing black leather pants with a matching bodice, along with knee-high boots with at least three inch heels. A large *Tsipor* demon is perched on her shoulder, which fits in with her Gothic apparel.

What surprises me even more than her outlandish outfit is the black feathery wings that protrude from her back. They flutter gracefully, whispering to the air. Her entire appearance portrays a major contrast, her whole outfit a huge demarcation to her overall look. Blanched eyes unblinkingly glare my way. Her red lips twist into a malicious snarl.

The three pawns remain placid and hollow, their expressions vacant of any emotion or feeling. When Livian lands next to them, they don't acknowledge her presence, and vice versa, which strikes me as weird. Isn't she supposed to be their mother figure?

My palms burn and glow red as she takes a couple of steps forward, her heeled-boots slapping viciously at the hardwood floor. A voice inside my head screams for me to run, but I stand my ground. Lifting my chin, I glare right back at her, my hands balling into fists. She stops only a couple feet away, tilting her head to the side, apparently sizing me up.

The smell of death is dancing all around, clinging to the air with its abrasive reek. I try breathing through my mouth so as not to snort the noxious stench.

"Hello, Clarity. I am Livian." She bows her head, the whole while keeping her white eyes focused on mine. A peaky tone harbors her voice, her words coming out gentle and slow. And just as Christopher had pointed out, her voice is enchanting. His voice echoes between my ears:

Her voice sounds like a chorus of angels, which she uses to entrance unsuspecting humans.

"Hey!" I call out strongly. "Halloween was a few months ago, but I can see you celebrate year round!"

Why did I say that? Why did I open my mouth and let that snarky but true comment slide from my lips? And where is all the bravado I'm experiencing coming from? I'm not brave at all – I'm quivering in my boots ... literally!

Her lips curl into a sneer. "You do not approve of my attire, Seer?" She ruffles her long white eyelashes.

"Uh..." I can't think of anything to respond with, so I say, "Not ... really?" That last part comes out like a question.

Surprisingly, she throws her head back and laughs, expressing, "I like you, little *Ra'ah*. You stand here and disrespect me, knowing who I am and what I'm capable of, but yet you are not afraid ... well, at least on the outside you show no fear."

She pauses, her smile fading and her eerie white eyes tapering to thin slits. "You can fool your human counterparts, but you cannot fool the unseen. *We* can see what lies inside of you, and what lies there is a frightened little girl who wants nothing to do with the unseen, spiritual realm." She takes two steps forward, her glare unrelenting and vile. "You want to go back to the way it was before. Go back to a time when you were blind to the spiritual war surrounding you. You want to be unenlightened about angels and demons, but most of all, you want to forget who you really are."

"I'm not afraid of you," I softly reply, praying that the tremble in my voice will go unnoticed.

She sniffs the air, then grins. "Oh, yes you are, little Seer. I can smell the fear rolling off of you like waves in the ocean. Your terror feeds me, keeping me solid. You see, I gain strength from human fear and pain, and yours is intoxicating." Tilting her head to the side she continues to study my face. "Ah, and the rapid pitter-patter of your heart is a sweet sound to my ears, thrumming like humming bird wings. A dead giveaway that you're in a panic here. Only a fear so heavy and thick can cause a human heart to sputter out of control."

Everything Livian speaks rings true. Fear has trapped my body in its evil clutches, and my heart is thudding so fast I feel I might pass out at any moment.

Mustering up a small amount of courage, I spit out, "You

can't hurt me."

"Yes, yes, I know." She sighs, then starts pacing a circle around me. "The power of the Creator is within you, protecting you, holding you close. That disgusting bright light I hate with a bitter passion resides inside of you, though you don't know how to ... *use* it."

"I used it well enough on Lukus," I point out defensively.

Her eyebrows raise. "Yes, I know. I talked to him. What you don't understand is that I'm way more powerful than he could or ever will be."

She stops pacing and stands right in front of me, so close I can feel and smell her repulsive breath. "Yes, you're protected. I cannot touch you, though there is one thing I *can* do."

"Oh yeah?" I snarl. "What's that?"

"I can take away your speech," she utters. An ill grin daubs at her lips.

Opening my mouth to retort, I find that my tongue no longer works. It's weird. My brain is formulating words but they can't be released. They're stuck in my mind with no way out.

So, Livian had been telling the truth – she *can* take away my speech.

"Also," she says in fierce authority, her feet circling me again, "I can take hold of your muscles, immobilizing you where you stand."

As soon as those words leave her mouth, every muscle in my body cramps and tightens, my will to move effectively stripped away. The pain is horrible, not letting up for even a second. A scorned frost rushes into me, my breath hitching in my lungs. Every part of my body is paralyzed where I stand.

Again she stops pacing, getting within inches of my face. "You've faced demons before, but not ones as strong as I. Fear is my fuel. Desperation is my drug. I can use both to my advantage."

I can't breathe. I can't move.

God, help me.

"That's enough, Livian."

Livian hisses and flies backward, almost knocking over the three pawns, who still appear zombified.

The moment she backed away, the hold she's had on me

releases. I drop to my knees, gulping in deep, long breaths. A gentle hand clamps over my shoulder, sending immediate relief to soar through my body. Looking up, I find that Sam has come to my rescue.

"T-Thank y-y-you," I stutter, still trying to catch my breath. I stand to my feet, my legs wobbly. He hugs me, holding my body up until I'm able to regain composure. The strong smell of fresh lavender overtakes the air, flushing out the decaying stench of Livian.

"I've told you a million times that I'm always with you." He smiles.

"Oh, how nauseatingly *sweet!*" Livian spits, baring her teeth. They've grown longer and sharper, like vampire fangs. Her voice has deepened and is filled with hatred. "You broke the rules, Guardian! You were not inv – "

"*You* crossed the line," Sam sharply interjects. "She is protected by The Light and you will not touch her."

"Oh please!" scoffs Livian, her body tense and rigid. "You weak, meaningless celestial. The *Ra'ah* is my mission, though another has peaked my interest in this town."

"What are you saying, demon?" wonders Sam.

She frowns as she paces around her pawns. "There's another soul in this town other than Clarity's that I'm willing to bargain for. Out of all the souls in this town, there's only one I hope to keep."

"Wait a minute," I say in confusion. "If you're not after me, then who are you after?"

Her face softens, making her appear angelic. "It is not who I want – it is who my David wants."

"Who your *David* wants?" My face scrunches up as a ball of perplexity barrels into me.

"Yes," she gently says. With her fingertips, she caresses his cheek, as if petting him. "Yes, my sweet David wants someone." Turning sharply my direction, trapping me in her steely gaze, she adds, "And what my David wants ... he gets."

"Really?" I cross my arms at my chest, glaring icily at General Livian. "So, who does your David want?"

Smiling, her sharp incisors gleaming, she responds, "My David wants Kora."

Chapter Twenty

Sam

Livian is playing Clarity. There is no negotiating with a demon. None whatsoever. Livian's using Kora as a bargaining tool to trick Clarity into believing that she will leave her and everyone in town alone, as long as Kora becomes one of her pawns. The only problem is, Livian has no intention of leaving this town alone.

No matter what, Livian won't back down until she has destroyed Clarity. After all, she's the demon General's main target.

Studying my Charge, I raptly listen to her thoughts as her brain processes what Livian has said. She's taken back by the demon's proclamation, confused by the bargaining attempt being made on Kora's life.

Turning her gaze on me, Clarity says, "Sam, you once

told me that a battle is coming, one that only I can fight – is this the fight you were talking about?"

I nod my head, answering her question.

She flips her attention back to Livian. "What kind of deal are you wanting to make?"

"One you cannot possibly turn down," she mysteriously replies.

"That doesn't answer my question." Clarity sighs and shakes her head. "Just tell me the deal ... using *words*."

Clarity is becoming annoyed. Her heart rate is speeding up, evoking her blood to rapidly rush through her veins. All the while her brain is working overtime, trying to explicate an escape plan. By reading her thoughts, I realize that she's not on the right path to freedom out of this old gym, and definitely not away from a demon General.

Livian crosses her arms. As she does, her fingernails grow to three inches long.

"Very well, little Seer," Livian jeers, "I'll tell you, but you must take into consideration the gravity of the situation at hand before you make your final decision."

Clarity glares at her and says, "Go ahead. Speak."

Livian gets right down to business. "Would you sacrifice one of your own to save many?"

"Uh..."

Clarity is stumped, so I decide to intervene.

"You don't have to answer that, Clarity." I step in between Livian and my Charge, my stance strong and defensive. "Quit this head game, Livian."

Livian chooses to ignore me and continues talking. "Here is my deal. I'll leave this town and you alone, in exchange for Kora's soul."

Suddenly David collapses, dropping hard to his knees. He grasps his head in his hand and whines, "Kora, Kora, Kora..."

Livian touches a finger to his forehead, and instantly this stops his continuous cries. His whole body stiffens, then goes slacks. Passing out, he falls the rest of the way to the ground.

She looks at Clarity and I, remarking, "Lovesick, the boy is. Kora has broken his heart."

Clarity retorts boldly, "I don't care if he's lovesick and

brokenhearted. I will never hand over Kora – or anyone in this town."

Livian stands up straighter, placing her hands on her narrow hips. "So, that's your answer. You cannot sacrifice one for many. You are too selfish and prideful to think about anyone else."

"I'm not selfish, nor am I prideful," Clarity notes. "The answer to your question is I will not let you have any souls at *all*. Not only that, but I'm also going to kick your tail all the way back to Hell."

Livian locks eyes with me. "She's a feisty one. Very, very amusing. I almost feel bad that I have to destroy her." She pauses, cutting her gaze sharply to my Charge, baring her long fangs. "*Almost*."

"You will not touch her," I order, allowing my wings to spring from my back. I spread them wide, sheltering Clarity with my angelic flanks. In return, Livian's entire visual aspect transforms, displaying her true self.

"We will see about that!" growls Livian, her voice deepening.

A gasp escapes Clarity's lips as Livian morphs into the

beast she truly is. Shiny black feathers cover her pale skin, her white eyes glow yellow. Bones make cracking sounds as her body twists and alters. By the end of the transformation, Livian is a twelve-foot tall monstrosity.

The demon lets out a brutal inhuman shriek. The floor underneath our feet starts to rumble, causing the windows to rattle all across the gymnasium. Basketballs roll across the floor, and the old desks that were stacked in the corner come tumbling down.

My gaze falls on Clarity. She's terrified – beyond the chasm of fear. Her brown eyes are wide, her heart is catapulting sharply against her chest.

When she finally pulls her eyes away from the demon, I warn, "Be prepared. This is just the beginning."

Clarity

This is just the beginning – five horrendous words that either make or break you. There are many beginnings in life, but when you watch a demon from Hell transform into a monster that no horror film can match – *that* kind of beginning I can do without.

David is still unconscious on the ground, while Darren and Danielle's zombie visages seem to be frozen on their pale faces. They look as if nothing major is happening, like a mini-earthquake isn't attacking the gym.

What kind of hold does Livian have on these teens?

Right when I think I've seen it all, a black cloud forms above the demon General's head. It grows bigger and darker with every passing second, like the first churns of a storm, until...

What is *that*?

Little *Tsipor* demons crawl out of the grumbling clouds, too many to count. They circle above us like vultures hovering over a meal. I've been seeing these things for weeks now, but I'm still not used to them. Their long fangs drip with thick saliva, and just like Livian, their bodies are covered with shiny black feathers and their eyes glow like yellow fireballs in their sockets.

"I hate these things," I tell Sam.

Sam replies with a, "Yep."

Abruptly, Livian commands, "Attack!" On cue, her army of *Tsipors* dive from the air like torpedoes, their targets Sam and I.

"Sam!" I yell over the storm of flapping wings.

Immediately, Sam twists around and wraps his wings around my body. His blue eyes glow powerfully, staring deeply into mine.

"Look at me, Clarity," he orders. He's shielding me from the outpouring of demonic beings. "Don't look at them – look at *me*."

A bright light starts to emanate from him, showering me with his warm calm and lavender goodness. Gazing into his eyes, I relax, my nerves chilling out. I know I'm safe, and that everything will be okay. No matter what happens, I'm safe and secure in the arms of my Guardian.

Suddenly an explosion sounds, grabbing our attention. Two beautiful angels have crashed through a window directly above us. Tiny shards of glass rain down to the ground. The angels, both blonde and female, outstretch their wings and stare down the demons with glowing blue eyes. A celestial light, like the one Sam harbors, flows strongly from them.

A couple of Livian's demons try attacking the two angels. They do not succeed. The angels simply lift their hands and touch them with their fingers. Astonishment washes over me at this wondrous sight. Just by touching the demons with their fingertips, the demons immediately explode and turn to dust.

The metal doors slam open behind us, sending us spiraling around. Two people, a boy and a girl, stroll into the gym. They're dressed in black, appearing confident and strong.

In very fast and fluent movements, they jump and flip in the air above. They land right in front of us, crouched in defensive stances. Whoever they are, they harbor some *mad* skills. I can't tell much about them, only that they are tall, collective ... and know exactly what they're doing.

As the *Tsipors* target them, the newcomers attack first. They use no weapons – only their hands.

That's when I figure it out.

"S-Sam," I stammer, my voice quivering.

"It's okay," he says.

"Are they – "

"Yes, they are."

A great rush of adrenaline flows through my veins. My hands are on triple fire.

Seers. Yes, Seers! They are Seers and they have shown up at a perfect time – to rescue my butt.

The mutated bird demons attempt to get close to the Seers, but they fail. They never touch them, thanks to the power in the Seers palms. With hands lifted high, palms out, a white light shoots out and traps the demons within the beams. Instantly, they are turned to dust.

I gape at them in total awe. Will I be able to do that? Will I actually be able to shoot lights out of my palms and defeat the enemy?

"Clarity Miller!" the boy shouts in a deep voice.

Snapping out of my awestruck reverie, I reply, "That's me!"

With the two walking backwards in unison, the boy yells, "Run!"

Run? Why do they –

"You can trust them," Sam assures.

"Why do they want me to run?" I wonder, staring into Sam's radiant orbs.

"There's too many to fight," he informs. A bright glowing sword appears in his hand as he nods his head. "We got this."

Following his gaze, I find that the other angels have swords, and are using them quite well. *Tsipor* demons are falling all over the place – well, what's left of them, anyway.

"You coming or not?" the girl questions. They've already made it to the exit door.

Still in complete disbelief, I reply, "What?"

The girl frowns. "Get the cotton out of your ears, the lead out of your feet, and *move!*"

The two Seers flee out the doors. I follow directly behind, not wanting to leave my Guardian's side. However, I know I'll be okay. I can trust them. Sam said I can, so what do I have to fear?

When my feet hit the outside world, the wind nearly takes me off my feet. Lightning is everywhere, allowing sight into the sky. I'm amazed and appalled at what I see.

Tsipor demons are everywhere, weaving in and out of the lightning. Too many to count. There has to be thousands flying in the supernatural storm above us. For a moment all I can do is stare, my body frozen in place. A living nightmare – that is what I'm observing. Only I'm not asleep. This is reality … *my* reality.

A hand latches onto my arm.

"Come *on*!" the girl orders, sounding irritated. "We've got to get out of here!"

She drags me to an old beat-up truck. Slinging the door open, she pushes me inside, then slides in next to me. The boy is already in the driver's seat. The engine turns over a couple of times, then roars to life. Before I know what's happening, we're lurching forward, the tires of the truck throwing gravel into the air.

"Where do we go, sis, where do we go?!" the boy yells hysterically to my left.

To my right, the girl shouts her reply. "Just *drive*!"

We tear down the road, going way above the forty-five mile speed limit. Lightning flashes all around us. Trees on the edge of the woods are being tossed to and fro by the heinous winds, some bending at extremely odd angles. A few tree limbs break loose, falling onto the road in front of us. Thankfully, the boy driver has killer driving skills.

A loud bump sounds on the roof of the truck, seizing our attentions.

"W-What's that?" I ask, my voice shaking with worry and adrenaline.

The girl shifts her eyes to me and grins. "Relax … we got this."

Without taking her gaze off mine, she lifts her palm to the roof, laying it flat. I allow my eyes to drift upward. A bright light forms from her palm, the brightness illuminating around the outside of her hand. The loud screeching that follows fills the truck cab.

My eyes fall back on her. She's still staring at me, and still grinning.

"Told ya so."

"How do you do that? How do those lights shoot from your hands?" The shock factor I'm experiencing is continuing to elevate.

Confusion scrunches her face. "You mean you don't – "

Suddenly, the truck starts to rock back and forth.

"What the...?" The boy sounds nervous, which in turn makes me nervous.

Like a dark shadow clouding out the light, the truck becomes swarmed with *Tsipor* demons. The windows are covered over with these nasty beings, even the windshield. Only the yellows of their eyes can be seen.

As the truck goes into a tailspin, the three of us do what anyone else in this situation would do.

We scream.

We go round and round, my stomach churning and my heart pounding. I close my eyes, waiting for this to end. It can't end well.

Behind my closed lids I see brightness. Opening my eyes, I'm surprised that the whole truck cab is bathed in white light. It becomes brighter and brighter. We continue to scream as we watch the demons explode to dust, all at one time. The truck is still out of control, and we are still screaming.

The bright light is gone, except for the headlights of the truck. Eventually we come to a halt, stopping directly in front of Trina's Diner. Right in front of the diner's door.

My heart is hammering like crazy. I'm totally shocked that we're alive. Every nerve in my body is frayed and unhinged. I'm at a loss, I'm speechless, I'm hyperventilating...

"I'm starved!" the girl exclaims. "Hey, look, a diner! Yum, yum, yum..."

I watch, slack-jawed, as she opens the door and springs out. Looking to the dark-headed boy, he shrugs his shoulders.

"As soon as your heart stops spinning out of control, come join us." He jumps out, then turns back to me. "Take all the time you need." He closes the door, then walks into the diner, whistling the whole time.

Time.

For some reason, I feel like I'm running out of it.

Sam appears next to me, his lavender scent spiking the air. His hand touches mine, and instantly my heart calms.

Sighing, my head rolling lazily on my shoulders, I look him in the eye and ask, "What was all that about?"

"*That*," he says with a grin, "was the Squint twins."

Chapter Twenty-One

Clarity

Trina's Diner was built in the 1950s, and had been one of the nicest places in town. However, as the years have gone by, no one has taken the time and effort to update its décor. Now it's just another greasy pit in a pathetic setting with artery-clogging food.

After talking with Sam, and calming myself, I'm now walking through the doors of the oldest diner in town. It's not hard to find the Seers, since they're the only two patrons other than myself. They'd chosen a booth in the very back. Both are causally talking and sipping drinks.

Walking down the aisle, my eyes on them, a bizarre feeling rushes through my mind. How can they sit there all nonchalant, talking and laughing together? Don't they remember what just happened? The gym, the demons, the truck spiraling out of control...

"Hey, she made it!" The girl pats the seat next to her. "Hop a squat, girlie-o."

As I sit, I take a quick moment to look them over. The girl has curly black hair that sits just below her shoulders, and her skin is a caramel shade. The boy has the same dark hair, except it's cut short. He also harbors the same skin color. They both have bright green eyes; actually, they look exactly alike.

What had Sam called them? The Squint twins?

"Yes, we're twins," the girl says.

My jaw drops. "How did you – "

"Easy," she interjects. "I can read the questions written all over your face, so let me answer them – yes, we're twins, yes, we're biracial, and yes, we're *cool*."

"We get that look all the time," the boy laughs. Reaching across the table, he shakes my hand and says, "My name is Matty, short for Mathew, and the bubbly girl sitting next to you is my twin, Marty, which is short for Martha."

"Nice to meet you," Marty tells me, shaking my hand as well. "And let me go ahead and get it out – we're half Caucasian and half Hispanic, and no, we aren't bilingual. Not only that..." She pauses and frowns. "Never call me Martha. *Ever*."

"Uh, okay," I react. I'm not exactly sure how I'm supposed to take that, so I don't push it any further.

"That's our angels," Matty points outside. "Their names are Hope and Faith." I follow the direction he's pointing and see the two blonde angels talking with Sam. They're standing next to the old beat-up truck, all three talking animatedly.

"They look just alike, too," remarks Marty. With raised eyebrows she adds, "Sort of ironic, isn't it?"

I shrug my shoulders. "I guess so..."

"Oh!" she suddenly exclaims. "I ordered you a coke – also a burger and fries. I hope that was okay."

"Yeah, that's fine." I give a slight smile, though it's forced. My mind is reeling from everything that's happening. I'm both shocked and excited. I'm finally around other Seers – *my* kind, so to speak.

Matty leans over and says, "You'll have to excuse my sister. She's a bit of a control freak."

"I am not!" argues Marty, with her hand raising to her chest.

"Yes you are!" Matty fires back. "You always have to

have your way. For instance, take tonight for an example – *I insisted that we wait on Clarity so she could order her own food, but noooo*! What happened instead?" He changes his deep baritone voice to a squeaky, nasally tone and says, "*Matty, please, we're in the middle of Hicksville! Everyone drinks sodas and eats burgers and fries here! It's, like, tradition or something.*" He ends the rant and leans back in the booth, his green eyes full of amusement.

Turning to me, Marty rolls her eyes and shrugs. "He's such a drama queen, all because I'm the oldest – "

"By three minutes and forty-two seconds!" he points out.

Again, she rolls her eyes. "He always brings that up."

Someone clears their throat. The three of us glance up. The waitress stands there, carrying our food with one hand, with her other hand sidled up her hip.

"Am I interruptin' somethin', or do y'all want this food?" She views us through tired eyes, her frowning face giving her a wrinkled-up prune look.

"N-No, you're not interrupting," I quickly assure the waitress. "Yes, we're ready for our food."

She places the burgers, fries and drinks in front of us, still unsmiling, then walks away. Apparently she's wishing that she was anywhere other than this old decrepit diner.

Don't blame her, really.

Marty watches the waitress walk away, then turns to me and asks, "Is all the folks in this town that outgoing and spunky?"

I smile, replying, "You wish."

Sam

"I am glad you are here," I tell Faith and Hope, my fellow Guardians. "She's been waiting on bated breath for this night to come."

"We came when the time was right," says Faith.

"Yes," Hope adds. "There is a place and time for every moment on earth."

I smile, shifting my gaze to Clarity, who is sitting in the diner with fellow Seers. "Yes, I know. Every situation has a time and a place. And the Father's time is always perfect."

"Yes," the two angels echo together.

"So," I say, turning and facing them, "do you have any information that could be useful in defeating Livian?" They look at each other, then back to me.

"We do not know much," says Hope.

"We only know that more pain and suffering is coming," adds Faith.

Shaking my head, I glance back at Clarity, who seems to be conversing with the Squint twins.

"Yeah, that figures," I mutter.

Clarity

Matty and Marty quickly dig into their meals. I pick up a fry and nibble on it, not really tasting it.

"So, where are you guys from?" I ask in attempts to getting to know them more.

"Atlanta," Marty responds through a mouthful of food. "We grew up at the Seer Society, where *you* should have grown up, too."

"*Marty*," Matty speaks, also with a full mouth. I can't be

too sure, but I think there's a hint of warning saturating his voice.

"What's the Seer Society?" I ask, my inquisitive side sparking to life.

"We'll explain later," Marty responds after swallowing a bite of food. "For now just eat."

We eat in silence, our chewing and gulping the only sounds in the place. In the end, the twins have all but licked their plates clean, while my meal is only half-eaten. I'm too restless and antsy to eat.

"You guys sure were hungry," I note, not hiding my astonishment.

"Yeppers," Marty expresses. Taking her napkin, she wipes ketchup and grease from the corners of her mouth. "Kicking demon butt is extremely strenuous on the body, and us Seers always need to refuel, because another battle can happen," she dramatically snaps her fingers, "just like that."

"Yeah, I was famished," agrees Matty, who's slurping his coke loudly. "And now I'm stuffed. This food is actually pretty good."

"Oh, I concur," Marty says in a sarcastic tone. "I can

actually feel the grease flowing through my veins as we speak, possibly causing a heart attack in my near future – why, it's simply invigorating!"

"Don't speak death, Marty," Matty warns. Marty sticks her tongue out.

I ignore her sardonic words and force a smile. "Yeah, this used to be the happening place a couple of years ago. When my friends and I were younger we were here all the time..." My words screech to a halt as a flood of memories scuttle through my brain. I place my entwined hands on the table and stare down at them, praying that I don't start crying in front of the Seers.

"You've been put through the ringer, haven't you?" Marty sincerely inquires.

I nod. "That's putting it mildly."

Matty smiles. "Why don't you tell us about it."

Sucking in a breath, swallowing the ball of nerves stuck in my throat, I tell them how my life has been the last few months.

I tell them about when I met Sam and how he explained that I was a Seer. I tell them about my first encounter with demons, and of Lukus and his Hellhounds. I tell them about the night of the dance and how it had changed the town. I get them caught up to the present, about Livian, her pawns, and her plans.

"Wow," Matty expresses. He leans back with his hands laced behind his head. "You've been through a lot, and ... and you just found out that you're a Seer."

"That's why you looked so weirded-out by the lights shooting out of our hands." Indignation colors Marty's face as she suddenly explodes, "You don't know what you're capable of! You have no idea! I mean, we knew that you were a newbie, but we had no idea that – I can't believe you just found out about your Seer heritage!"

"It's not my fault – " I try to argue, but it seems Marty doesn't hear my voice.

"Oh, man ... do you know how long it's going to take for you to understand the basics? Not only that, but that demon General is going to want a rematch, and soon!" She sucks in a breath, then adds in a more calm tone, "Clarity, do you realize how many hours, days, weeks, *months* it's going to take to get you up to code with your Seer abilities?"

"It's not my fault," I say again. "I can't help that I don't know what I'm doing!" Frustration leaks out with the next words I speak. "I know I have a bunch to learn, but you don't have to cram it down my throat!"

"Okay, okay, okay," she repeats over and over again. Closing her eyes, she takes a few deep breaths, letting them out slowly.

I watch her, fascinated. "What are you *doing*?"

"Cleansing breaths," responds Matty. He still appears at ease, with his hands laced behind his head – as if Marty's *freak out* is a normal occurrence. "Marty always works herself up in a tizzy. Once you've been around her awhile, you get use to it. Trust me, I know – I've been around her for eighteen years."

"Okay," I say slowly.

After a few strange moments, Marty finally settles down.

"Alright, I'm better now," she tells us, opening her eyes. "Clarity, I'm sorry. It's just that this whole situation makes me so angry!"

"Don't be upset," I tell her. "I know that I have a lot to learn, but it's not the end of the world."

She leans her elbows on the table, dropping her face in

her hands.

"I can't believe your aunt kept this from you," she murmurs into her hands.

Whoa – what did she – *huh*?

"What did you say?" I ask in stunned confusion. She peeks through her hands, not dropping them from her face.

"Marty, shut-*up*," Matty mutters under his breath.

"Wait just a minute." Looking from Matty, then back to Marty, I inquire, "What does my aunt have to do with any of this?"

Silence coats the air, thick and heavy. So heavy I fear the ceiling and everything around us will collapse at any minute. Marty and Matty glare each other down, as if sending soundless messages through their eyes. Eventually Marty drops her hands … and the silence.

"Matty, she was going to find out sooner than later."

"What? What am I finding out?"

An uneasy sigh escapes her lips. Gazing strongly and steadily into my eyes, she says, "There's something you need to know…"

Becoming irritated, I exclaim, "Tell me!"

Marty's face becomes expressionless as she reveals, "Clarity, your Seer heritage came from your parents. They were Seers."

Chapter Twenty-Two

Clarity

My heart falls to my stomach as I yelp in disbelief, "What?!"

Matty leans forward and grabs my hand. "Your mom grew up at the Seer Society. Your dad attended a college nearby. That's how they met."

"It actually a pretty cool story," Marty jumps in. "Your dad was getting attacked by some low-class demons and – "

"Not now, Marty," Matty states sternly. Looking back at me, he presses forward. "As I was saying, she met your dad at a nearby college. They got married. Not long after that, God blessed your father with Seer abilities."

"As I was saying," Marty says, shooting her brother a nasty aspect, "your parents have been, and always will be, an important part of Seer Society history. Their extraordinary meeting is one they put in the books. You see, most Seers marry fellow Seers. That's how it had been generation after generation – until your mom broke that so-called, man-made rule." She pauses and smiles. "She fell in love with your father, who wasn't a Seer. Since Seers generally have visions or dreams of whom they'll marry, it was hard for the Elders to go along with you mother's choice."

"The Elders," Matty interposes, "are the ones who *control* the Seer Society. At that time they didn't believe your mother when she told them she'd dreamed of your father. They thought she was making it all up to defy their rules and regulations."

Marty nods and grins. "Yep. Believe it or not, you mother was a rebel – that's why the Elders didn't believe her. She always pushed their buttons, most of the time on purpose – at least that's what our parents told us."

"She'd claimed in a dream that Jerry Miller was fighting alongside her in battle," Matty informs. "Even though he wasn't a Seer, he was there. That's how she knew that he was to be her husband."

Marty sighs. "It's really a romantic story."

I shake my head slowly, having trouble comprehending what's being told to me.

My parents had been Seers. My *parents* had been *Seers*. Not only that, but it appears that Marty and Matty, who are complete strangers, know more about my parents than I do.

Also, the fact that A.C. has failed to let me in on this family secret has my nerves jostled and fried.

"Is my aunt a Seer as well?" I ask, my voice trembling with emotion.

"No," Matty quickly replies. "The Seer gene comes from your mother's side, not your father's. Though God can choose anyone He wants to carry Seer abilities."

"Which makes their story so unique," proclaims Marty.

"To make a long story short," Matty presses on, "the Elders forbid your mother from marrying Jerry Miller. So one night the twosome ran away together, got married, and *voila*! Jerry became a Seer, proving the Elders wrong, and rocking the whole Seer world and its traditions."

"Ever since Eloise Thrasher rebelled and married a "normal" human," Marty makes quotations marks using her fingers, "Seers and non-Seers have been falling in love and getting hitched. I like to think that God had this planned all along, to show the Elders that they needed to ditch their man-made traditions, and to also quit being stuffy and superficial."

"Marty, oh *please*." Matty rolls his eyes at his sister.

"Don't *oh please* me, little brother!" snaps Marty. "You know as well as I that the Elders are old school jerks, and..."

Marty continues ranting about the Elders – whoever they are – but I stop listening. I kind of zone out, letting the whole conversation sink in. With all the new information being flung in my face, I still haven't jumped the first hurdle of all – my parents being Seers. And it's not just that. The fact that my aunt knew the whole time...

Jumping up, I announce, " I have to go talk with my aunt."

Marty and Matty both stop talking and glance up at me. Comprehending expressions shine from their countenances. Matty reaches in his pocket and pulls out a piece of paper.

"Here's our cell number," he says, holding it out for me. "Call us when you need to talk, or ... start *training*."

Taking the paper I say, "Training?"

"Girl," snorts Marty, "we've got a lot of work to do. And we ain't leaving until you're ready to take on that demon

General."

I nod, gingerly taking in her words. "Thanks."

Spinning on my heels, I walk down the aisle and out the door. When I pull the car keys out of my pocket, that's when I remember that my car is parked at the school.

"Great," I mutter.

A rush of wind hits my face, along with the sound of flapping wings.

"Need a lift to your car?" Sam inquires, smiling. Obviously he's been reading my thoughts. He's been reading them the whole time.

I sigh.

What would I do without Sam?

***

The drive to the hospital takes forever and a day, though it's only ten minutes away from the school. Sam had dropped me off at my car, disappearing just as fast. I was okay with him leaving me alone. I needed some time to think – some undisturbed time.

I grip the steering wheel tightly, my knuckles white. Tears of anger and despair, mixed together with frustrated perplexity rains down my face. My thoughts have been captured in a whirlwind spin, going round and round at a dizzying pace.

How could A.C. keep this from me? How could she keep such crucial information locked in a vault, kept from her brother's only daughter?

I pull my rust bucket of a Honda into the hospital parking lot, choosing a spot between a pick-up truck and a shiny red sports car. Slamming on my brakes, I come to a screeching halt. Throwing my door open, I almost dent the blemish-free convertible. With my anger at full peak, I whip the door shut, so hard I hear the window crack.

Sprinting up the walkway and through the doors of the hospital, a sick feeling overtakes my body, knocking me over with heavy waves of nausea. Stars explode behind my eyes, and I start feeling lightheaded. I head to the restroom, where I drop to my knees in front of a toilet and unload all the food in my stomach.

After the vomiting episode is over, I stagger over to the sink, splashing water on my face and rinsing out my mouth. Glancing at my reflection in the mirror, I'm surprised at the person staring back at me. My skin is sickly pale, my eyes are red from angry tears, and my hair is a tangled mess.

What am I going to say to A.C.? Where do I begin? Right now I'm so mad at her, so hurt that she's kept this secret from me. The person that raised me the last five years had left me completely out of the loop. The fact that my parents had been Seers was buried into an unknown abyss of secrets. With all these emotions and thoughts rolling in my brain, my anger seethes, as rage flows vastly in my veins.

"Don't be too hard on her."

Sam's reflection appears in the mirror. He has materialized behind me, his lavender smell scenting the air. His hands are shoved in his jean's pockets. He looks sadly at me, his face set in a grim expression.

"Why?" I ask, my tone severely obstinate. "Why should I pretend to be okay when I'm not? Actually, *nothing* is okay. I mean, look at the facts – if I'd known about my parents, maybe I'd be a little more prepared, and life would be different. Sam, tell me … why should I not be angry with her?"

"She has her reasons for not telling you," he responds, his gaze unblinking.

"Yeah, and I'm about to find them out." I walk to the door, then stop. Peering at him sideways I ask, "Why didn't you tell me, Sam?"

He closes his eyes and leans his head back against a locked stall.

"I couldn't tell you."

"Why?"

"I just couldn't."

Understanding shakes me to the bone. "You didn't have clearance from the Throne Room, did you?"

He opens his eyes, his gaze finding mine. "Right."

I turn, facing the door, and lean my head on its cool surface. "What about my parents?" I whisper.

"What about them?"

Taking a deep breath, releasing it slowly, I wonder, "Why didn't my parents tell me?"

He blandly answers, "They had their reasons, as well."

I shake my head and mutter, "Right. Typical."

Exiting the bathroom, I make my way to the elevator and

head up to the third floor. The door opens, and the first person I see is my aunt. She's busy chatting with her fiancé Doug, along with a few others that have congregated at the nurse's station. As I approach, it takes all the self-control I have to lightly tap her on the shoulder. Without said control, I might have punched her between the eyes.

A.C. swings around. Surprise lights up her face when she sees that it's me. A cheerful smile tugs at her lips.

"Clarity, what are you doing here?" The smile on her lips withers away as she gets a good look at my face. "Oh, no, you've been crying! What's wrong?"

"I need to talk to you privately," I say icily, my expression stone cold.

"Can it wait?" she wonders. "Doug and I are about to go downstairs and grab a bite – hey, what are you doing out past midnight?"

"This can't wait any longer," I say, ignoring her question. Crossing my arms at my chest, I know that my harsh tone is the reason I've gained some bewildered looks from her coworkers.

A.C. bites her lip, viewing me with suspicion. No doubt the dusty wheels in her brain are creaking and spinning to life.

"Okay," she finally replies. Glancing at Doug she says, "Go on down. I'll catch up."

"I'll be waiting." Doug bends down and places a kiss on her cheek. Then turning to me he says, "Good to see you, Clarity."

"Yeah, good to see you, too," I tell the tall, blonde-headed EMT worker. I watch as he and the other hospital workers walk away. A.C. shoots me a perturbed look, but I shrug it off.

"Follow me," she orders. "Let's go to the waiting room. It's empty tonight."

I follow her into the unpleasant waiting room that stinks of scorched coffee and disease. Chill bumps rise on my arms. I'm thankful for the hoodie I'd pulled on at the last minute.

A.C. closes the door and locks it. She motions for me to sit down. As I sit, she takes the seat directly across.

"What's up?" she starts investigating. Closing her eyes, she rubs her forehead. "Is something going on with Kora?"

"No, this has nothing to do with Kora."

"Does it have something to do with school?"

"No."

"Work?"

"No."

"You and Brenton – you're not pregnant, are you?!" Her eyes widen, regarding me with fierce alarm.

"No!" I exclaim, adding, "This is about Mama and Daddy!"

Her expression becomes wooden. "What about them?" she inquires.

I swallow a bundle of nerves, then ask, "A.C., why didn't you tell me they were Seers?"

Chapter Twenty-Three

Clarity

A.C. says nothing, leaving her expression vacant. I watch as her face turns ashen, the darkish blue circles under her eyes becoming more defined. Her breath hitches in her throat, then she smoothly lets it out. Suddenly she looks much older than she really is. We sit in complete silence, the clock hanging on the wall *tick-tocking* the seconds by. We stare at each other, wordlessly, until I can't take it any longer.

"Are you going to answer me or not?" I ask, my tone drenched with vexation.

She opens her mouth, then snaps it shut. Standing to her feet, she walks over to the water cooler and makes herself a cup of water. She drains it immediately.

Facing the water cooler, her back to me, she asks, "You want some water?"

"No," I readily respond, keeping to the seat. "All I want is some answers – *now*."

Her shoulders slump at my reply. A speck of regret filters through my system, but I push it to the side. I can't let her defeated edge knock me off my anger ride, because what she's done is wrong, plain and simple. She should have told me the truth about my parents, which in turn would have told the truth about who I really am.

"You're right," she admits. "I've been keeping the truth from you for way too long." Slowly, she walks over and takes the seat across from me, her eyes focused on the linoleum floor. "I'll tell you all I know. You deserve that much."

"Yes, I do," I agree.

Her tired eyes rise and meet mine. "How did you find out?"

"No, A.C.," I say, shaking my head. "I'm the one wanting answers, not you."

She nods. "Okay, ask whatever you want. I'll answer the best I can."

Quickly, I get down to the main event. "Why didn't you tell me?"

"I wasn't sure ... I didn't know if you would receive the *gift*." She spits out the last word as if it leaves a bitter taste on her tongue.

"Why wouldn't I have the same gift? Both of them – "

"Your dad didn't have it until he met your mom!" she strongly interjects. "The very night they got married was the night he met his Guardian, and your mother's Guardian."

Intrigued, I ask, "What were their angel's names?"

She ponders that question, then replies, "Rachel and Arthur."

"Did he know about her?" I carefully question. "Did Daddy know that Mama was a Seer, and did she know he was a normal?"

She arches an eyebrow. "A *normal*?"

I sigh. "A new term I learned tonight, right after I was attacked by demons. Luckily two Seers showed up and saved my butt." I pause, feeling a bit of satisfaction by her horrified expression. "Yeah, that's right. I met two Seers tonight and somehow they know more about my parents than I do."

"You really see angels and demons?" Her eyes are red

and brimming with tears.

"Yes," I say softly, lifting my palms. "I have marks that verify that, though you can't see them."

"How long have you been able to see them?" she questions, cautiously looking at my hands.

"My marks?"

"No," she sighs. "Angels and ... and *demons*."

My hands fall to my lap as I reply, "Since September."

"Does Kora and Brenton know?"

"No."

"Is my Guardian here, like, right now?" she whispers, her eyes widening even more.

I chuckle. "I'm sure he or she is, but I don't see them all the time. I see them only when they want to be seen."

She drops her head into her hands, her elbows resting atop her thighs.

"Oh, Clarity," she says, her voice muffled. "I'm so sorry. I've really messed up."

Tears sting my eyes, but I will them away. "Just do me a

favor and start at the beginning."

"The beginning?" she states, her hands descending to her lap.

"Tell me everything you know."

"Okay, give me a minute to gather my thoughts."

Crossing my legs, crossing my arms, I tolerantly wait for her to start. In a way I feel bad that she's stressing out, especially since she's planning a wedding and is so high on life at the moment. Though when I think back on the last five months, the pity train slams its brakes.

"Don't be hard on her," says Sam, who has manifested in the seat next to me. I cut my gaze over to him.

"I'm not going to be," I tell him. "If you haven't noticed, I'm waiting patiently for her to gather her thoughts."

"What?" A.C. says. I turn back her direction. A mask of confusion has snapped onto her face.

"Oh, nothing," I reply, shrugging nonchalantly. "Just talking to Sam."

"Sam?"

"My Guardian."

As I explain, another angel has appeared, sitting next to her. An extremely handsome, blonde-headed angel. He's dressed in jeans and a white tee. Vanilla must be his scent. It mingles well with Sam's fresh lavender.

"Your Guardian just appeared in the seat next to you – he smells like vanilla."

"You're making this up," she jeers.

I shake my head. "Nope, he's there. And for some reason angels smell. Sam smells like lavender, Kora's angel smells like fresh cut grass, and your angel smells like vanilla. They smell way different than demons. Demons just ... *stink*."

Though A.C. can't see her Guardian, she turns her head slowly, her breathing heavy. She's looking right at him, though she can't see him. He gazes lovingly at her, his hand lightly touching her face. A shiver ruptures through her.

"What's his name?" she asks, her voice as light as a feather.

"Taylor," he says in a beautifully deep tone.

"Taylor," I communicate for him.

She smiles. "Hello Taylor."

"Hello," he whispers, his smile grand.

"He says hello," I inform. "Now, let's get back to my parents, please."

"Clarity," Sam scolds, rolling his eyes.

"What?" I charge back, annoyed.

He grins. "Take it easy." This time I roll my eyes at him.

A.C. blinks, her eyes wandering my way. "S-Sorry. Got a little side-tracked."

"No problem. Now talk."

She tilts her head, studying me. "Did you know that your dad and I grew up in Tennessee?"

"No," I answer. "I've always thought our roots were here in Georgia."

She shakes her head. "No, we come from Tennessee, and your mom grew up in Atlanta, super close to the college your dad attended.

"The summer Jerry left Tennessee, everything changed. He'd moved into an apartment with two of his friends, and just like every teenager having their first taste of freedom, they went all out, partying and hitting the clubs." She clears her throat, then continues. "One day, out of the blue, he called and told me that he'd met the most gorgeous girl in the world – your mother, Eloise Thrasher."

A smile graces my lips as my mother's image crosses my mind. Her long brown hair, her dazzling smile – in the looks department, she would have ranked up there with the beautiful angels.

"He said she was different," A.C. continues, "that something about her changed his outlook on life. He told me he knew she was the one he wanted to spend the rest of his life with. Of course I was skeptical at first, since he'd been such a player ... you probably didn't want to hear that, did you?"

"Not really," I answer, scrunching up my face. Nobody wants to hear that their dad was a player in his day. Gross and *eeew*.

"Forget I said that," she laughs. Looking to where Taylor is sitting she inquires, "Is he still there?"

"Yes," I say, throwing Taylor a smile. He grins as well, his bright blue eyes never leaving his Charge.

A.C. blushes, nervously placing an unruly strand of hair behind her ear.

"Sorry," she looks back to me. "All this is just so weird..." She trails off, then says, "To continue, from the moment he laid eyes on Eloise, Jerry was genuinely smitten, and I was happy for him, but our mom and dad, your grandparents, didn't share the same enthusiasm."

"Why?" I wonder. My parents and A.C. never spoke about Grandma and Grandpa Miller. I'd never seen any pictures of them, either.

"Because they wanted him to concentrate on his studies instead of girlfriends, and when he told them he was going to marry Eloise, they disowned him. They told him he was on his own."

"That's terrible!" I exclaim, feeling sadness for both my parents. They had fallen in love and had absolutely no support from two very important people.

"It was," she agrees. "After that, I didn't hear from Jerry much, not until Christmas Eve. That's when he phoned home to announce that he'd married Eloise, after knowing her a mere six months. He told us he would be living at a place called the Seer Society. Not long after that, his transformation began."

"Transformation?" I dubiously speak.

"When God gave him the gifts of a Seer, it opened his eyes and showed him a whole new world. Your father changed completely. He tried explaining it to me, about his new life, what it was about and what the Seer Society stood for, but no matter what he said, I just didn't get it. I couldn't comprehend that there was an unseen world teeming with angels and demons battling over human souls. Though I didn't turn my back on him like our parents did – he was my only sibling. So I accepted his new life and his sweet wife. However, your grandparents could not accept any of it."

"Then what happened?" I eagerly inquire. "I know Grandma and Grandpa are dead, but – "

"They're not dead," she intervenes. "They're alive and well."

My mouth drops. "They are *alive*?"

I can't wrap my overworked, distraught mind around this info. I've been completely swept away in a sea of mental rejection. My hand slaps to my forehead as a sudden pain surges in my brain.

"You mean not only did you keep my parent's secret from me, but you also kept me in the dark about my grandparents?"

A brand new rage rifles through my veins. Sam quickly grabs my hand, instantly sedating my nerves. Taylor touches A.C.'s shoulder, no doubt attempting to keep her chill. It seems to work.

"Clarity," she begins, sounding jaded, "it's a sore subject. Your parents would have eventually told you everything, but they didn't get the chance. I know you think you've been kept in the dark, but your parent's only concern was protecting you. That's all I've ever wanted to do, as well."

"That doesn't explain why my grandparents disowned their own flesh and blood." I entwine my hands together, laying them in my lap.

A.C. traces her tongue over her teeth, her brows furrowed. "The reason they have nothing to do with me is because I chose to believe my brother. You see, Clarity, my parents – your grandparents – are atheists. They don't believe in God. They don't believe that any higher power or deities exist. So when their only son started talking about God, the Holy Bible, angels and demons, they told him to leave and never come back." A tear slides a burning trail down her cheek. "And since I chose to support my brother, they told us both that we were orphans and on our own. That's when I moved to Atlanta."

Tears of my own spill down my face.

"Unbelievable," I whisper.

"Believe it," she whispers back.

"But why didn't you guys tell me all this? And why did we leave Atlanta and move to this crap-hole of a town?"

"Because," she says, with a small sob causing a break in her voice, "your parents and I were not positive that you'd get the gift, so moving to the country, away from other Seers, seemed to make the most sense. At the time, that is. And we didn't tell you about your grandparents because we didn't want you to get hurt. If they can disown their own children, what would they do to a grandchild?"

"Are you saying..." I can't finish my statement – I'm too disgusted.

My stomach contracts with a queasy feel. This discussion, this whole *evening,* is simply glitched. How cruel my grandparents had been to disinherit their children because of conflicting beliefs. How cruel they *still* are, since they're still alive.

"Clarity, I'm sorry you had to find out this way," she honestly expresses. "But you must understand – I was only trying to protect you, and even though I chose to believe my brother, support his decisions, and to believe in God … it doesn't mean I understand it all."

I glare at her with stormy eyes. Oh, how I want to scream at her, but reading the sincerity, regret, and pure love in her eyes – the ice that had frozen my indignant heart instantly warmed, melting into a sea of compassion.

Reaching over, I lay my hand atop hers. "I love you, A.C., and though I wish you'd told me sooner, I understand now why you didn't. Thank you for finally telling me. I forgive you."

I walk out the doors of the hospital feeling a tangled-up ball of emotions – relief, fury, sorrow, edginess, delight, tension and comfort. Yes, a large trash bag of wound-up energy continues to pile up inside of me, yet at the same time it feels like an overwhelming ton of weight has been hoisted off my shoulders.

Finding out my parents had been Seers gives me an elated feeling, though keeping it a secret was all kinds of wrong. As for my grandparents … what they'd done was just plain despicable. The lowest of all lows. Maybe one day I'll meet them, though at the moment I have no desire to do such a thing.

Yanking my cell phone from my pocket, I find the paper

with the Squint twin's phone number. Marty answers on the first ring.

"How's it going, slugger?"

"Just swell," I sarcastically reply.

"Did your aunt fill you in on everything?"

"As far as I know." Taking a moment to think, I clear my throat and add, "I'm ready."

"Ready for what?" asks Marty on the other line.

"To train," I clarify. "I want to know everything. I want to be prepared."

A few thick ticks of silence pass before she curiously wonders, "You're sure you're ready?"

"I've never been so sure of anything in my life," I tell her honestly.

I can almost hear the smile in her voice as she says, "Welcome to the team, Miller."

Livian

The Seer gets in her car and drives off. I watch her car from the top of the hospital, watching until the darkness swallows it up. Lightning flashes above me, while rage begins flaring in my veins.

I hate her. With every fiber of my being, I hate that *Ra'ah.* Throughout my entire existence I've never met a Seer that could crawl so deep under my skin. Something is different about this one, and now that two other foot soldiers for The Light have come to help guide her, one important fact has to be faced.

This assignment will not be as easy as I thought.

Monty releases a groan. I pet the little demon, trying to soothe his nerves. He feels my irritation, my disdain for this human.

"Monty, it's okay," I say. "We just need to be patient and wait for the opportune time."

Gazing to the sky, I see my army dancing in the dark clouds. They're awaiting my command, though it will be a little while longer before the entire army will be released. Tonight was just a taste of what's coming. Not even half of my army had shown.

Failure is not an option. I will not be defeated.

"When the time comes," I speak aloud, "they will not know what hit them."

Chapter Twenty-Four

Kora

The nightmares are unrelenting. They just won't stop. The lady with white hair is a monster, and nightly I'm chased by things I cannot even describe. I sweat through my clothes, soaking my sheets, waking up cold and scared. For the first time in my life I feel true fear, which is ridiculous – dreams can't do any harm, so what do I have to fear?

For weeks I've been tortured nightly in my sleep. Ever since I broke it off with David, who has fallen off the face of the planet, along with his brother and sister.

Clarity and I go to church every Sunday. I ask God to forgive me for whatever I've done to deserve such heinous, sleepless nights. I pray that He will help and protect me from my troubled mind, and from the monsters in my dreams. He doesn't answer, though. To me He feels a million miles away.

Pushing the covers to the side, I stand and put my robe on. Walking across the hall, I notice that Clarity's door is slightly ajar. Not bothering to knock, I slowly open the door the rest of the way … and nearly jump out of my skin. Someone is standing in the corner of her room. A darkened shadow.

Quickly I realize what it really is. Clarity's stupid punching bag.

I still don't know why she has it.

"Clarity," I whisper, gently shaking her shoulder.

"Hmm," she murmurs, slightly opening her eyes. A shocked look crosses her face as she sits up straight and exclaims, "Kora! Are you okay? What's wrong?"

"Shh, Clare, I'm fine. It's just … can I sleep in here with you tonight?"

Confusion lurches across her features. "Sure, but I have to ask … *why*?"

I hesitate before replying, "I'm having nightmares. Like, every night. I just don't want to be alone."

She gives me a sympathetic, yet knowing look. Then, scooting over and patting the mattress, she says, "Slide on in."

I do exactly that. Punching the pillow, getting it just right, I lay my head down and sigh. Warmth spreads through my body and finally I feel peace. Maybe enough to get some dream-free sleep.

"Want to talk about the dreams?" Clarity asks softly.

"No," I promptly respond. "I just want some rest."

A moment of silence passes before she says, "Okay, but I want you to remember something."

"What's that?"

She yawns, then responds, "I'm always here for you, no matter what."

A smile touches my lips. I know what she speaks is truth – she's always been there for me, even when I was at my lowest. Throughout the years she's always been a comfort to me. When I'd met Kevin and started going to church, I'd learned that we weren't supposed to put our hope and trust in mankind. Only Jesus could be our comfort, our support, our healing – our *everything*.

I once believed that Jesus held me in His arms, but now...

I don't know where He is.

Clarity

The next three months passed by in a fevered acceleration. February melted into March, March blew into April, and April rained its way into May. Springtime has hit Garlandton with all its beauty and splendor, with summer hovering just beyond the horizon.

All of us seniors have an unbearable itch to graduate and get out of town, though we can't scratch it just yet. With less than a month left of school, everyone was getting antsy.

Being so close to the end of school also meant that prom was around the corner. Usually all dances were held in the school's gymnasium, but the administrators thought holding a dance where a student was gunned down would be in poor taste.

This year the prom will take place outside, right in the middle of Garlandton Square. Brenton and I have no desire to attend the prom – we have our own plans made.

Dinner and a movie sounded better than some lame-o dance. It's really more our style. Kora decided that work would be more fun than dredging up old dance memories. She'll be working a double shift at the movie theater.

The only people out of our little group attending prom is Casey and Janey, who in the past couple of months decided to give their relationship another shot. I pray that it will work this go around.

Three weeks until graduation. Three weeks, and I'll be headed to New York with Brenton, kissing Garlandton goodbye. That is, if the Squint twins let me.

The Seer Society is set up in a private location somewhere in Atlanta. Marty and Matty want me to live with them at the Society. Not only can I master my Seer abilities there, I'll also be able to earn a degree. The twins had told me that college classes were available, anything from teaching to doctoring.

I don't know what to do. On one hand, if I choose the Seer Society, I'll be around people like myself; people who know what it's like to be different. On the other hand, there's Brenton, Kora, and A.C. – the people who keep me grounded to normalcy. Also, I've been looking forward to getting as far away from Garlandton as possible. Atlanta may not be far enough.

The police were stumped over the vandalism of the old

gym a three months back. No fingerprints, no leads, nothing at all to go on. They told the town that it appeared to be some bored teenagers with nothing productive to do (I prefer that scenario to what really occurred). The gym vandalism is still under investigation ... they should just give up now.

After the run-in with Livian and her army, Marty and Matty started training me in all the ways of a Seer. They know (and so do I) that we must prepare for the battle ahead. Livian will come back and fight, bringing her three pawns and her grotesque army.

David, Danielle, and Darren had vanished. The school did an investigation, only to find that all their paperwork had been forged. Social Security numbers, birth certificates, names and addresses turned out to be impressive fakes. The car I'd seen Danielle drive had been left abandoned in a field just outside of town. No tag or registration was found.

With their disappearance, and Livian's absence, I've been able to really focus on my training. I feel like I'm finally getting used to the new Seers in my life, but it's hard keeping them a secret. When Kora works, we train at my house. When Kora's home, we train in the woods behind Barney's Hotel, which is the hotel the twins are staying at.

Yes, Barney's Hotel. That's the owner's name. Barney.

"Your hands are you strongest weapons," Marty had told me one day in their hotel room. "Your marks contain your power, the power that is within you at all times. *You* and only you can grab that power ... you know, that white light that burns through your entire body? That's the power of God. He fills your every pore, energizes your every nerve, all the way through to the marrow of your bones with this heavenly power. To catch hold and control it, you must first complete one step."

"And what step is that?" I'd asked her in complete fascination.

Her lips had curled into a grin, while her hand tapped her chest. "Listen to your heart. Once you hear the voice of God, and feel His spirit, that's when you've got hold of the power stored inside you."

Her answer had perplexed me to no end, but after the first month of training, her answer gradually became clearer. My Seer gifts and abilities are becoming less foreign. My soul and mind is starting to work together with God's plan. I'm feeling comfortable in my skin ... my *Seer* skin, to put it bluntly.

The burning in my palms and seeing into the spiritual realm (AKA angels and demons) has become a normal function in my life. I feel wholly normal, which has been absent from my life for quite some time. I feel truly...

Blessed.

Tonight the school's prom will commence. People are, this very afternoon, shuffling things into order, such as hair appointments, limos, dinner reservations, ectera, ectera. As for myself, I'm in the middle of training. In a sparring match with Marty Squint.

My date with Brenton wasn't until seven tonight, so the twins thought it best to indulge in a couple hours of sweating. We're behind my house, and Matty is supervising the match, making sure that it doesn't get out of control. Not that Marty and I dislike one another. It's just that she talks smack the entire time, which, at first, troubled me deeply. However now that I've been spending loads of time with her, I've absorbed a lot of her attitude. Not only am I learning to fight, I'm learning how to be the fastest mouth in the south.

"Are you even trying?" I chuckle as I swiftly duck her punches. "My grandma could whip your tail with one hand behind her back!"

Before I know it, she kicks my feet out from under me. I fall flat on my back, the air launching from my lungs.

Peering down at my face, she counters, "Wait a minute … your grandma? Didn't she, like, disown you or something?"

Springing to my feet, I shrug off her toxic comment. After my talk with A.C., I'd told the twins everything we talked about, and now I'm paying for it. When Marty finds herself on the losing end of the match, she doesn't think twice about throwing that *tidbit* in my face.

About to unleash another round of verbal smack, a voice halts my tongue.

"Uh, Clarity?"

Flipping around, I face the person with the voice. My breath becomes ensnared in my lungs, while my stomach drops to the ground. Two people stand there, with mouths agape and expressions shocked.

"B-Brenton?" I stammer out, completely floored. "Kora? What are y'all doing here?"

Nervous laughter escapes their lips, both of them staring me down. They act as if a great big ball of *whoa* has rolled on top of them.

"Uh," Kora starts, "I forgot my wallet, so I came home to get it." She's wearing her work uniform, black pants and burgundy button-up shirt.

"Oh," I say. "Did ... you get it?"

She waves it in the air. "Yeah, so..."

"So..."

"I'll talk to you later," she says. "I've, uh ... yeah. Later."
She spins on her heels and heads to the front of the house.

Marty and Matty are still as statues, with aspects of total
disarray frozen on their tanned faces. Their mouths hang open,
and their green eyes are unblinking. Clearly they are at a loss for
words, not knowing how to handle this situation. I'd been
keeping them a secret for months.

They are secrets no more.

Turning around, I walk over to Brenton and kiss his
cheek. "You weren't supposed to be here until seven," I point
out.

"I wanted to surprise you," he explains, his eyes focused
on the twins. "But it appears that I'm the one surprised." He
wraps his arm around my waist. "Are you going to introduce us
or what?"

"They're, uh..." I gulp, shooting the twins a despairing

look. Yes, my tongue is officially *tied*.

"We're Clarity's cousins from the north," Marty speaks up. She walks over and extends her hand to Brenton. "My name is Marty, and that's my brother, Matty."

Brenton shakes Marty's hand, his visage incredulous. "Really – *cousins*?"

Matty walks over, shaking his hand as well. "Very, very distant cousins," he notes.

Brenton releases a shaky breath. "Well, it's nice to meet you guys. I'm Brenton, Clarity's boyfriend."

An uneasy silence falls around us. The only sounds come from birds chirping in nearby trees. Brenton stares at the twins, still trying to comprehend that I'm somehow related to them. The twins stare back, both blushing, and both speechless.

Though I'm not related to them by blood, I am by my Seer heritage, so...

Still. Yeah. Awkward.

"Marty, we better go," Matty tells his sister. "We've got that ... that *thing* to do, remember?"

"Oh, yeah!" Marty anxiously agrees. Looking to Brenton

she says, "It was nice to meet you, Brenton." Then at me she whispers, "See you later ... *cuz*."

"See ya later," I reply, watching as they pass by.

With Brenton looking the other way, Marty catches my eye and mouths *He's hot*.

As their truck revs up and peels out of the driveway, Brenton remarks, "Cousins? I thought Caroline was your only living relative."

"Evidently not," I counter. I had yet to tell Brenton about my family and Seer gifts. Deep down, I know that I'm running out of time. I'll have to tell him, and soon.

"Who found who?" he continues to investigate, he eyes narrowed.

"What do you mean?"

"I mean, did you find them or they find you?"

"Oh," I avoid his eyes, "they found me." It's the truth, even if they'd had help from angelic beings.

We walk to the front porch, side by side.

"Where are they from?" he softly inquires. Something in his voice tells me he's hesitant to broach the subject.

"Atlanta," I reply.

"Oh." He runs a hand through his hair – a nervous habit – and says, "I'm a little confused about what I saw. You know, fighting and all that..."

"Oh, that!" I interject, laughing. "That was them teaching me some self-defense moves. They live for stuff like that." They do, they really do.

"That's cool." He twists around, halting my steps. I bump into him. He pulls me close. "So, I thought we could start the date early."

"Sure," I say, "but I need to take a shower."

"Yes, you do." He grins, wrinkling up his nose. "You're kind of sweaty."

I smile. "Give me twenty minutes."

"Sure." I start up the porch steps when he calls out, "Hey!"

"Yeah?" I stop and turn, my sweaty ponytail swishing around.

He grins. "Bring an extra change of clothes."

"Why?"

He places a finger to his lips and answers, "It's a surprise."

Chapter Twenty-Five

Clarity

"So, our date is starting at the swimming hole." I look at him with raised eyebrows. Bemusement swirls in his chocolate brown eyes.

"Yeah!" he exclaims energetically. "Cool, right?"

Staring out the truck's passenger window, I take a grand sweep of the plush landscape.

The swimming hole is made from a natural spring, located in what us Garlandtonites call the *boonies*. Wildflowers are in full bloom, their purple, white, yellow, and red colors dotting the green grass. Huge pines and weeping willows pave a path to the spring. The sunshine glistens off the clear water, casting a lovely, peaceful shade. Honeysuckle vines wind up and down the trees, their sweet concoction breezing through the sunroof.

Brenton hops out of the truck and closes the door. I do the same, watching him curiously. He's up to something. I just don't know what that something is.

"Want a sandwich?" Brenton asks. He picks up a picnic basket and blanket from the back of his truck.

Tilting my head to the side, I wonder, "What are you up to?"

"What do you mean?" He spreads the blanket out, placing the basket on top of it.

"This." I gesture around the swimming hole. "The water, the food, the change of clothes – " I stop talking. I stop using words. His facial expression speaks volumes.

"Brenton," I say, taking a couple steps back, "whatever you're thinking, don't – "

Too late.

Before I can stop him, he picks me up and runs toward the swimming hole. He sloshes through the icy water until both of us go under. If any of my senses had been asleep, they're awake now. The water is a big glacier of *cold*, even though it's May.

For a moment I feel like we're kids again, goofing off and playing in the water. At one point he picks me up and throws me into the deepest part of the hole. Forcing my way to the surface, I jump on his back in an attempt to dunk him. He laughs in return, which causes me to laugh. Then he loses his footing, and the both of us go under again. We sputter and gasp for air when we hit the surface.

"Rope swings?" He points to the oak tree that houses two ropes.

I grin. "Rope swings."

Swinging back and forth on the ropes, with the wind breezing through our hair, we let go at the same time, plummeting to the water below. He pretends he's Tarzan, doing his best impression of the jungle guy. Kind of cheesy, but I find it enduring ... and hilarious.

Eventually we tire ourselves out. He walks over to his truck and retrieves two towels – he'd planned this so well. Wrapping the towel around my shoulders, we sit down and eat turkey sandwiches and cut-up fruit.

After awhile, we lay back on the blanket and stare at the blue sky. My head is on his chest, listening to the beat of his heart. Everything about this day is perfect. The trickling water of the spring is peaceful, and the fresh air where summer and spring mingle is a complete delight.

For the first time in months, our relationship is normal. Like we'd never gone through a friend's death, a few fights, a break-up – *we* are finally back to normal.

To some people this would be the lamest of all dates, but for us it's simply perfect.

"When do you want to get married, Clarity?"

His question catches me off guard. "What did you say?"

"You heard me."

Rising up to a seated position, I stare into his eyes. His face holds a serious edge, though his dimpled grin is shining bright.

"You're ... *serious.*"

"As a heart attack," he counters, his brown eyes searching my face.

"Brenton," I begin, trying to get my thoughts in order, "I know we've talked about it, but ... this is a big step."

Nope. Can't get my thoughts together. The roaring of my heart is stealing most of my attention.

"We're planning on going to New York together, and I think a one bedroom apartment is more economical. Plus..." He plays with a strand of my hair. "I want to start off right – I want us to be married."

My breath snags in my throat. He feels exactly how I do about marriage and doing it God's way.

When I'm able to breathe again, I ask, "Are you saying you want to elope?"

He nods, leaning up on his elbows. "Clarity Elise Miller, I'm ready to start a life with you. I've already told you – you have my heart, and you will forever. The question is this: Are *you* ready to start a life with *me*?"

I stare at him, at a complete loss for words. I take in his smile, his caring eyes, his expression of love and sincerity.

What do I do? Is this the moment I've been waiting for? The moment I unload all of my secrets; the moment that Brenton finds out that I'm a foot soldier for The Light. I love him, want to be with him. I want us to get married, and have children one day, but...

Would he accept me?

"Clare-Baby?" he whispers, cupping my cheek with his

palm.

I open my mouth to speak, but no words form. Instead of talking, I bury my hands in his thick hair and kiss him.

Kora

Today has been the slowest day in the theater's history. There's no new movies playing, and with the prom starting in a couple of hours, there will not be a teenager in sight. Sitting behind the concession stand, bored out of my mind, I listen to the *tick-tock* of the clock hanging on the wall. It's one of those cat clocks, where the cat's eyes and tail move along with each passing second.

I hate that clock.

With no one around, I take the time to think on the nightmares I've been experiencing. The dreams are always the same. I'm continually being chased by the lady with white hair, by disgusting monsters, and sometimes David and his siblings. The weird thing is, I'm not alone. I know that someone is running next to me, though who it is, I can't tell. At first I thought it was Kevin, but a gut feeling had told me it wasn't him. It's someone else, someone who knows me well.

Maybe talking with Clarity would help. Nah, probably not. If I tell her, she'd tell A.C., and then I'd be back in the psych ward at the hospital.

No, I'll just keep my dreams to myself...

"Kora, didn't you hear me?"

A voice cuts into my thoughts. It belongs to Steve, the evening manager and all around jerk-wad.

"Sorry, Steve, what did you say?"

"The garbage," he snaps, pointing at the over-stuffed trash can. "It needs to be taken out."

Steve is a tall, lanky guy with dark hair, thick coke-bottle glasses, and, for some reason, loves to wear suspenders. He also loves to make the people beneath him feel inferior.

I bite my tongue, holding back a very nasty comment. Believe me, I have tons of comments I could sling at him. Like, he's a thirty year old gamer whose greatest joy in life is picking on his teenage underlings. What keeps me from hurling mud is the sad fact that I need this job. If I let my guard down and told him how I really felt, then he'd go cry to the owners. Then I'd be fired, and he'd most likely get a raise.

Life is so unfair sometimes.

Glancing at the trash, I turn back to him and exclaim, "Steve, that bag is full and bigger than I am. Can't you get Grant to do it?"

Steve smirks. "Grant is getting ready for prom, which leads me to wonder – why aren't you going? No date for the mentally disturbed orphan girl?"

His words sting – a lot. Tears burn the back of my eyes, but I don't allow them to break loose. Rather, I clamp down on my tongue and attempt to let his empty words roll off my back.

Silently, I walk over to the garbage can and tie the trash up. Then, with all my might, I pull the bag out of the large plastic can. It's heavy, but I'm able to get it out. Steve watches me the whole time, wearing a smirk on his dumb face.

Hefting the black bag of trash onto my back, I look at him and say, "You are so mean."

He flinches, as if my words slapped him across the face. Then, with a sneer and a grunt, he spins around and walks away.

It takes me a few minutes, but eventually I make it to the dumpsters behind the theater. I'm nothing if not determined. After a few tries, the gigantic bag finally drops into the big green dumpster. Releasing a breath, rubbing my hands together, I turn around … and gasp with surprise.

Glaring at the person in front of me, I ask, "What are *you* doing here?"

Clarity

Brenton and I lay on the blanket in one big cuddle. The sun is in its early stages of setting, blessing the earth with orange and red hues of light. Crickets and frogs sing together as they prepare to close the door to the day, in turn swinging the door wide for nighttime. We've had a blessed afternoon spending time together. Now with evening approaching, our dinner and movie date will commence.

"You want to go to dinner now?" I question lazily.

He laughs, the sound rumbling in his chest. "I'm kind of liking this right now."

Closing my eyes, I sigh, loving the steady beat of his

heart. I'd almost spilled the beans to him about my Seer gift, but my lips had other plans. Instead I'd kissed him, then the rest of the afternoon we held each other in a tight embrace. At one point I think I fell asleep – that's how peaceful this day has been. So, so peaceful.

The caustic ring of my cell phone sounds from my purse, which was laying in the cab of the truck. I sit up, but Brenton pulls me back down.

"Just let it ring," he whispers.

"Answer your phone."

I jerk my head toward the voice, nearly clocking Brenton in the chin. Sam stands by the water's edge, his expression stiff and rigid. His blue eyes glow fervently. As always, with his sudden appearance, a hint of lavender coats the air.

"Answer your phone," repeats my Guardian, adding a strong, "*now*."

Pushing Brenton lightly on the chest, I say, "Sorry. Better answer it."

Brenton sighs and closes his eyes. Standing to my feet, I glance at Sam. His eyes never leave mine, and by his defeated countenance, I immediately know that something is wrong.

Something has happened.

What's going on? I ask, using my thoughts.

Sam replies, "You're about to find out."

Reaching into the truck cab and pulling out my phone, I answer, "Hello?'

"Clarity! Oh, thank God!" I cringe at A.C.'s strident tone.

"A.C., what's wrong?"

Brenton hears the worry and concern in my voice. Hurriedly, he jumps to his feet and runs to my side.

A.C. continues, "You've got to come to the hospital right now!"

Dread-filled shivers cover me from head to toe. My palms warm up with that familiar heat.

"What's happened?" I whisper, my eyes pinching shut.

"It's Kora," she frantically speaks. "She's been beaten up – beaten to a pulp." She pauses, a sob escaping her chest and releasing into the phone. "I … they don't know if she's going to make it."

Sam

Livian has gone too far. She's used one of her human pawns to hurt another human being, which has officially crossed the line. And because of this, a soul is hovering between life and death.

"Clarity, what is it? What's going on?" Brenton questions. He's following Clarity around, picking up the blanket and picnic basket, then throwing it in the back of the truck.

"Just hurry and get in," she responds, flying into the passenger seat. "I'll tell you on the way to the hospital."

Opening his door and sliding in, he reacts, "The *hospital*?"

They tear down the dirt road. I prepare to follow, but I'm stopped in my tracks.

"I'm gathering up the troops, Sam." Gabriel stands by the water next to me, his arms crossed at his chest.

Glaring at him, I say, "So I assume you've gotten

word from the Throne Room?"

He nods, then says, "Stay with your Charge. Don't leave her side."

With that, my wings release and I fly up into the sky.

I don't need to be told twice.

Chapter Twenty-Six

Clarity

The drive to the hospital is near unbearable. Thoughts of Kora bruised and broken creep across my mind, leaving in its trail a muddied existence. I can't stop the hard beating of my heart, which not only pounds in my chest, but also in my head. My flaming hands are impossible to ignore.

What has *happened*?

"She's going to be okay, Clare," Brenton tries assuring. He rubs my shoulder, attempting to console me.

Nothing he can say or do will help – only Heaven can soothe my unease.

As we pull up to the emergency entrance, I swing the door wide and jump out of the moving truck. Brenton calls after me. I don't acknowledge him. My brain is too focused on finding my best friend. I am too consumed with worry and regret.

I pass by people, shoving them out of the way. The reception desk comes into view, so I head there. A girl, maybe a couple of years older than me, sits behind the desk. She's flipping through a magazine and chewing her gum loudly.

"I'm looking for Kora Dodd," I tell the young woman. Her eyes lift from the magazine. Annoyance flares across her face.

"Who?" Her eyebrows lift, wrinkling her forehead. Apparently she's confused by my request.

Becoming peeved, I lean forward, my face inches from hers.

"*Kor-a D-odd,*" I enunciate slowly and carefully. In return, I get a go to *you know where* look.

"How is she?" Brenton breathlessly inquires. He gives my shoulder a squeeze.

Facing him, I reply, "I don't know! This chick doesn't comprehend the English language or – "

"Clarity!"

Hearing my name, I twirl around. A.C. is rounding the corner. Tears are streaming down her face. Shaking off Brenton's hand (the squeezing was getting on my nerves), I race down the hall.

"Where is she? How is she?" I interrogate. She throws her arms around my body, gracing me with a full-on bear hug.

"Follow me," she orders. Hooking my hand with hers, she pulls me down the hall. "She's hooked up to a few machines. One of her eyes is swollen shut and she's got cuts and bruises all over her body. Five of her ribs are broken – that's all I know right now." Brenton trails behind, his expression flushed with concern.

I gawk at her. "A.C., the cuts, are they..."

"They are not self-inflicted," she races out.

Tears burn my eyes, my palms on fire. "Is she going to make it?"

"They're not sure. They've taken some X-Rays and other tests. She has another concussion, and the fact that she had head injuries a few months ago – it's a waiting game, Clarity." We stop in front of a door, the number searing into my brain. Room 167. "She's in here."

I place my hand on the doorknob. It's freezing cold against my hot hands. Tears roll down my cheeks.

"What can I do?" I whisper.

She gives me a pointed look. "Talk to Heaven."

I nod, her statement making complete sense.

Twisting the knob and opening the heavy door, a gasp expels from my mouth. Taken back. That's what I am – I'm taken back by what's in front of me. No words could ever prepare me for this moment.

Kora, *tiny* Kora, lying in a hospital bed. Hooked up to various machines, each one beeping a different tune. Her head is wrapped in white bandages, her face is a swollen, bruised wreck. Underneath all the black and blue, her skin is the palest I've ever seen.

"Kora," I croak out through trembling lips. I take her hand in mine. It's cold, so cold. Brenton walks up behind me.

"She's going to be okay," he says softly. "She's stronger than she looks."

"Yes, she is," I concur. "I just don't understand. Why did this happen? Who do it?"

Right after I uttered that last question, the scent of freshly cut grass saunters below my nose. Christopher has materialized on the other side of Kora.

"One of her co-workers found her behind the theater," Christopher informs, his hand caressing her forehead.

My eyes find his.

Did Livian do this?

I think of Livian, the demon General. White hair, white eyes, and black wings. Anger swells my heart, the need for revenge aching in my veins.

"No," he answers, then adds, "though she used one of her pawns to act it out."

Who?

His blue eyes glow as he replies, "The girl. Danielle."

An image of Danielle traverses across my mind. Her blonde hair, her pale skin, her blue eyes, her perkiness...

Her ignorance to the fact that she's a puppet being used by the evil one.

While Christopher and I have our little back and forth, Brenton is oblivious that there's a celestial being in the room with us. Instead, he continues to gently rub my shoulders, most likely thinking he's helping me stay calm.

It's not working. I'm anything *but* calm.

A knock at the door jolts me from my vengeful thoughts. A.C. walks in, her face a pallid shade. Her hair falls free from its ponytail.

"You guys are going to have to leave," she whispers, her gaze on Kora.

"No," I speedily return, tightening my grip on Kora's limp hand.

A.C. sighs. "I know you don't want to leave her, hon, but the doctors want to check her out. They want to make sure there's progress."

Still, I stay silent, gazing down at my best friend. Christopher continues to stand next to her, his eyes no longer glowing but keeping steady on Kora. His love for his Charge is unrelenting.

"C'mon, Clare-Baby," says Brenton. He has to physically take my hand from hers. "Let the doctors do their job. Kora needs to get better."

Reluctantly I cave, allowing Brenton to pull me away. We walk down the hall, somehow making it to a waiting room. It reeks of stale coffee.

I sit down on a hard chair, my nerves jittery and chaotic.

"You want to talk about it?" Brenton wonders.

"No," I say. My eyes fall down to my entwined hands resting on my lap. A familiar ringing bounces off the walls of the small room. It doesn't register that it's my own phone until Brenton points it out.

"Clarity – your phone."

"Oh." Shaking the cobwebs from my threadbare brain, I reach into my pocket and retrieve the phone.

"W-What?"

"We heard about Kora," a voice says on the other end.

"Marty? Is that you?"

An unreadable expression passes over Brenton's face. He leans his elbows on his thighs, resting his chin on his balled-up fists. His brown eyes watch me, unblinking.

A very dramatic, Marty-like groan touches my ear.

"Uh, *duh*! Who else would it be?"

I roll my eyes. "What do y'all want? I'm at the hospital –
"

"We need to talk," she hastily pushes. "Like, right now."

"I can't!" I protest, appalled at the thought of leaving Kora. "I can't just *leave*! Kora needs me."

"Trust me, Clarity," she says in a direct manner. "You *want* to hear what we have to say."

Lavender specks the air as Sam appears beside me.

"Go," is all he speaks before he disappears.

A nauseating feel clenches my stomach. I have no other choice but to go.

"Meet you at Trina's?"

"We're already here!" she exclaims. "It's all you can eat helper night. Oh, and just so you know, I already ordered for you … is that a problem?"

Livian

The Seer's boyfriend paces the hall of the hospital. He's experiencing an unrest that he can't explain. He has noticed that Clarity's been acting strange for a long time, and it's driving him nuts.

Why did she have to leave suddenly to meet with her "cousins"? Why was she lying to him? Anyone with eyes can see that there's no way they swim in the same gene pool.

Well, I can help him find out the truth. Not only that, but helping *him* will help *me* in the process. He's in my way if he stays here.

"Go to Magnolia Road," I whisper in his ear. "There you will find the answers you seek."

"Magnolia Road," he says aloud. The wheels spin in his brain on hearing my voice, though he believes it's his own thoughts.

"Magnolia Road," I repeat.

With that said, he turns around and sprints to the elevators. I smile, pleased with myself.

Now I can retrieve what I came for.

Clarity

On entering Trina's, I spot the twins in their usual booth in the back. They're both chowing down on some kind of meat and noodle dish. A plate full of the same lumpy stuff sits across the table from them, most likely my dinner – a dinner I will not be able to digest.

Sliding into the booth, a coke sits next to the plate of mush. Condensation pools around the bottom of the glass. The air conditioner is turned way low, making me so grateful that A.C. let me borrow her purple sweatshirt. When she'd noticed my clothes were a little damp, she had insisted I take it.

"Where have you been?" Marty speaks through a mouthful of food. "We've been waiting for nearly an hour."

I pick the coke up and sip at it, my mouth suddenly dry.

"Sorry," I mutter, "but it took some time to convince Brenton I'd be fine coming alone. A.C., though, was more than willing to let me drive her car."

Swallowing a bite of food, Marty asks, "Does Brenton know about, you know..."

I shake my head. "No, not yet. I was going to tell him earlier, but it … I couldn't." Changing the subject I ask, "So, what did you want to talk about?"

"Well," Matty says uneasily, glancing sideways at his sister, "it's more like something we need to show you."

On cue, Marty brings out a manilla envelope. Reaching in, she pulls out three 8x10 sized pictures. Carefully, she separates the pictures in front of me. Her eyes are watchful, as if gauging my reaction.

Tearing my eyes from her observant gaze, I allow them to drift down to the pictures displayed before me. My breath draws in, though it's quite hard for my lungs to push the air back out. I'm basically shocked stupid, which is quite a feat considering all I've gone through lately.

Three pictures, three people – David, Danielle, and Darren. However, the names underneath the pictures are different.

Above each picture, the word **MISSING** is broadcast in giant bold lettering. I stare at that one word, unblinking and speechless, for an entire minute. The sounds of pots and pans are busy clanging in the background. I try to speak, but no words come forth. To put it plainly, I'm irrevocably and utterly mystified.

MISSING.

Marty points a chewed down, nubby nail at Danielle's picture. "Her real name is Bethany Key – she's from Tennessee." She points to Darren. "His real name is Anderson Kirkland. He's from Mississippi." Then lastly, David. "His real name is Timothy Jones, and he's from Kentucky."

A vast array of shades and colors swirl in my line of vision as I fight to process this new plethora of information.

"Why are y'all showing me this?" I whisper, my eyes glued on the images the photos hold.

Matty replies, "This is the type of people Livian hunts – people like Kora." He pushes his plate to the side. "The weak, the depressed, the rejected, the suicidal – "

"The broken," Marty adds softly.

"We've done some research," continues Matty, "and we have found that these three individuals come from very similar backgrounds."

I lift my eyes. "How?"

He lets out a shaky breath. "Bethany's parents divorced, and her father moved to California. Before she ran away, her mother had turned to alcohol, which caused her to lose her job and their home. Bethany has been missing for seven months."

"Anderson's story is about the same, except he ran away from an abusive father." Marty takes a quick sip from her glass.

"He's been missing for nearly three months."

"And Timothy has been missing for over a year," Matty says, rubbing his tired green eyes.

"They are all under full possession," Matty adds with a cringe, his tone lamentable. "It will be hard to detach the evil from them."

"Which is exactly what we must do," Marty proclaims, matter-of-fact.

My body slumps deeper into the booth, my heart and soul dispirited. "How can we save them?" I wonder. "We don't even know where they are."

"That's where Kora comes in," Marty responds.

"Kora?" I shake my head, perplexed. "How can Kora help?"

"Her angel said that she was talking with Danielle before the attack, right?"

"Yeah, but – wait, how did you know that?"

Marty's eyes roll. "Angels. Seers. *Conversing*."

"Oh, yeah..." Well, duh.

"So," Marty presses on, "when she wakes up, we can interrogate her. She can tell her side of the story." A satisfied grin diffuses across her dark features.

A distressful breath eludes my mouth. What she's just spoken stabs into me, like an icepick to the heart. Matty is the first to notice my troubled expression.

"What's wrong, Clarity?" he questions. His eyes have narrowed, studying me closely.

A nasty taste builds on my tongue. I force it down with a sip of coke.

Staring him right in the eye, I say, "*If* she wakes up."

All the color drains from his face, and his body becomes tense. A shaky breath evades his lips.

"What are you saying? That she ... that she might..." He pauses, rubbing a hand down his face. "What are you saying?" His tone becomes calm, though I'm able to detect the slight quiver in his voice.

"Matty," his sister says firmly, lifting a hand to his shoulder, "she's going to be fine."

He looks over at her. "How do you know that?"

"I just know," she whispers.

I watch this back and forth, astonished and confused. What's happening here? Why does Matty care what happens to Kora?

"Wait," I hold a hand in the air. "What am I missing here? Matty, why are – "

I halt my questions when I notice that every word I speak produces white cottony rings in the air. The twins breath is also producing little smoke rings, only it's not smoke. There's been a change in the diner's temperature. It feels like someone has turned the air conditioner to below zero.

Frost starts crusting over the windows, like the windshield of my car in the wintertime. The twins stare behind me, taking in fast gulps of air. Something is obviously disturbing the two.

Slowly, I turn around in my seat to see what's so disturbing. Automatically, my hand flies to my mouth to muffle the scream building in my lungs.

Chapter Twenty-Seven

Clarity

The waitress stands frozen, mid-stride, her mouth set in its usual deep scowl. A ticket is clenched in her hand, her waitress uniform is bunched slightly around the hips. Shifting my gaze to the kitchen, I'm floored once more. The cook holds a pan in the air, frozen in the middle of hanging it on a hook. It seems that the entire diner is frozen in time ... except for us Seers.

The burning sensations in my palms intensify, pulsating red. Rotating back around, facing the twins, I see that their palms are blazing just like mine. They stare at me, and a deep understanding streams between the three of us. As a unit, we rise to our feet, readying ourselves for battle. No demons are in sight, but there's demonic activity brewing in every nook and cranny of the diner.

Icicles have formed, hanging from the ceiling, chairs,

tables, doorknobs – all over the small building. We hold our hands in front of us, palms out, preparing to do some damage. Instead of inflicting pain, the voice of a demon General sounds.

"Little Seers, little Seers, let me in."

Livian's taunting voice booms through the diner. Her laughter shakes the floor beneath our feet.

Marty snorts, unmoved by the demon's presence. "How *lame!*"

"Show yourself, demon," demands Matty, his voice filled with authority.

"Oh, I will," she replies, her tone musical. *"Come to the abandoned church on Magnolia Road. We'll be waiting for you in the cemetery, along with your darling Kora."*

Livian's words cause my stomach to cramp. My heart restricts mid-beat in my chest. Dizziness rams into my gut, and my legs threaten to give out.

I'm not the only one affected. Matty, who is by my side, flinches and becomes tense.

"You're lying," I say loudly.

"You mean you don't know?" she asks, sounding surprised.

When my cell phone goes off inside my pocket, she cackles. *"Ahh, now you'll know."*

With a shaky hand, I take out my cell phone and answer, "H-Hello?"

"Clarity!" A.C.'s clamorous voice is close to piercing my eardrum. "I-I went to Kora's room and … her window was open and … and..."

"Is she there, A.C.?" Sadly, I already have the answer.

"She's gone. She's gone. We … can't find her!"

The phone drops from my hand, falling to the brown-tiled floor. Rage and hopelessness folds together within me.

"What is it?" Matty grabs my shoulders and shakes me, his voice close to hysterical. "What's happened? Where's Kora?"

I hear him, but I don't reply.

"Please … don't hurt her," I whisper, tuning Matty out. My voice cracks with despair.

"Tell me what's happened!" orders Matty. Staring into his wide eyes, I'm still in complete shock.

"She's got her," I say in disbelief. "Livian *has* her."

"No." His hands drop from my shoulders, his arms falling to his sides.

Livian's malevolent laughter stings my eardrums. *"You want her? Come and get her, but be warned – your deaths are inevitable!"*

"Don't hurt her!" I scream, just as an invisible wind whips and batters us. We hover together, creating a protective circle.

When the wind ceases, the waitress unfreezes. She scoots past us and slams the check on the table. Then she walks around us again, ignoring the fact that we're standing in the middle of the diner, huddled in a tight circle. Sounds begin filtering through the air. Loud banging and clanging come from the kitchen. All life in Trina's Diner has woken up. Reality has shifted back to normal speed.

A few seconds later, we wake up ... well, Marty wakes up.

"Snap out of it!" she shouts, slapping her brother across the face. "We've got work to do."

He blinks. "I-I don't get it. Why is this happening to her? To me?"

"Matty," she says through clenched teeth, "if you want to help her, you've got to get a hold of yourself. Freaking out is not an option."

"You're right." He shakes his head, running a hand through his short hair. Reaching into his back pocket, he takes out his cell phone and starts dialing. "Marty, you and Clarity go to the hotel. I'm sure Hope, Faith, and Sam will be there. I'll pay the tab and get a few Seers on the phone." Teary-eyed, he looks at his sister and says, "We've got to get her out of this."

Marty hugs him tightly. I'm surprised by this act of love. I've never seen them embrace before.

"Don't worry," she consoles, releasing him from their hug. Seizing my hand, she pulls me out the doors and into the darkness.

Sam

"I can't get to her!" yells Christopher, his tone clearly frustrated.

We stand on top of the hospital. A few minutes before, Livian and her pawns had broken in, taking an unconscious

Kora with them. She'd kept Christopher busy in battle, which allowed her pawns to unhook Kora from her machines. As soon as she was free, Livian wrapped all four humans in her wings and flew away. Christopher had tried to follow, but Livian's army of *Tsipor* devils kept him at bay, and now...

Their whereabouts are unknown.

"We will find them, Christopher," I say. "The Father has a plan, and – "

"It's not fair!" he interjects. "Kora didn't choose a life of suffering and pain, but it's found her. It always finds her! Our jobs as Guardians are to *guard* them. But how can we guard if we don't know the future of their souls."

"Settle down there, cowboy."

We shift our attention to Gabriel, who has dropped in front of us.

"How can I settle down," Christopher seethes, "if I can't find my Charge?"

"It's the enemy," Gabriel points out. "All of his followers have a certain level of power. Livian has an entire army of demons rallying behind her, and she's using them well."

Christopher looks at me, then back to Gabriel. "How is this helping *anything*?"

Gabriel sighs. "Your Charge will not die tonight, though her life is about to change tremendously." Nodding at me he says, "Sam, they need you at Barney's Hotel. Something has just gone down. Go to your Charge. I need to speak with Christopher alone."

Immediately I fill up with tension.

"What's happened?"

"Go." Gabriel's eyes flash brilliantly. *"Now."*

Clarity

The night air is sticky and hot as we run across the street to Barney's Hotel. My thoughts are scrambled and clustered together. Questions ... so many questions. And I ask them the whole way across the street.

"What's going on? Why is Matty so concerned about Kora? Why was he nearly crying? Why is he getting Seers on the phone? What are we going to *do*?"

Arriving at the entrance of their room, Marty rips the key from her pocket, totally ignoring my queries. Ramming the key into the lock, she unlocks the bolt and swings the door open, pushing me inside. And just like Matty had said, our Guardians were there. The mixture of roses and lavender welcome us with a sweet-smelling embrace.

"Where is Matty?" inquires Hope.

Slamming the door, Marty answers, "Across the street, paying the tab, calling for backup."

Before she has finished the response, Hope has disappeared, no doubt materializing beside Matty.

"Clarity, have a seat. All we can do is wait for Matty." She situates herself on a couch, her knees pulling to her chin. Closing her eyes, she seems to be praying, her lips moving wordlessly.

I sit down on the edge of one of the full-sized beds. They're covered with orange comforters, the whole outdated room set in the seventies. Focusing all my attention on a praying Marty, I almost don't notice when Sam plops down next to me. Lavender covers my senses with strong tranquility, but I still have questions that need to be answered.

"Why won't you tell me?" I softly ask.

"Tell you what?" she retorts, her green eyes opening and staring into empty air. Faith has taken a seat next to her.

"You know what," I angrily snap. "Tell me what's up with Matty. Tell me why he's so concerned for Kora. He talks like he knows her, which I know he doesn't."

Her eyes drift over and catch mine. A tiny speck of uncertainty flashes in her gaze. An awkward quiet has settled in the room, so strange that I have to force myself not to scream and pull the hair from my head.

"Go ahead, Marty," Faith speaks, her voice light and airy. "She needs to know the truth."

"No," Marty shoots back in a defiant tone. "I promised my brother I wouldn't say anything. Not a word."

Faith smiles and takes Marty's hand. "It's okay. It is *time* for her to know."

"It's time?" I bristly exclaim. "It's time for me to know what?"

Marty releases a loud, defeated sigh. Glaring at her Guardian, she says, "Fine. I'll tell her, but I'm blaming you if

Matty becomes angry."

Faith continues to smile. "Trust me – he will not be angry."

"Okay." Marty straightens her legs, stretching them out. With her green eyes on me, she declares, "I hope you can handle what I'm about to tell you."

I roll my eyes. "Just spill it."

"Remember," she starts, "when we had that conversation about how Seers dream or have visions of their significant others?"

I nod.

She narrows her eyes. "Well, Matty dreamed of Kora ... four years ago, when we were only fourteen."

My heart does cartwheels in my chest, shortening my breath.

"Are you saying..."

"What I'm saying is that Kora Dodd is my future sis-in-law."

I gape at her. "No way."

"Yes way," she nods. "Kora Dodd is destined to be Kora Squint. Matty didn't realize she lived in this town, or that she was your best friend – until earlier today."

I hear what she's saying, but still, it's hard to swallow.

"Unbelievable. Matty dreamed of – "

The door suddenly bangs open. Matty strolls in, with Hope following behind. Without a word, he stands in front of the nightstand, placing his wallet, phone, and spare change on it. He waits to speak until he's facing us.

"Alright, so a few Seers from the Society are on the way, so I – " He hesitates two seconds, catching drift of our flummoxed expressions. "What's happened now?"

Marty stands, straightens her shoulders, and looks at him, her countenance indecipherable. "She knows, Matty. The dream, the Kora – Clarity *knows*."

"How could you?" he questions, with betrayal painted on his face. "I trusted you with this huge secret and – "

"Faith made me tell!" Marty reacts, pointing to the angel, who shrugs in return.

Matty shakes his head. "You have got the biggest mouth

– "

"Guys," I jump in, getting in between the two, "it's nothing to fight about." To Matty I say, "I think it's awesome that you dreamed of Kora. It's the best news I've heard in a long time. You ... don't have to worry about me saying anything."

Relief falls over his face like a veil. "I was afraid that you wouldn't approve. Plus, we had no idea she lived here."

"And you know how angels forget to tell you certain details." Marty crosses her arms.

"Marty, don't start." Faith lets out an exasperated sigh, flinging her blonde ponytail. "You know the rules – some details you must – "

"*Find out for yourselves,*" Marty cuts in, completing the sentence. "Yeah, been hearing that one all my life!"

"So now you understand why Kora is so important," Matty presses, keeping the conversation geared on Kora. "I saw her so clearly in my dream, though in the dream she had longer hair and..." He pauses as a blush creeps across his face. "Just promise you won't tell her, alright? I don't want to freak her out. You know, before she gets a chance to know me."

"I promise I won't tell." I say these words softly while

my heart swells with joy for my best friend.

He grins. "Thanks."

"Okay, guys," Marty abrasively cuts in. "Have you forgotten what's waiting for us on Magnolia Road?"

"She's right," I agree, glancing at the door. "Let's pile into the truck and haul – "

"Whoa, stop right there," Marty smirks. "We're not taking the truck."

"Why?" I inquire.

"Because we need to get there fast, dependable, and as discreetly as possible. The truck is not fast, not dependable, and definitely not discreet."

Confused, I ask, "So how are we going to get there?"

I turn to Sam. A sly smile overtakes his lips. Dread ices my blood as I realize what he's thinking.

"Fly," he says smugly. "We will fly."

Chapter Twenty-Eight

Clarity

"I can't believe you hate flying!" Marty yells over the flapping of angel's wings. Laughing, she adds, "You're such a *dork*!"

I hang on tightly to Sam, my arms wrapped around his neck and my legs tied at his waist. Without a glance or opening my eyes, I shout, "Shut your pie hole, Marty!"

Burying my face as deep as it can go into Sam's chest, I try to let the steady flutter of feathery wings coerce me to tranquility. Unfortunately, Sam's warming calm and lavender scent does nothing to ease my fear of flying.

Happy thoughts start reeling through my head. Kissing Brenton, holding his hand, hanging with Kora, the swimming hole – anything to force my mind off the present.

However, those thoughts are overtaken by the present

situation, causing queasiness to explode throughout my body. All the *what ifs* float by in a sea of doubt and brokenness, leaving my mind one big mass of uncertainty.

What if we're too late?

What if we can't help Kora?

What if we can't save the three possessed?

What if...

What if we're defeated?

Sam's comforting voice shakes me from my disturbing *what ifs*. "God didn't give you a spirit of fear and timidity, but one of power, love and self-discipline."

"Quit reading my thoughts, Sam."

"Worrying accomplishes nothing," he continues. "Worry is the opposite of faith."

I don't say a word – I don't have to. Sam speaks the truth – he always does. I already know that worry doesn't accomplish a thing. The real problem is my faith – I've always had a problem with it. I think it boils down to trust, and that's another problem I have. It's hard for me to trust. That's something I've been working on, and will probably work on the rest of my life.

After a few minutes, or maybe just a few seconds, Sam says, "Clarity."

"Hmm?"

"We're here. You can let go now."

Peeling my eyes open, I turn my head, finding that Faith, Hope, and Matty are busy scanning the dark environment we've landed in. Only Marty stands there focused on me, her arms crossed with her mouth possessing a smirk. I'm also still latched onto Sam, holding on for dear life, even though we're on the ground.

"Well," she remarks, tapping her foot loudly on the ground, "I see we've overlooked an important part of our training."

I drop my legs and arms, feeling a bit shaky from the celestial flight. Before we'd left, I'd borrowed some of Marty's clothes. The black jeans were way too long, so I'd had to roll them up a couple of inches. The black shirt fits a little too tight around my chest. Still, it's way better than a damp tank top and shorts.

The twins are dressed the same, wearing combat boots on their feet. They look like soldiers, only they carry no weapons. Tonight the only weapons we harbor are our hands, the deadliest of all weapons against demons.

"Are you sensing anything, Sam?" inquires Hope.

Sam has his eyes closed, as if in deep meditation. A few seconds later, his eyes open wide.

"They are here," he announces. His eyes are the brightest I've ever seen, glowing like two blue dots in the stark darkness.

The only light available is the moon hanging in the black sky, its shine casting eerie shadows on the depressing landscape. The glow illuminates the Guardian's white wings.

We stand in the middle of an old cemetery, with a burned-down church in the background. Empty beer bottles and trash litter the ground like a decomposing blanket. Two charred walls of the church stand, riddled with graffiti. Pews still sit where the sanctuary used to be, just like they did when the church had been painted a cheerful white.

I'm sure, in its prime, this church had been a peaceful place to worship. However, now it was used for teenagers to hang-out, make-out, and party – evidence of all three are scattered among the ground.

"Where are they, Sam?" I whisper, looking toward my

Guardian. He doesn't reply, though he continues to survey the landscape. His angel eyes glow, vibrant and consistent. Another question is on the tip of my tongue, but it never comes out, all thanks to Marty shouting into the night.

"We're here!" she screams. With her arms outstretched, she jumps onto a tall, crumbling headstone. "Come and get us, *Livian*! We're right here!"

I open my mouth to hush her up, but Sam takes my hand and gives it a squeeze. Our eyes meet. He shakes his head, a silent gesture telling me not to interfere.

We stand in silence, listening out for any supernatural activity. The rustling of leaves falling from dying trees and the quiet *hoo-hoo* of an owl is the only noise we hear, which is strange. Usually crickets, frogs, and a variety of nocturnal animals sing into the night, but tonight it's like they know...

Something hangs in the air, and it's all wrong.

Again, Marty cries out in an attempt to stir the demons from the darkness.

"Where are you? Don't tell me you're *afraid*!" She barks out a condescending laugh. "That's it, isn't it? You're too afraid of three Seers and three Guardians because you know that – "

The ground begins to shake, knocking Marty off the tombstone. She's unfazed by the mini-earthquake embarking on the cemetery, as if this is an everyday occurrence. Maybe in her life, it *is* an everyday happening.

Landing as graceful as a cat, Marty stands in defensive mode, palms up and out.

"Hold steady!" Matty yells. His eyes are wide and darting all over the place.

The air around us grows thick and cold. So cold. I'm thankful for the incessant heat burning in my palms, even though at any moment we will be face to face with evil ones.

Each breath we respire creates white clouds in the frigid air. The wind swirls the leaves off the ground. The dead trees twist and dip at odd angles. Then, right before our eyes, a tornado of black and gray touches the ground. The rumbling funnel feels like its trying to pulls us into it. When the wind becomes too intense for comfort, I reach out for Sam, but that's when the funnel dissipates and figures – *human* figures – become visible.

At first they appear as black, human-shaped blobs, but then, like a vesture being lifted off our vision, we see the figures clearly. Darren, Danielle, and David, whose real names are

Anderson, Bethany, and Timothy, stand side by side. To my horror, their eyes are completely white, announcing the stronghold over them. Their minds are mislead, clouded with devious and deceitful thoughts. Directly behind them, a figure emerges from the darkness. My stomach and heart flip-flop at the sight.

Livian, dressed in a long, flowing black dress, lands a few feet in front of her pawns. The shine of the moon glistens against her glossy black wings. Her pale skin, white hair, and white milky orbs are in stark contrast to her Gothic ensemble. A large *Tsipor* demon, the same one that I'd found sitting on Kora, is roosting on her left shoulder.

The smell of rotted meat hangs thickly in the air. I have to fight the urge to gag. Seeing her brings fear and angst, troubling my tattered nerves. Though what really frustrates me is what she holds in her arms – *who* she holds.

Kora, still in her hospital gown and bandages, hangs limply in the demon's arms. Her eyes are closed, one I know is swollen shut. I take a strong step forward, but Sam quickly pulls me back.

"Wait," he says. His glowing eyes never leave the demon.

"Yes, my little *Ra'ah*, listen to your angel." She grins, sporting sharp, pointy teeth. "We have much to discuss."

Christopher appears next to Sam, his countenance empty of any expression. Hope and Faith walk up beside them, their blue eyes piercing through the darkness.

"Give them up, evil one," Faith speaks with authority.

Hope adds, "Yes, demon. Let the young ones go."

A hiss escapes through Livian's gritted teeth. "Why, Hope and Faith, do you not call me by my name? Do you not remember how close we used to be? As close as sisters, if I remember correctly."

"We remember," Faith counters sadly. "However, that was before you defied the Father and fell."

Livian cackles. "Don't you see what Lucifer did? He freed us from bondage!"

"There is no freedom in death," Sam says, his tone strict.

"And what do you Guardians do?" continues Livian, who obviously ignores Sam's remark. "You spend eternity guarding the puny human race, who daily kills each other – who daily is dying and going to Hell! They could care less about God and Heaven. They could care less about angels and demons. They just don't *care!*" Standing straight, with Kora still in her arms, she lifts her chin and says, "You know I'm right, and if you say you haven't thought this before, then you're liars."

The angels stand firm, stand strong, unblinking.

"You are the liar and the deceiver," Hope points out. "And you are no longer our sister. You haven't been for a long time."

"You are the enemy," Faith says. "Now, leave the humans alone and leave this town."

Livian frowns, shaking her head. "I am sorry, but I cannot do that." Livian's arms go limp, which drops Kora in the process. Her body hits the ground, hard. She doesn't wake up. I cry out, wanting so badly to run to her side, but Sam steps in front of me and blocks my way.

Tears fall from my eyelids at the sight of my best friend's fragile body, all bruised and beaten. I glance at Matty and see that he also feels powerless at the moment.

"She will be okay," Christopher whispers. Matty and I look to Kora's angel. He looks at me, then at Matty. "The Father has this under control. Trust Him."

"You see," Livian begins, grabbing all of our attentions, "I can't leave this town alone. It calls to me, beckons me, *feeds* me with its delicious sin. True, I was sent here to annihilate the Seer, but now … this is personal. There are many souls in this town aching to be perverted, torn up and defiled. There are so many unsuspecting humans living in wickedness, especially the young ones. The ones who are at the age of accountability, who know right from wrong, but choose darkness. Those are the very souls my master longs for." She pauses, glaring at the Guardians. "However, I am willing to turn my back on this town. I am willing to negotiate."

"On what terms?" Sam questions.

"What I offered in the beginning," she replies, her lips curling. "One soul for many. One soul, and I'll leave this town and all its occupants alone … including the Seers." She laughs. "Of course, I can't stop my army from destroying the town. They have their orders, and, well, those are non-negotiable. But I, who can do the most damage, will leave."

"Wow," Marty whistles. "That's one sucky negotiation right there."

"You will not have Kora," Christopher speaks up. "Also, you will leave this town. If you don't, we will be forced to make you leave."

She grins. "Christopher, so good to see you again. Say, did you lose something, or someone?"

Christoper doesn't reply.

"No," Matty says, strong and firm. "You can't have Kora."

"That's right," I back him up. "You can't have her or anyone in this town."

"Never," adds Christopher. I can't see his face, though I'm pretty sure it's cast over with fierce determination.

Livian's eyes blaze bright yellow, narrowing to tiny slits. "That's your final decision, *Ra'ah*?" Her question is directed at me. "You'd rather die than allow one soul to be taken? You'd rather die than let me have Kora?"

Glancing at the twins, then at the angels, I look back to Livian and answer, "Yes."

Marty chuckles. "Looks like you lose, demon."

"You fools! You are making a grave mistake!" Livian growls as black feathers spread all over her pale skin. The *Tsipor* demon shrieks, flying off her shoulder and into the night. She lets out a vicious howl as she grows taller and taller. Her nails grow sharp and long. Lightning streaks the sky. We look up...

And all Hell breaks loose.

Chapter Twenty-Nine

Sam

The sky becomes congested with Livian's demon army. Not hundreds, but thousands fly through the air. The veil to the spiritual realm has been unzipped, letting loose the evil onto the earth.

I look to my fellow Guardians. We nod, coming to a silent understanding. With a flash of light, our swords appear in our hands. They're golden and touched by the hand of God. We lift them to the sky as they glow a bright white.

With one last glance at the Guardians, I yell, "By the grace of God!"

"We will be victorious!" they yell back in unison.

Bending at our knees, we jump into the night, directly toward the cloud of darkness. We unleash Heaven's power, waging battle against the enemy.

Clarity

The flapping of many wings mingling with Livian's evil cackle pierces through my brain like tiny shards of glass. Right then and there I know that it will take years to drain this moment from my memory. That is, if we live through this insanity.

Sam and the other Guardians have taken to the sky, their golden swords of light slashing down any *Tsipor* demon that's in their path. I'm amazed at their stealth and grace.

Matty stands to my left, Marty stands to my right. Their eyes are solely trained on the battle in the sky. With hands firmly at their sides, lifted slightly, their Seer marks are as plain as day and bright red. Just like mine. I know what they're thinking – eventually the battle in the sky will be making its way to us.

Livian starts stomping her way over, but is halted when a blonde-headed angel hops in front of her.

"Good evening, Livian," the tall, broad-shouldered, pony-tail wearing angel greets.

A sneer forms on Livian's face. "Gabriel."

With a sword of light appearing in his hand, the angel grins. "Shall we dance?"

Livian lets out a deep, inhuman howl, then leaps at the angel. The angel's wings burst from his back as he takes to the skies. Angered by the move, Livian follows right behind him.

"Wow," remarks Matty. "That was..."

"*Weird*," Marty finishes.

Suddenly an intense pressure churns and rolls in my gut, causing my heart to spasm out of control. My hands burn, as if I'm holding lit firecrackers. They ache with the need to release the fierce pressure that has been building up for months. My entire being is a bundle of wrought-out chaos.

Marty must sense my unease, because she shouts, "Clarity! Just like in training!" She has to holler over the loud beating of demon wings.

"This is nothing like training!" I retort in a yell.

"Concentrate, Clarity!" adds Matty. "Close your eyes and concentrate. Clear your mind of all fear and doubt. Grab hold of the power God has gifted you with. Grab hold and take control!

When the pressure becomes too much, release and let it go!"

"Remember," Marty says, "you hold the power in your heart – set it free!"

Though it's hard, I close my eyes and try catching hold of the heavenly power that's burning through my bloodstream. However, it's hard to concentrate with Livian's hellish wails, the beat of many demon wings, and the howl of the tempestuous winds that batter the cemetery.

Even though I'm experiencing the most uncomfortable pain thus far in my young life, I surprise myself by detecting the power. I feel it settling in my heart, like a ball of fire laying in my chest. Popping my eyes open, excitement and anxiety rushes crazy hot in my veins, taking over all synapses within my body.

"I've got it, guys!" I joyfully cry. "I have found – "

The sounds of swords swishing in the air cuts off my jovial rant. My heart thumps arduously as I catch sight of the angels in brutal combat with the demons. It appears that a few other angels have joined the battle, some I've never seen before. Each slice of their glowing blades tear down demon after demon, turning them into dust. Squeals of pain and anger fill the air. I'll never forget those sounds, those horrifying sounds.

I've never seen Sam so swift and ferocious! He and his fellow Guardians are taking down the *Tsipor's* numbers tremendously, and for a brief moment I think that the twins and I are not needed. That thought expires after about two and a half seconds. We watch in dismay as demon upon demon piles on top of the angels, covering them with their disgusting, grotesque bodies. At that precise moment we see our first dose of evil ones. They're hurdling themselves toward us, displaying their fangs, hissing as they drop from the sky.

Yellow beady eyes blaze through the darkness of night. That's all I'm able to see as of now. Fear clamps over my heart, and I fear the power I'd just grappled onto may flee. Luckily I have Marty to snap me out of my delirium.

She slaps me across the face – she really loves doing that.

"Clarity, don't look at them! Instead, hold your hands out in front of you, palms out! They're almost on top of us!"

My face stings from the slap, but I do as I'm told. I mimic their movements, with my eyes strictly on the enemy. The pressure in my chest slowly starts to recede, all the power within me gathering in my palms. A bright white light starts shining in the center of my hands, sluggishly overpowering the redness. The painful burn is getting close to unbearable, my whole body a huge tremble.

"Guys!" I holler, not daring to reel in my gaze from the sky. "When do we let it go?"

"Wait for our signal!" Matty replies.

"What?!" I counter. The urge to release the power is getting stronger.

"On three!" clarifies Marty. "One!"

A line of demons are headed straight for us. My body shakes with a strange and awkward anticipation. Don't know what to expect, but something is about to happen, something that will change my life even more than it has already.

Don't know how I know. I just … *know*.

"Two!" Marty continues.

The evil ones are drawing nearer and nearer. So close I can feel the air from their beating wings. So close I can see every detail on their faces. I'm amazed at how human their faces are, harboring sneers and snarls … though the claws, their hairy bodies, and wings are evidence of how *inhuman* they are.

"Marty!" I scream. A few more feet and the demons will be right on us.

"Three!"

The celestial lights the twins possess flash, capturing demons in the heavenly brightness, immediately reducing them to dust, and I...

Do nothing.

Absolutely nothing.

The light that had been growing in my palms, and the intense burn, is gone. I shake them, rub them together, clap – but nothing works. They don't turn back on. The burning pressure has fled.

"Clarity, you can join in anytime!" remarks Marty. She takes a demon down, its dust falling in her face.

Dumbfounded I confess, "I c-can't."

"What?!" Marty reacts without a glance my way.

"The power, the light, it's … *gone!*"

This catches her attention. She finally looks at me, her charged-up expression falling to alarm.

"What did you do?" she questions, seemingly appalled.

I gawk at her. "Nothing … *something*. I don't know..."

"Get down," she orders, pushing me to my knees and hovering over me. Turning to her brother she says, "Matty, help protect her."

"What?" Matty's too busy flashing down demons to look.

"It's Clarity! She's lost – OW!" Marty nearly falls on top of me. Hurriedly, she stands to her feet.

Spying her face, I gasp. She has three claw marks on her left cheek, bright and angry. Blood runs freely down her face and neck.

"Oh, Marty! Your face! Are you – "

"I'm fine," she says, though her voice is weak. Bending down to one knee, she places her hands on my shoulders and glares at me. "Matty and I will keep fighting, but we need you. We need you badly. Look!" She points upward. The demons spilling from the sky are innumerable. "They are going to keep coming. Concentrate, find that power, and use it!" Releasing my shoulders and rising to her feet, she raises her palms. Light shoots from them, destroying two more demons. As she's facing the evil I hear her pray, "Lord, God of heaven's armies, please help her find that power. We need her, Lord."

The wind whips around us as a demonic growl roars

through the air. On my knees, I watch the angels tear down demons left and right, but the evil ones continue to come. Like Livian had a never-ending supply of these ugly dudes stashed away, hidden in a hole in the atmosphere.

The twins are swamped with demons, able to take some out, though getting clawed at the same time. Blood drips from their wounds, but they push on. Thriving. Like the pain is fuel, their ceaseless determination keeping them set ablaze.

Closing my eyes, I cover my face with my hands and start to weep. Weep like an infant.

Why is this happening, Lord? I'd felt the power you gifted me with, but it's gone. It left me. Why? Why did it leave me?

CONCENTRATE, MY CHILD.

I jerk my head up, my eyes fluttering open. A breath I had no clue I was holding rushes through my lips. That voice, that strong voice ... I've heard it before. Even in the middle of a war zone, it's a comfort to my soul.

"I tried," I say aloud, "but I failed. I can't do it."

CLARITY. CONCENTRATE ON THE BEAT OF YOUR HEART. THERE YOU WILL FIND THE POWER IN WHICH

YOU SEEK.

"I don't know how!" I scream out.

TRUST ME. HAVE FAITH, MY CHILD.

Again, I close my eyes, trusting the voice that speaks. I know who it belongs to.

Desperately, I attempt to block out everyone and everything that surrounds me. It's hard, though eventually I succeed. I fold into myself, aware of the world around me, but at the same time able to peer inside my heart – at least, I think that's what I'm doing.

Maybe God is allowing this to be seen, paving the way toward the power He's bestowed upon me. That's the only logical explanation I can come up with. Can't be too sure, since I've never done this before.

The power that eluded me just moments before is there, smack dab in the middle of my heart. That burning white light shines, beckoning me to come closer. The pressure is intense, a heavy weight just begging to be freed. Lifting my arms high above me, raising my head to the sky, I concentrate on the pressure that is slowly spreading through my body. I wait for it to settle in my palms, but it has other plans. Instead of the burn in my hands, it filters throughout my entire body. A pain like no other touches every cell and nerve my body holds, causing my heart to throw itself against my chest.

Opening my eyes, I start to panic. I feel like a raging wildfire is consuming my existence, the heat becoming unendurable. A bright light forms, swallowing me whole. The light is so brilliant I'm afraid I may go blind from its sheer radiance.

Not able to stand the fire progressing within my body, I begin to scream. An instant relief follows as the celestial power surges out of me. It's the most strange yet exhilarating feeling I've ever experienced.

As it flows out of me, my entire being becomes electrified. It feels like I'm dreaming, but that feeling disintegrates into a fine mist as the power leaves and reality rains down on me.

Well, something's raining down.

I fall to the ground, completely and utterly drained of energy. I can't even lift my arms.

As I lay there, empty and burnt-out, I become cognizant of the fact that everything has gone silent and still. Forcing myself up on my elbows, I find that a couple pairs of eyes stare down at me – a couple of very stunned and bewildered eyes. I try to ask what's up, but I'm too weak to move my mouth.

A few weird seconds tick by before Marty inquires, "How did you do that, Clarity?"

"Do what?" I'm finally able to talk, though my voice hovers just above a whisper. Then shock grabs my throat. "Hey, what's all over you guys? Where are all the demons?"

Matty and Marty are covered with a grayish dust, from head to toe. Their green eyes appear vibrant against their dusty skin. Looking down at myself, I see that I'm also covered with the ashy gray stuff.

Matty bends down to one knee, studying my face. "You really don't know, do you?"

"Know what?" I ask in a trembling voice.

Marty sits down next to me. "Clarity, you just dusted thousands of *Tsipor* demons single-handedly. This," she tugs at her shirt, "is all that's left of them." I watch as fine silvery dust particles floats off her shirt and into the air.

My jaw drops. "You mean..." I have no words to describe what I'm feeling.

"I've never seen any Seer do what you just did," says Matty with a grin. "You are a powerful warrior of God."

Marty agrees. "You were drenched in light! We only get the light in our palms, but you … it *emanated* from you, just like the angels! You were one big ball of light." The amazement on her face would have been funny if the situation had not been so confusing.

"Maybe it's because she's held it in for so long," Matty states aloud. "Maybe she's had a build up over all these years."

Marty nods, chewing on her fingernail. "Maybe."

"I – I *killed* them?"

"That's right," Marty says. "Sent them back to Hell. And it was totally awesome!" She lets out a holler, giving her brother a high-five. They talk excitedly, and I'm so transfixed on them that I almost don't notice Livian hovering above us.

"Guys, look out!" I warn.

Both Marty and Matty turn around, facing the demon General.

Chapter Thirty

Clarity

Livian hovers above us, and she is not happy. Her usual silky white hair now resembles a tumbleweed of tangles. The fancy dress she wears is in tatters. A permanent snarl has taken over her lips. Her white eyes glow a bright yellow. She's angry, and for good reason, too.

"You've killed my army," she growls. "You've sent them back to Hell. Now," she reaches back a clawed hand, "it's time for you to meet your Creator!"

An inhuman shriek sounds from her mouth as she lunges for us. Though before she can rip our heads off, she freezes in place. We watch as her yellow devil eyes bug from their sockets. A look of shock and surprise parades across her pale face. Slowly, her body turns gray. It looks as if she's turning into a statue, frozen in a dreary eternity. We scream when she explodes. Gray, silvery dust rains down, covering our bodies with the remains of the demon General Livian.

Marty spits besides me. "Yuck, it got in my mouth."

"Mine, too," I say, wiping my mouth with my hand.

"My mouth was closed, so..."

We glare at Matty. He only shrugs.

As the dust clears, we spot our Guardians, Sam, Hope, Faith and Christopher. The foursome had all stabbed her with their swords – the swords that carry Heaven's Light.

"That. Was. *Awesome!*" exclaims Marty.

Allowing my gaze to meander upward, I'm shocked to find that angels still hover in the dark sky. They hold unreadable aspects on their faces, their glowing blue eyes on me. One of them sticks out among the rest. Blonde, broad-shouldered, ponytail-wearing angel. What had Livian called him? Gabriel?

Becoming self-conscious, I ask Sam, "Why are they staring at me like that?"

As if they heard the question, they turned their eyes away from me. One by one, light envelops them. When the light recedes, they are gone. *All* of them.

"They are amazed by you." Sam drops to his knees

directly in front of me. "There's never been a Seer able to accomplish what you just did."

"Sam," I whisper, feeling deflated, "I don't even know how I did it."

A small moan sounds off to the side. We shift our gazes and find Kora attempting to sit up. She's waking up from her nightmare – I hope.

Pushing myself up, standing on wobbly legs, I make my way over to her. Half-way there I lose my footing, falling to the ground. With my energy level being near zero, I crawl the rest of the way.

"Kora," I say softly, placing her head in my lap. "Don't move. Relax."

One of her green eyes stares up at me – the other eye is still swollen shut. Confusion has settled deep in her pupil.

"Clare, is that you?"

"Yeah," I answer, forcing a smile.

"W-Where are we?"

I hesitate before replying, "It's a long story. I'll tell you about it later."

"My head hurts, Clarity," she whimpers. A single tear escapes her eyelid. "Actually, everything hurts. Hurts so bad..."

I swallow a hard lump in my throat, working hard not to show any sadness or fear. "You're going to be okay, Kora."

Christopher leans down and places a hand on her head. Matty, Marty, Sam, Hope and Faith follow over, creating a circle around Kora and I.

"Kora will be fine," Christopher tells us.

"How do you know?" I ask.

He answers, "Because The Father said so. He has big plans for her."

"Hey," Kora slurs. She lifts an arm, pointing a shaky finger at the twins. "I've seen you two before."

Matty grins. "Yeah, behind your house. We're ... friends of Clarity's."

"Yeah," she smiles lazily. "Why are you cut up and bleeding?"

"We got in a little fight," Matty replies, puffing his chest out.

"He got his butt kicked," Marty tells Kora.

"Did not!" Matty reacts. Marty only smirks.

"*Oh-Kay*." Then, lifting her chin, she wonders, "Who are all the gorgeous and handsome models?"

A giggle bubbles up and out of me. "What? You think Matty and Marty are models?"

She shakes her head. "No, not them – *them*." She lifts her eye toward the angels.

"What ... you can ... see them?" Comprehension swims through my veins.

"Well, *duh*, Clarity," she responds, sounding more like her usual self. "They're standing all around us, and they're all *hot*! Who wouldn't notice them?"

I glance up at Sam, the twins, Hope, Faith, and lastly, Christopher.

"How is this possible?" I ask of her Guardian. He only grins.

"Well, it's kind of obvious," Matty says, staring at Kora with wonder. "Kora can see angels."

"*Angels*?" Kora stares at him like he's grown an extra pair of limbs. "What are you, on drugs or something?"

Marty slips out an exaggerated sigh. She spins around on her heels, rubbing at her temples, remarking, "Oh, you've gotta be kidding me!"

After Marty's comment, five black sedan-looking vehicles pull up. They surround Anderson, Bethany, and Timothy – I'd forgotten all about them.

All three appear disoriented and dazed. Men and women, presumably Seers, walk up to them. They begin talking with them, wrapping blankets around their shoulders and handing them bottled waters. Their Guardians, Lara, Zachary, and Rebecca, appear next to them. Glancing at us, the angels smile, then all their focus is placed on their Charges. Now that they're no longer controlled by darkness, the angels can reach out and comfort them.

"They're from the Seer Society," Marty informs me. "They'll take care of them."

"What's going to happen to them?" I wonder.

She smiles. "Don't worry. They're going to get the help they need."

Before I can get more information, Kora pipes in, "Will someone *please* tell me what's going on?" She gazes up at us with her good eye.

Christopher rests on his knees, his hand touching her head. A relieved sigh presses through her lips.

"I'll tell you everything you need to know," he promises.

A lazy grin spreads across her face. "Yeah … okay."

I stand up, leaving Kora and Christopher to talk. I walk over to the twins, who appear in deep conversation. Thankfully I'm regaining some strength, though my legs are still a bit rickety.

"What are y'all talking about?" I ask, wearing a broad smile on my face.

"We're just talking about Kora," Matty answers excitedly, "and how awesome it is that she's seeing angels! Think about it … I dreamed of her, found her here, and now she can see angels. Isn't that great?" He grins from ear to ear.

I continue to smile, but when Marty's countenance changes from joyous to befuddlement, a small amount of nausea hits low in my belly.

"Marty, what? What is it?"

"Take a look for yourself." She lifts a shaky finger,

pointing directly behind me.

I swish around ... and almost barf.

Walking up to us is Brenton. He appears afflicted and stressed, his eyebrows a straight line.

Before I can speak, he asks, "What ... the *heck*? Why is Kora talking to herself over there? Who are those people in black cars talking with Danielle, Darren, and David? What were you doing a few minutes ago? Why are your so-called *cousins* scratched up and bleeding? What's the gray stuff all over you? What ... is going on?"

He's quite hysterical, and for good reason. I wonder how much he's seen – everything, I suppose, except for the battle itself. A pounding in my skull commences after all of his questions, and I know there's only one thing I can do.

With a sudden burst of energy, I snatch his arm.

"We need to talk," I express.

With my grip tight on his arm, I pull him into the woods located behind the debilitated church. Thankfully the moon is full, its grand shine lighting our path. We come to an opening in the woods. A huge oak tree has fallen, right in the center of the opening. I drag him over and we both take a seat on the tree.

Brenton's eyes are on me, studying my face. His facial expression is a mixture of perplexity, caution and tension, all rolled into one over-stuffed burrito of madness. The ticking of many strained seconds pass before I finally give in, unable to keep my secrets under wraps.

"I've got a lot to tell you," I begin, working overtime at keeping my voice calm and unshakeable. "A lot of crazy, dysfunctional, *unbelievable* things. I was going to tell you earlier this afternoon, at the swimming hole, but ... I chickened out. I-I can't go another minute like this. I just can't."

His expression softens.

"Go on, Clare-Baby," he whispers. "Tell me what's going on. Help me understand what I just saw."

"Well, what exactly did you see?" I ask cautiously, tightly watching his reaction.

A jittery laugh eludes his lips. "I really honestly don't know. I pull up and you and your cousins have your hands held above your heads, slapping and hitting at empty air. I watched your cousins getting scratched, their blood pouring from their wounds, but ... I didn't see anything that could cause the wounds. And then ... you look up at the sky and scream a horrible scream. After that a windstorm or something happened all around you guys. Gray, dusty ash started floating everywhere – why are you guys in a cemetery? Why are you even *here*?"

A thought pops in my head. "Wait, how did you know we were here?"

"I don't know," he says, rubbing a hand through his hair. "In the hospital, I thought I heard a voice tell me to go to Magnolia Road." He pauses, gazing into my eyes. "So I did."

He drops his head to his hands, breathing heavily.

"Clarity," he whispers, lifting his head, "tell me I'm not going crazy."

"You're not crazy," I tell him.

The last few months have been building up to this very moment. There is no going back – this was the moment of truth, the moment I would find out just how much Brenton could take … and how much he truly loves me.

The time is now.

"We were battling demons, Brenton. *Tsipor* demons, which are bird slash human looking demons. Very nasty, but easy to defeat – sort of. A General in Satan's army named Livian brought these things to our town, and also three human pawns. Danielle, David, and Darren, whose actual names are Bethany, Timothy, and Anderson, were her pawns.

"Her intention for coming was all because of me. She'd been sent to take me out, but she didn't want to stop there. She'd decided that she wanted Kora, all because David – er, Timothy had fallen in love with her. Long story short, we sent Livian and her army back to Hell with the help of our Guardian angels.

"The cuts and blood you saw appearing on the twins were from the demon's talons, and the dust you saw – well, can still see because it's all over me, is the remains of the demons. When I screamed, it's because I'd finally grabbed hold of the power God has given me, and for some reason I was able to take out thousands of demons at one time, which surprised me, as well as the twins and our guardian angels.

"The windstorm – I really don't get that yet. I only know that demons tend to conjure up wind during battles. Also, Matty and Marty aren't my cousins, which I'm sure you figured out. But we do have one thing in common."

"And what's that?" he asks, his tone disconcerted.

"We're Seers, Brenton," I answer. "And the people you saw talking to the three new students – they are Seers, too."

Brenton stares at me through stormy eyes, his face wearing an unreadable shield. Abruptly he stands, pacing a line back and forth directly in front of me.

"Okay," he says, still pacing, and again running his hand through his hair. "If all this is true, and you guys really were battling demons, why couldn't I see any of it?"

I draw my knees up to my chest, hugging them close. "Because you are not a Seer."

He stops pacing, his dark eyes burning into mine. Walking over, he kneels on the ground, placing his hands on my legs.

"Tell me, Clare-Baby – what's a Seer?"

That one question opens the door of my heart. I begin revealing all the secrets that I've kept bottled up for so long, starting with the day I met Sam.

I unload everything, from Nick being possessed and abusive toward Daria, to Lukus and his Hellhounds, and also their involvement in the Thanksgiving dance shooting.

Bringing him to the present, I tell him all about the Squint twins, the truth about my parents, and the tiny bit I know of the Seer Society. With each word I spit out, ten pounds of tortured silence lifts off my shoulders, with much needed repose replacing it. By the time I utter the last piece of secrets, I feel as light as a feather, beyond happy to have it all out and in the open. The light, high feeling doesn't last long, though, as a silence falls bitter and heavy upon us.

Brenton's face twists into anger. "You knew that Kevin was going to get killed, and you did absolutely nothing to stop it."

His abrasive words stab my chest, penetrating my heart.

"Brenton," I breathe out, "I had just found out about it all. I didn't know Kevin would be killed that night, I promise you." I wipe at a tear that's stinging down my cheek. "I didn't ask for this life, this supernatural gift. But I've found out that this life needs *me*. God has blessed me with a special gift, a purpose –"

"But I don't have a purpose, right?" he interposes.

"What? Of course you have a pur – "

"You lied to me." He rises to his feet. "You've been lying to me this whole time."

I mimic his moves, reaching for his hand. "I didn't mean – "

"Don't touch me," he snarls, his jaw clenched. He yanks his hand from mine.

I gape at him, disbelieving how he's acting. "Brenton, *please...*"

He glares at me with eyes I no longer recognize. "If what you're saying is true, then where was Kev's angel the night he died?"

"His angel was there," I reply, "but it was his time."

"I don't believe you." He shakes his head, backing away. "This is nonsense. None of it makes any logical sense." He starts walking away.

No. This can't be happening. It just can't...

Catching up to him I ask, "Brenton, where are you going?"

He stops, and I bump into him. Turning around, he places his hands on my shoulders, his chocolate brown eyes peering deeply into mine.

"Clarity, I..." He trails off, closing his eyes.

My heart is pounding as I wait for him to continue. I don't know what's swirling around in his mind right now, though I know it's been completely blown away. This is the moment of truth. This is the moment I'll know how much he can and cannot take, and if he can't take it, then...

"I need a breather." He opens his eyes and gazes down at me. His face is drenched with a sadness so profound, my heart begins to crumble.

"You need a breather from what?" I bite my lip and close my eyes, not entirely sure I want the truth.

His next words slice my heart in two.

"Us," he replies.

Somehow I find the courage to open my eyes and look at him. "Us?" My voice comes out small and weak. *Defeated.*

"I can't handle all this. I ... don't think we can be together anymore."

"Brenton, don't say that ... *please.*" My heart has exploded into a million tiny pieces. "You can handle this. I promise, you can – "

He shocks me by crushing his lips to mine, wrapping his strong arms around my body. We stay in a lip lock for a minute, maybe two. In this time my heart starts taping itself back together, my hope being that he's changed his mind. That he's not giving up on us.

When he breaks the kiss and touches my forehead to his, a sense of optimism sprints through my veins.

"You'll always have my heart, Clarity," he whispers. "I've always loved you – I *do* love you, but there's no way this will work. No way."

My heart shatters again, its sharp fragments penetrating my soul.

Giving it one last try, I plead, "Don't give up on us." Tears spill down my face, dripping with heavy emotion.

"Don't cry," he whispers, his voice breaking.

"Please..."

"I've gotta go, Clarity, I've ... gotta go." He walks backward, the whole time looking at me. There's tears in his eyes, threatening to flow at any moment. Before they fall, he swiftly turns around and walks away, deserting me in the dark woods.

The feeling of rejection settles powerfully onto my weakened bones. My legs tremble and fail me. I fall to the ground and cry. Just cry. My life just walked away. My life and future just walked away, taking my heart along with him.

Lavender surrounds me as strong, warm arms pick me up.

"Clarity," Sam breathes, "I've got you. Everything will be okay."

Gazing into his eyes through thick tears, I shake my head. "No. Nothing will be okay. Nothing. I'm alone."

"In time, everything will be fine." His blue eyes glow as he says, "I am where you are, Clarity. You are *never* alone."

Taking to the skies, we fly away, the moon bathing us with its splendor. I don't even mind that we're flying. I feel no fear at all.

Maybe I'm healed from the fear.

As for my heart...

Chapter Thirty-One

Clarity

Brenton Sparks left town that night. He told his parents that he needed to get away from everyone and everything, and that he would be in touch. His parents had questioned me about his leaving so suddenly, but I had no answer to give. The look in their eyes told me everything I needed to know.

I was to blame.

Three days later, Kora was discharged from the hospital, her injuries healed, though her ribs would take a while longer to fully mend. The whole drive home she conversed with Christopher, her angel. A.C. had been amazed when she found out this information. However, the twins and I are still confused. How can Kora see angels, but not have Seer marks?

Little did we know the next night would change her life forever.

Sam

"It's about to happen," Christopher tells me.

We're standing in the hallway of Clarity's house. Kora was busy getting ready for bed, while Clarity was already in bed.

"Yes," I tell him. "I can feel it in the atmosphere."

"Is Clarity doing any better?"

I frown. "She's brokenhearted, but she will endure. I believe something good will come out of her troubles. I just don't know what."

"What is she doing now?" he wonders.

I smile. "She's sound asleep, but that's about to change."

Yes, a *lot* of things are about to change.

Kora

With only the glow of the moon shining through the

window, I stare at my reflection in the bathroom mirror. It's only been four days since they discharged me from the hospital, and boy, does it show.

The eye that had been swollen shut is now open, but still as black as ever. It will take a lot of make-up to cover up that monstrosity on graduation day, that's for sure.

Clarity had told me all about Seers, and David and his siblings. In reality, they had not been siblings, or who they said there were. A demon named Livian – the lady from my nightmares – had orchestrated the whole vile predicament. I'd gotten beat up by Danielle, who is actually named Bethany, and I still don't understand why.

Though Clarity, and my Guardian Christopher, (still in amazement on the angel, demon, and Seer thing) had explained that Livian wanted to possess and take me away with her "clan", I still don't understand … why?

In such a short time my life has changed, from one extreme to another. In less than a year, I'd fallen in love, lost that love to a bullet, lost my mother, had a cutting incident, gotten together with a guy possessed by a demon, almost got possessed myself, found out that my best friend was a Seer who battles demons, and now I can actually *see* angels – no one can make this stuff up!

Sighing, I walk over to the bed and lay down. My eyes stare up at the ceiling as I pray.

"Lord, I've been through a lot. I've loved, I've lost, I've sinned, and I've been forgiven. Thank you for your mercy and grace. Not only that, but thank you for being patient with me. Thank you for blessing me with Clarity and A.C., and thank you for my Guardian, Christopher." I pause as emotion starts to ruffle my nerves.

"God," I whisper, "I will trust you from now on. My faith has grown. Whatever happens next, I will rejoice. Yes, I will rejoice."

Suddenly a burning sensation takes over my body, mostly in my palms. Lifting my hands to my face, I start to scream...

Clarity

Kora's scream pierces my eardrums, as if she's laying right next to me. Falling out of the bed onto the floor, I stumble back up and out the door. I cross the hall, passing by Sam and Christoper. They're leaned against the wall, not bothered by Kora's yelps of pain.

"Why are you just standing there?" I ask, baffled.

"Just hanging out," Sam replies. He wears a sly smile on his lips.

"She's okay," Christopher says, in his no-nonsense tone.

Shaking my head at them, I push open the door. I find Kora in the bathroom. The light is on, and she's standing directly in front of the sink. The water is on full blast. She's no longer screaming in agony – now she's just sobbing.

"Kora!" I exclaim, hurrying to her side. "What's going on? Are you – "

My words drop off a cliff of surprisal, falling into an abyss of drifting questions. She looks at me through wide eyes, then back down at her hands under the rushing water. They're shaking and ... and *marked*!

"Oh, wow, Kora," I stumble out, still amazed by what I'm witnessing.

"What is it?" she questions. "Why are my hands burning so bad and ... what's up with the crosses, wings, and crowns?"

I grin, showing her my palms. "They're marks, Kora. *Seer* marks. And as you can see, they're just like mine."

She stares at my hands, then back at me, open-mouthed, her expression that of horror.

"Clare," she whispers, "I'm freaking out."

I laugh, then say, "Sorry, don't mean to laugh. It's just … let me get Christopher."

Once in the hall, I glare at the two smiling angels.

"You knew," I figure out. "You knew she was getting marked."

"What was you first clue, Clarity?" wonders Sam sarcastically.

I don't get angry by his sardonic question – I'm way too happy to be angry.

"I've got to call the twins," I tell them, walking into my room. "Oh, and Christopher..."

"Yeah, I'm going," he says.

Picking up the phone, I try dialing the twin's number. My hands are too shaky with excitement to dial the numbers.

Eventually, I get it done. Matty answers on the first ring.

"Clarity, what's up?"

"You want to know what's up?" I laugh. "Get a load of this..."

***

Graduation day finally arrives, us seniors happily throwing our tasseled caps in the air. A small sense of accomplishment saturates the hot Georgia air. Everyone is excited to get on with their lives.

Some are moving across the Unites States, while others are staying around to attend Garlandton Community College. Some are joining the Army to further their education, while others simply just don't care where they end up.

As for Kora and I, we will be traveling to the Seer Society in Atlanta. When are we leaving? The day after graduation, which is today. Right now.

The week before graduation, A.C. and Doug surprised everyone when they left for a weekend getaway and came back married. She left a Miller and came back a Cox. Caroline Cox. Nice ring to it, right?

Now, as Kora and I busy ourselves with loading our stuff in my brand new, four-door Jeep Wrangler with hard top (no more rust bucket), I take one last look at what I'm leaving

411

behind.

I'll be leaving my parent's white house on almost thirty acres of land, which I gifted to A.C. and Doug. In their will my parents had left the house to me, but I feel it's more prudent to give it to the newlyweds. After all, A.C. has been my provider the last five years. She deserves to have this nice home. Plus, there's plenty of room for a couple of kids.

Lifting my gaze to the roof, I look at my bedroom window. I can't count the number of times I've sat on that roof at night, stargazing and wondering where life would lead. I'll miss the nights wrapped up in a blanket, enjoying God's beautifully constructed masterpiece.

I'm leaving Casey and Janey, two good friends who are giving their relationship another shot and attending the community college together. If you saw them walking down the street, you'd know right away that they love each other. I really hope they make it. I really, really do.

I'll be leaving behind a cashier job at Baker's Supermarket, a dingy old movie theater where I'd watched numerous movies with my friends, a bowling alley where I used to get drunk, and Granny Mae's Creamery who, in my opinion, has the best ice cream in the south.

I'll be leaving behind an old school and an old red barn that will forever hold bittersweet memories. I'll be leaving a school gym where one of my friends had been killed, his life cut short by a jealous, possessed teenager, I'll be leaving acres upon acres of fields that hold a gazillion bales of hay – my childhood playground.

Many, many memories, good and bad, I am leaving behind. However, the worst part about leaving is knowing that Brenton won't be leaving with me.

Technically, I'm not leaving him, since he'd skipped town nearly four weeks ago. No one, not even his parents, know where he has gone. All the plans we'd made had been placed in a shredder and thrown in a wayward wind, separating and scattering into a million different directions.

As hard as it was, I'd written him a letter and placed it in an envelope, along with the ring and sunflower necklace he'd given me. In the letter, I told him that no matter what he chose, we'd always be friends. I've forgiven him for leaving. I still love him, and I always will. An empty space where he used to reside in my heart aches nonstop.

Wherever he is, I know he's not alone. I know his Guardian is with him.

A horn blares, honking its way into my thought train. Turning around, I see Matty and Marty's truck bounding down the driveway. It comes to a screeching halt next to my cherry red jeep.

"*Sweet!*" Matty whistles loudly as he jumps down from his truck. "You like driving in style, don't you, Clarity?"

I laugh. "I don't know about that. The only other car I've had was a rusted-out piece of junk."

"Hey, watch it!" Matty jokingly warns, his palm tapping the hood of his truck. "Don't let the rust fool you – *this* rust-bucket can be a real monster."

Marty walks around the jeep, asking, "How did you afford it?"

"It's kind of a gift from my parents," I reply, not at all taken back by her question. "In their will they had specifically put in that they wanted me to have a brand new car for my graduation."

"Oh," she says, piercing her lips together and nodding her head. Her puffy, curly dark hair bounces with each nod.

"Let's go!" Kora yells as she jumps into the passenger's seat.

"And here comes our newest member." Marty sighs. She climbs back into Matty's truck and shuts the door.

Matty walks over to Kora, leaning against the door with his arms crossed. I can't be too sure, but I think I see a blush creeping across his tanned face. Kora still doesn't know about Matty and his dream – I won't be the one to tell her.

"A little eager to leave, aren't you?" His smile is bright and sincere.

"Eager to kiss this town goodbye," she quickly replies, adding, "You know, the old me would've mooned the town and everyone in it goodbye. Thankfully God has changed me."

Matty's blush deepens. Kora has rendered him speechless. Turning around, he walks to his truck and gets in. I snicker, knowing that he will have to get used to Kora's antics. It will take him awhile, of that I'm positive.

As soon as I turn on the Jeep, Kora blasts the air conditioning. I shoot her a look, arching an eyebrow.

"Sorry," she says, her face burning crimson. "It's just, I've never been in a vehicle with air conditioning." She reclines back in the black leather seat.

"Neither have I," I confess. Placing the Jeep in drive I

ask, "You sure you want to do this? Atlanta is going to be a huge switch from Garlandton."

Lazily, she lolls her head to the side, placing huge white sunglasses on her face.

"The real question is," she says mysteriously, "is Atlanta ready for *us*?"

Looking at each other, we laugh, deep down knowing we're making the right decision. Leaving this town is definitely putting us on the right track.

We drive down my long driveway and pull onto the road. We pass Garlandton High, and pass through the small town square. We pass the road that leads to the swimming hole. We pass the road that holds Kora's old trailer. We don't say a word as we pass by the sign we thought we'd never see:

You are now leaving Garlandton.

Drop back in soon!

***

Evil wears many faces, takes many forms. That much I have learned from my mistakes. It can spread like wayward thistles flying in a gentle breeze, and when it comes upon its target, it doesn't want to let go. Once evil takes root in a human soul, it's a fight to the finish. Wickedness is unrelenting, painful … and everywhere. The only way to get rid of darkness is to allow the light in. That is the way to defeat the darkness – let the light shine.

Just like evil, love spreads and tries to take root in a human soul. It fights the battle that wages deep within us, and it's a tough battle. However, the decision is up to us.

Do we take the path to darkness, or let love show us the way to light?

My eyes had been closed when I'd met Lukus and the Hellhounds, but I was ready for Livian when she'd shown up in the small town of Garlandton – more than I believed, anyway.

Most likely Livian thought I was an easy target, and that the town would be an easy take over. She overlooked one very important fact.

Seers are determined individuals.

With the help of many Guardians and two fierce Seers, we were able to defeat Livian and her army. The light that overtook me sent the *Tsipor* demons back to Hell, where they belong. Of course, they'll be back. They always come back.

I'm not alone. God has shown me that. He came through for me in the midst of all my troubles, going as far as lifting me out of the dark watery depths. He's also blessed me with a very powerful gift, and I will use it and give Him all the glory.

Even with a broken heart, I see the light weaving its way into my life, and also in the lives of my loved ones.

Driving to Atlanta, headed to the Seer Society, I tell myself that I will never be fooled by the devil again. I tell myself that I will never let evil embed within my soul, taking over my light. I promise myself that I will never, ever get hurt again. That I will never fall in love with anyone ever again. I will guard my heart until the day I die – only God is allowed in my heart. He is on that throne.

Of course, I have a feeling, this premonition...

I'll be wishing in the next few months that I'd never promised myself a single thing.

Epilogue

Brenton

The photo is starting to fade. I stare at it way too much. The edges are bending, and my fingerprints have smudged it. I don't know why I keep looking at it – I've already memorized every detail.

The way her brown eyes appear lighter in the summer, but darker in the winter. The way her brown hair falls in waves down her back. The way her smile completely captivates me, melting my heart. The smell of her perfume...

This is all I do. Sit in this hotel room, lay on an uncomfortable mattress, and stare at the only photo I brought; the only photo that mattered.

Clarity.

Just thinking her name brings tears to my eyes and sorrow to my heart. What have I done? Is she thinking of me?

Does she hate me?

Well, I don't hate her. Not at all. I love her. I want to marry her.

Why did I leave her?

Nausea builds in my stomach. It's been happening more and more as the days pass. Quickly, I jump up and race to the bathroom. I hover above the toilet and wait, thinking at any moment I'll be sick.

Nothing happens. The sickness doesn't come. Only the burn. The burn in my hands.

Walking to the mirror, I stare at my reflection. I've lost some weight. I've lost some sleep.

I've lost my love.

Twisting the water on, I place my hands under its cool flow. Then, glancing down, I look at my palms, staring in a heavy mystification.

Crosses. Wings. Crowns.

Lifting my gaze, I nearly stroke out. In the reflection of the mirror, a girl stands behind me. She's wearing a white dress and has long light brown hair. A familiar scent plagues the air …

honeysuckle, maybe?

I don't say a word. The foreign marks on my hands came late last night, and have been there ever since. They're not going away, and neither is the mysterious girl who has appeared in the hotel bathroom.

I'm not afraid. I'm not shocked. I could be dreaming, maybe hallucinating, but I can't be too sure. I'm not sure of anything anymore.

When the girl's eyes glow blue, my heart struggles in its confinements.

"Hello, Brenton," she greets with a smile. "I'm Sarah."

Author Thanks...

Thank you to my Lord and Savior for birthing in me an imagination and determination to write. No glory is mine. It's all Yours.

To my mom, thank you for the support through these years, and all the years of my life. I love you. And to my dad in heaven, thank you for being a great father while you were here. I miss you so much. I love you.

To Rocky, my husband and best friend, thank you for supporting me, and for handling all the formatting/cover designing and all that goes with it. I love you to the moon and back.

Ryder, Wyatt, and Sarah – best children in the world. Mama loves you!

My Lifeline family – thank you for accepting my weirdness. Thank you for the support you've given. God's about to open doors that no man can shut! Love you all!

To my readers and fans, THANK YOU! Get prepared for more, my friends.

Remember...

God loves you.

www.ingramcontent.com/pod-product-compliance
Lightning Source LLC
Chambersburg PA
CBHW070614260626
47161CB00007B/2435